CLEAR
BLAKE BRIER
BOOK 7

L.T. RYAN

WITH
GREGORY SCOTT

LIQUID MIND MEDIA

For information contact:

Contact@ltryan.com

https://LTRyan.com

https://www.facebook.com/JackNobleBooks

THE BLAKE BRIER SERIES

Blake Brier Series

Unmasked
Unleashed
Uncharted
Drawpoint
Contrail
Clear
Quarry (coming soon)

CHAPTER 1

JIM BRIER GASPED. His eyelids fluttered open.

Inside the windowless room, buzzing of the fluorescent ballasts mixed with the groans of a few others who'd likely also come to the realization that it was a brand new day.

Jim stared up at the underside of Freddie's bunk. The heavy wire mesh squeaked and heaved before Freddie's legs swung over the side. His bare feet dangled next to Jim's head.

"You mind putting those things somewhere else?" Jim's voice cracked. He coughed to clear the frog from his throat. "They smell like Muenster."

Freddie hopped down and leaned against the edge of Jim's mattress. "Maybe if you got out of bed in the morning—"

Jim lifted his knees, then let his legs fall straight. "I'm working on it."

"Okay, old man." Freddie smiled. "You keep working on it."

"Just wait. In five years, you'll be right where I'm at."

Once upon a time, Jim would have already been "up and at 'em" as his wife would say. Now, at seventy-two years old, nothing about him was "up," never mind "at 'em." Each morning, his ritual started with a full five minutes of creaking and cracking before his joints limbered enough to stand up. While his body would have liked to stay stretched-out on the lumpy little mattress, it wasn't an option. The overhead glare said it was time to go to work.

There were no light switches inside the barracks. Controlled by timers, the two rows of fluorescents were triggered at seven-thirty sharp each day. It gave them exactly one half-hour to get ready and report to their assignments. Even on Sundays.

This suited Jim just fine. Anything to avoid being trapped in there for a single minute longer than necessary.

"Gonna be a nice day out there today." Freddie shoved his fingers in along the bedframe, tucking the sheets in tight. He walked around to the other side to finish the job. "A little cooler than yesterday."

Jim threw back his top sheet and pivoted his body until his legs draped over the side. His bare feet touched the cool tile floor. "I wouldn't know."

As a condition of his remediation, Jim was assigned to the interior cleaning crew, while Freddie was one of those responsible for the grounds. Working alongside professional landscapers, the work was no doubt harder, but it came with hours of fresh air and sunshine. Not a bad trade-off.

Funny, Jim thought, how he had once sat at the top levels of the organization, and now? A janitor. It was enough to make anyone reassess their choices.

But it wasn't the menial job, nor the lockdown that had soured him against the Church of Clear Intention. That had been the fault of the Church itself. A consequence of its disjointed ideology and draconian acts. To think, he had once been an arbiter of such.

"I'll grab your coffee," Freddie said.

Jim nodded with a grunt and leaned over to stretch his back.

Around him, the room filled with light chatter and shuffling feet.

Between the men's and women's bunks, along the eastern and western walls, was a ten-foot-wide gap. At this time of the morning, it was akin to a ten-lane freeway.

People scurried to the bathrooms to catch a quick shower, brush their teeth, or change out of their linen pajamas. Mostly, they marched the shortest path to the four coffee pots lined up on the counter next to the inner door. The first one there was responsible for firing them up.

Like the outer fire door on the far side of the room, the metal inner door remained locked from dusk until dawn. A reminder, they'd been told, of their closed-mindedness.

"A narrow mind is the prison of the soul," the Sage was fond of saying. "To open doors, you must first open your mind."

In another context, it would seem like sound advice. Under the circumstances—a transparent ultimatum.

Of course, in case of an emergency, the door to the outside could be opened by pressing the bright red lever. But, as the decals warned, it would set off the alarm. It didn't matter, anyway. Once outside, there was nowhere to go. A high, spiked wrought iron fence guaranteed it.

"Here ya go, hot and black." Freddie handed over a steaming Styrofoam cup, then sat on the bed next to Jim. "How I like my women."

Jim threw Freddie a meager courtesy laugh.

Ah, Freddie.

Frederick R. Cook. Good for that same joke at least three times a week. But who was counting, right?

Jim patted Freddie on the thigh and held out his cup. "Thanks for this."

Current proximity aside, Jim and Freddie had been friends for over two decades. Both former members of the Echelon—a governance board formed to oversee the enforcement of policies, recruitment efforts, and physical expansion of the organization—Jim and Freddie shared a similar level of experience. And culpability.

Upon first glance, they could have been related. They had both long since gone gray; were both tall, from New York state, and on the outs with the Church. But their similarities ended there.

A widower with no children, Freddie was never in any hurry. He came across as simple, taking everything in stride, even while his words betrayed his discontent. In Jim's estimation, the man was every bit as simple as he seemed.

Why Freddie was there in lockdown, Jim couldn't begin to understand. Sure, he might have asked the wrong questions. Dared to point out the obvious. But in the end, Freddie would have done whatever was asked of him. It was in his nature to take the smoothest path. To avoid conflict.

The chance of him being any help was remote, but it couldn't hurt to keep trying.

"I was thinking," Jim said, "how well do you know the guys you've been working with? I mean, they're civilians, right? Maybe you can feel them out. They could get us a cell phone. Or maybe create a diversion. We could go back to the plan we talked—"

"Jim." Freddie sighed and looked down at his coffee. "It's too early for this. I swear you have a one-track mind."

"One of us has to." Jim stood and slipped his feet into his slippers, then turned to face his friend who refused to look Jim in the eye. "You say you want out. You say you're willing to do your part. But it really seems like you want to stay locked up in here forever."

"Don't be like that. I'm just saying, we need to bide our time. You know I'm here for you when—"

Unable to hide his disgust, Jim walked away without waiting for Freddie to spew any more empty promises.

As frustrated as he was, Jim couldn't hold it against the guy. If Freddie didn't want to rock the boat, it was his prerogative. Besides, there had to be others who wanted out and had the guts to do something about it.

Or, he'd figure out a way on his own.

"Help! Somebody help!" The high-pitched voice of young Sandy Jenkins pierced the mundane.

Jim jerked, both at the abrupt screaming and the sense of horror it carried.

"He's not breathing!" she yelled.

A small but frantic crowd gathered around the bunk of Garrett Brody. Jim hurried over to see for himself.

"Help me get him on the floor," someone said.

"I know CPR." Alex pushed through the group. "Check his pulse."

"Where's Yan?" Sandy hollered. "We need Yan."

The retired physician Zhào Yan was already working his way into the circle.

"Stop." Yan pushed on Alex's arm, preventing him from further dragging Garrett's stiff corpse off the bed. "He's dead. Has been for hours. There's nothing you can do."

"Oh my god!" Sandy burst into tears. "What happened to him?"

The crowd clamored. While some expressed their sadness, others whispered the mottled body was proof of a conspiracy. Jim didn't know what to make of it.

Garrett wasn't the most pleasant of people, but as far as Jim could tell, he was as healthy as an ox.

Only two days prior, Garrett had tried to walk out the front doors in a defiant huff, only to have security tackle him before he stepped one foot outside. He fought well for several minutes until three large men had pinned him to the ground—or so the story went.

Was that the cause of this? Had he suffered internal injuries at the hands of his wardens?

The irony was, Garrett would have been someone Jim could have used. Someone who might have been able to help him get his wife out. That was, if they hadn't despised each other.

Jim had accrued more than a few enemies by virtue of his former job. Garrett had happened to be one of them.

"I can't!" Cheri, a mousy little creature from Phoenix, bolted at the door as if she were going to plant a shoulder. She slapped the steel with both palms and screamed through it. "Open the door! Can anyone hear me? Come quick, it's an emergency! Please open the door!"

Cheri rested her forehead against the white painted metal. The tempo of her slaps waned to a sporadic rhythm, adding several more oily fingerprint smudges to the existing collection.

"Should we cover him?" Alex asked.

Jim looked back. He realized Freddie hadn't moved throughout all the commotion. Instead, he continued sitting, sipping his coffee as if nothing had happened. "You alright, Fred?"

"I'm fine," he said, without emotion.

The heavy door was flung open with a clang. The air seemed to be sucked out of the room as if they were in the pressurized cabin of a 747 at 30,000 feet, replaced by a pensive silence.

Losing her support, Cheri tumbled to the floor. Peter Hammond stepped over her as though she were an inanimate obstacle in his path and surveyed the scene. Two large security guards—wearing black polo shirts bearing the logo of the Church—waited for Cheri to crawl out of the doorway before filing in behind their superior.

"What seems to be the problem?" Peter stood with his feet shoulder width apart and his hands clasped behind his back.

The group parted, allowing Peter a clear view of Garrett's bunk.

"I see," Peter said.

The oldest son of the so-called Sage, Curtis Hammond, Peter had either been given the role of disciplinarian, or had just assumed it. He was an intense young man and, as far as Jim was concerned, a representation of everything that had gone wrong with the Church. Even though Jim had known Peter since he was a baby, Jim always considered it in his best interest to steer clear of him.

Peter sauntered forward. "Brothers and sisters, do not despair. While it is difficult for us to understand, nature is never disorganized. The universe seeks balance. We can only accept its energy, if we are open to it, but we can never control it." Peter reached out and grasped Garrett's lifeless hand, cupping it between his own. "Brother Garrett has shed his mortal bonds, this much is apparent, but we must have faith that his passing serves a purpose. A necessary component to the natural order of things."

Like father, like son, Jim thought.

"Take him." Peter motioned to the two guards, who hurried over and began lifting Garret by his feet and underarms. One looked over his shoulder as he walked backwards towards the exit.

"Where are you taking him?" Alex asked.

"Brother Garrett will be prepared for his family to receive him," Peter said. "Now let this not deter your progress on the road to redemption. Everyone, you will report to your stations in ten minutes. No excuses."

Peter stepped back through the steel door, letting it slam shut in his wake.

"Is he serious?" Sandy asked. "As if nothing happened? Garrett is dead. Doesn't anyone care what happened to him?"

"I do," Freddie raised his hand.

"So do I," Jim added. "If only to avoid being next."

CHAPTER 2

"YOU SURE YOU don't want to hang here, maybe lounge by the pool?" Blake stared out the back window, mesmerized by the gentle sway of the leaves. The sun's rays hadn't yet cleared the trees and roof, leaving a dusky glow on the patio. Despite the stagnant, climate-controlled air inside, he could almost smell the salty breeze through the glass. As always, it brought a sense of calm.

Behind Blake, Haeli dropped the blender pitcher in the sink. It clattered the silverware against the stainless steel, breaking him from his trance.

"You're not getting cold feet, are ya?" Haeli jammed a straw into the flimsy lid of a disposable plastic cup. As she sipped her fruity concoction, her pursed lips drew up into a mischievous smile. She extended her thumb and forefinger and squinted through the gap between them, as if taking a rough measurement of Blake's head. "You have to be a teensy-weensy bit excited to see them, after all this time."

"I am." The tenor of Blake's response was in contrast to Haeli's cutesy gesture. "I mean, I'm a little nervous. You know we didn't part on the best of terms."

Haeli gave a shrug and nodded. "Fair enough but hear me out. You know how sometimes we get in an argument and then a little while later, neither of us can remember why? This will be like that, I think.

Not that I'm implying this is trivial, of course. It's a different situation, and it's been years instead of hours."

"You're right." He thought for a moment. "But it's not only hashing out the past I'm nervous about. They're not answering or returning my calls. It's been days."

"Stop. They probably just changed their number. Who has a landline anymore anyway, right?" Haeli wiped a drip from below her bottom lip. "Doesn't mean anything. Anyway, we'll know what's going on in a couple hours."

"Very true." Blake moped back to his seat on the couch and pulled his laptop off the coffee table, and onto his lap. "I'll print the tickets as a backup. Are you all packed? We leave in thirty. And where's Griff? Have you seen him?"

"He's up. I heard him banging around upstairs." Haeli handed Blake a smoothie and then dropped down next to him on the couch, tucking her legs under her and resting her head on his shoulder. "I'm packed. Everything's set. No worries."

Blake clicked the trackpad. Across the room, the printer came to life, running through its ritual of clicks and clacks before deciding if it was ready to spit out a piece of paper.

"Look at this crazy shit." Blake pointed at the screen.

Haeli lifted her head from Blake's shoulder and straightened her posture. "What is it?"

"The Church of Clear Intention," Blake continued, "worth a little under a billion dollars in total assets. Mostly real estate. Can you believe that?"

"Is that your parents' church?"

Blake's jaw tightened and his head bobbed in the affirmative.

"Funny."

"What?"

"I don't know," Haeli said. "Not what I expected, I guess. When you said they got wrapped up with a cult, I was picturing a group of people chanting around a cauldron, drawing pentagrams on the walls in blood or something. Not a mega-corporation. And that name's ridiculous. What does it even mean?"

Blake laughed. "Who knows? I always thought the whole thing was ridiculous. When my folks first got involved I thought, 'this is going nowhere.' I mean, it was one guy with a handful of followers. I think they held their meetings in someone's living room. It was a joke."

"Not anymore, apparently," Haeli said.

"No, not anymore. Now it's a menace if you ask me."

"I'm sure it's harmless," Haeli said. "There are worse things for your folks to be involved with, don't you think? So they're into God and whatnot. More power to 'em."

"That's the thing—it's not about God. There's no God in the equation. This is who they worship—" Blake twisted the laptop to give Haeli a better view. On the screen was a picture of an older man with well-coiffed salt and pepper hair, bright teeth, a fancy suit, and a deep tan that could have been painted on with an airbrush.

"Hey now." Haeli nudged Blake. "Not a bad looking guy. Who is he?"

"Curtis Hammond. The founder." Blake straightened the computer on his lap. "And he's not your type."

"Rich and good looking. Yeah, not my type at all." Haeli smirked and pulled the screen toward her again. "So this is really The Guy? The Grand Poobah? Doesn't look like much of a prophet. If you asked me to guess, I would have said 'banker.'"

"More like a used car salesman," Blake said. "I met him once when I was a teenager. My parents hosted a backyard barbeque and invited him. Even then, I thought he was a tool. He had this arrogant, holier-than-thou attitude."

"Technically, he kinda is." Haeli smiled.

Blake grimaced.

"What?" Haeli laughed. "He's like their Pope. Can't get any holier than that."

"Pope, my arse. A con artist is what he is. Preying on the weak. Brainwashing them. Do you know how he keeps people drinking the Kool-Aid? He convinces them that all their problems are 'due to the influence of the toxic people around them.' And by toxic, he means anyone who doesn't buy his bullshit." Blake shook his head and folded his arms, continuing to stare at the man on the screen. "One of the first things members have to do to reach enlightenment or whatever he's selling, is cut off their friends and family. They're told that these people are holding them back from realizing their full potential. In reality, he didn't want anyone talking sense into them."

Haeli nodded. "And that's what happened with your parents."

"Yes, and no. According to Hammond, I was filling their heads with lies and I needed to be 'proscribed' as he called it—cut out of their lives completely. My mother performed her duty without question, but my father went against the rules and continued to call. But when he did, he would just try to bring me into the fold. He pleaded with me to 'come around,' and 'see the light.' For my mother's sake, he said."

"Sounds like it was breaking their hearts."

"Really? Because instead of saying no and walking away, the only thing they did was try to convert me. That's why I stopped taking his calls. I couldn't hear it anymore. I was never going to be enough. I was never going to come before the Church. Not for him, and definitely not for her."

Haeli reached over and rubbed Blake's upper back. "I'm sorry."

Blake could feel the anger bubbling up inside of him. It had been a long time since he'd let these memories affect him. They were part of the growing list of things Blake kept tucked away in the back of his mind, careful not to unpack. Like he had done with Anja. Like he would do with Ima.

Death and loss were woven into Blake's psyche. The same was true for Haeli, Fezz, Khat, Griff, and Kook. Anyone who had seen true conflict and survived.

Their experiences had changed them all in different ways.

For Haeli, escaping Levi Farr, then prison, seemed to give her a greater appreciation for her life, and her gifts. For Fezz, Ima's death seemed to have forced him to reassess what it meant to lead a fulfilling life. For Blake, it was Buck Novak's plight that drove him to seek a reunion. After losing both of his sons, Novak would have given anything for one more minute with his boys.

It was too late for Novak, but not for Blake. There was time to salvage the relationship. Maybe it was his short stint in therapy, or the wisdom that came with age, but for the first time in twenty years, Blake had begun to regret walking away.

"You kids ready?" Griff leaned over the railing at the top of the staircase. "We need to stop for gas."

Blake closed his laptop and slipped it into his bag. "Ready."

Griff moseyed down the steps, then snatched his keys from the kitchen counter.

"You gonna be able to manage without us?" Haeli asked.

"I was going to ask you two the same thing," Griff said.

Blake chuckled. "You and Khat can get some bonding time in."

"Yeah, sure," Griff huffed. "That's just what I need. Me and Mister Grouchy, all by ourselves."

"He's taking it hard." Blake said.

"He is." Griff threw his arms out to the sides. "I get it. It sucks. But Christ—"

Whether Griff wanted to admit it or not, he hadn't been himself since Fezz left, either. None of them had. As big a guy as Fezz was, he'd left an even bigger hole.

"Have either of you heard from him?" Griff asked.

Blake shook his head.

Haeli glanced at Blake and then back at Griff, shaking her own.

"Alright then," Griff sighed. He took the duffle from Haeli's hands and carried it toward the front door. "Let's get you to Warwick."

CHAPTER 3

"YOUR TURN." Ian planted his socked feet on the dashboard. "What is the longest word you can type with only your left hand?"

Fezz blinked away his glazed-over, thousand-yard stare. He glanced at Ian in the passenger seat and responded with forced exuberance. "Easy. It's 'howthehellamisupposedtoknowapus'".

"No." Ian chuckled. "That's wrong. You just put a bunch of words together. And there were nine letters from the right side, anyway."

"I was close though, wasn't I?" Fezz smirked.

Over the past several days, Fezz had learned a lot about Ian. For one, he never tired. It was as if his brain had a power source of its own. A mini fusion reactor, insulated from the conventional physics of the open road. What surprised Fezz the most, though, was the way he'd processed the news of his mother's death. He was emotional, but only for a few hours. Mostly, he asked a lot of questions.

Ian was driven by details. Logic. It was his coping mechanism. Everything sorted into its own little compartment. Fezz couldn't begin to understand it. He was barely holding himself together, despite a life-time dealing with death and disaster.

Luckily, they had each other. Even Fezz felt he needed Ian more than the other way around. Caring for an orphan, whether said orphan needed caring for or not, gave Fezz purpose. And, now, an actual destination.

After several days of aimless driving, roadside motels, and fast food restaurants, a goal had emerged. They began to see the forest for the trees, in a very literal sense.

For whatever reason, Ian had a fixation with the forest—that much everyone knew. Fezz was looking for a place for them to plant their own roots. A place where Ian could recapture however much of his childhood was left. Where they could be comfortable and, moreover, anonymous.

In central Indiana, a random discussion had turned into an epiphany. For Ian, Shangri-la, For Fezz, not so much. Nonetheless, it was decided. Coastal California. The home of the mighty redwoods. And they were already halfway there.

"Fezz?"

"Yeah?"

"Do you think when someone dies, they know it?"

Fezz gripped the wheel and swallowed hard. For as much time as they'd spent together, he still hadn't gotten used to Ian's blunt demeanor and endless curiosity. It was a simple, innocent question, yet a profound one. And one for which Fezz had no answer. "I don't know, bud. It'd be nice to think there's something after, but I can't say I believe that myself."

"Not after," Ian said. "Of course you don't know after. You're dead. You don't know anything, then. I meant, at the time. Do you think my Mom knew?"

Fezz sighed. "Yes, I do."

While Fezz left it at that, his mind swirled with images of the faces of fallen comrades. Ghosts who now lived in the world Fezz left behind. But Ian's question brought one face front and center. Bo Schaffer, or Boots as they called him.

Posted on the roof of what was left of a three-story building in Hraytan, outside of Aleppo, Boots had taken a round to the shoulder. By the time Fezz got to him, Boots had already dragged himself to cover and applied QuikClot to the wound.

A clean through and through shot, the bullet appeared to have missed anything vital. Bleeding had stopped and Boots exhibited no signs of labored breathing, loss of function in his arm, or shock. Even now, the memory of what happened next continued to haunt Fezz.

"Come on," Fezz had said, trying to scoop Boots to his feet. "Let's get you out of here."

"No need," Boots had replied, his voice measured and void of emotion. "I'm dead."

Fezz remembered laughing out loud. "You're not dead. You're perfectly fine. Now get up and let's go."

But Boots was right. Before Fezz could finish his sentence, Boots was gone. Just like that.

Somehow, Boots had known. He saw something Fezz couldn't have. And there was nothing anyone could do. What was even worse, they never found the shooter.

"Fezz?" Ian said.

Fezz shivered. He redirected his attention to the dashed lines whizzing through the broad beams of the headlights. "Did you say something?"

"I was just wondering how long 'til we get to California."

"It's going to be a while," Fezz said. "I tell you what, it's almost morning and we're not far from Denver now. Why don't we stop there? We can catch a nap, a bite to eat."

"I'm okay," Ian said, "but I think the truck needs a break."

"Why do you say that?"

"It's smoking." Ian twisted around and pointed toward the back window.

Fezz looked in his rearview mirror. The smoke trailing off the back hung in the glow of the taillights. "Damn it."

He pulled over a hundred feet past the exit for Route 181. As the pickup slowed to a stop, white smoke enveloped the truck.

Fezz turned off the engine and grabbed his cellphone. "Get out."

They both hopped out and moved several feet away.

"Smells like maple syrup," Ian said.

Fezz nodded. "Coolant."

A few minutes and thirteen tractor-trailer flybys later, the cloud began to dissipate. Fezz went to the driver's side, grabbed the flashlight from the center console, and popped the hood. Ian joined him at the front. "Let's take a look."

Lifting the hood released another small burst of smoke.

Ian coughed and waved his hand in front of his face. "Can you fix it?"

After waving the flashlight around the engine compartment, Fezz had to admit what he'd known from the start. He considered himself handy, but he wasn't MacGyver. They were in the dark, on the side of the interstate, with no tools. "I don't think so."

Behind the truck, the flashing blue and red lights of a Colorado State Patrol car cut through the darkness and the Dodge Durango's V8 wound down.

"Are we in trouble?" Ian asked, keeping his voice low.

"Not at all," Fezz said. "Just remember everything we talked about. You'll do fine."

A bright light rounded the pickup and illuminated Fezz and Ian. Fezz trained his own light at the trooper. His gold nameplate gleamed. *Baez.*

"Having some car trouble are ya?" Baez asked.

"Sure are." Fezz smiled. "Somethin' cracked. I think I'm burning off antifreeze. Always somethin', am I right?"

Baez nodded. "Where y'all comin' from? Rhode Island?"

Good work, Detective. "Plate gave us away, huh? Me and my son are taking a boys' getaway out west to take in the national parks. See the real America. Know what I mean?"

"Worth doin'," Baez said. "You got ID on ya?"

"Sure, of course." Fezz dug into his pocket and produced his Rhode Island license. Or one of them, anyway.

"Reynold Sutton?" the trooper read, as if it were a question.

"That's right. People call me Ray. This is my son Ian."

"Good to meet ya, young man."

"Yes sir," Ian said, "Good to meet you, too."

The trooper handed Fezz his license. "I'll call in for a tow."

"That won't be necessary," Fezz said. "We'll manage."

"Now look here, you can't be driving this thing and you sure as hell can't stay out here."

Baez wasn't wrong. Traffic on Interstate 70 was already picking up ahead of sunrise. It was a dangerous place to be. Especially for Ian.

"You're right. Thanks." Fezz put a hand on Ian's shoulder and ushered him into the grassy strip, off to the side of the roadway.

"Hang tight. I'll be right back."

It was five minutes before the trooper returned from his car and another eight minutes before the wrecker showed up. *Campbell Automotive*, it said on the door. *Byers, Colorado.*

The driver backed up to Fezz's pickup, then got out of his truck to make the connections.

"She yours?" the man asked. "She's a beaut."

"Thanks," Fezz said. "I'm Ray."

The man rambled over and extended his hand. "Ernie. Ernie Campbell." At around five foot-eight and maybe 170 pounds, Ernie was closer to Ian's size than Fezz's. He shook hands with vigor. "Damn, you're a big boy."

Straight out of a movie, Ernie was the guy you'd imagine showing up in a tow-truck in the middle of nowhere. His graying hair was unkempt, his flannel shirt and jeans were filthy, and his skin was leather. The only thing missing was a set of crooked yellow teeth. Instead, Ernie sported a gleaming white smile which, when he flashed it, gave him a charming quality.

"Hop in the front," Ernie said.

"Where you taking it?" Fezz asked.

"My shop's an exit up. I'll drop it there and me or my guy will take a look when we open at nine."

"What do we do until then?" Ian asked.

Fezz deferred to Ernie. "Is there a hotel nearby, by any chance?"

"Sure thing. Right off the exit. Budget Host Longhorn Motel. Best motel in Byers." Ernie laughed. "Only motel in Byers, if you don't count the other one."

"Works for us." Fezz helped Ian into the tow truck and followed him in.

Ernie joined them. "I'll drop you off first, then your truck. If you got a phone, just give me your number and I'll call you when I find out what's wrong with her." He handed Fezz a card and pulled a pen from the cupholder.

"Perfect." Fezz wrote his number. "How long do you think we'll be down?"

Ernie showed the pearly whites. "Like I said, I'll call."

As Ernie pulled into the lane, Baez's lights switched off.

"Byers, Colorado." Fezz put his arm around Ian. "As good a place as any."

CHAPTER 4

"COME IN." Curtis Hammond closed his laptop and sat up in his chair. When the door opened, he slumped again. "Oh, Peter."

"Who were you expecting? Gandhi?" Peter closed the door behind him.

"Evie. She's apparently been putting out fires at home. She's on the warpath." Curtis hesitated, trying to hide his annoyance at the unanticipated interruption. "Did you need something?"

Peter strode across the room and sat, teetering on the edge of the black leather sofa. His face was etched with concern as he balanced his elbows on his knees and clasped his hands together. Curtis swiveled his desk chair to face his son.

"Father, there's been an incident." Peter presented his palm. "Before your blood pressure skyrockets, just know it's under control."

"What's under control, Peter?"

"There's no way to sugarcoat it. One of the disconsolates has expired."

"Expired?"

"Died."

Curtis squinted. Two deep lines formed above his eyebrows. "Who? What happened?"

"Garrett Brody." Peter said. "Died in his sleep. Some of the others found him this morning."

"How could this be?" Curtis groaned. "Again? Really?"

"These things happen."

"Sure they do. My problem is, they keep happening here. We can't afford this right now, Peter. You know that as well as I do. Where is he now?"

"In the loading bay. My guys moved him as soon as we found out."

"I'm sure the rest of them were going berserk," Curtis said.

"It doesn't take much to set them off."

"Exactly." Curtis said. "They're big enough pains in my ass already."

"They're in line. As much as usual, of course. But that's not saying much."

Curtis stood and paced. "I'll notify Garrett's family. This time, we're going to have to call the authorities."

"Hold on," Peter said. "Don't do that yet. Or, what I mean to say is, don't do that at all. Let me take care of it."

"This isn't like the others, Peter. People will be looking for Garrett. And there was a whole group of witnesses. In case you've forgotten, the reason they're in remediation is because of their big mouths."

"They have no access to the news," Peter said. "They won't know the difference. I'll be discreet, just like before. The guy had a heart attack, or whatever. There's nothing we can do for him now. It's better than calling attention to us."

"I've got the Feds breathing down my neck." Curtis's face had turned as red as the side of a barn. "This is not the time. We need to play by the book here—from now on. You know they're looking to crucify us." He forced a deep breath, then let out a throaty snarl. "Goddamit!" In a fit of rage, Curtis swiped the lamp from his desk with enough force to send it flying across the room. Cord catching, the lamp's trajectory shifted straight for the floor. The shade exploded on impact, sending green glass along the hardwood in all directions.

Curtis took another deep breath and tried to slow his pulse. Lately, it seemed the cards were all stacked against him. For so many years, things had run without a hiccup. People had been loyal. They'd believed in the mission.

He wasn't sure when it'd happened, but somewhere along the way stress fractures had begun to form. The hairline cracks were turning into fissures. Curtis could feel it in his gut.

The IRS was out to get him, that much was clear, but it seemed like the universe itself was in cahoots. People dropping dead was a sign. If he believed in God, he might have thought he was being smited.

Maybe he was getting old. Losing his edge. His powers of persuasion.

It didn't matter. He would fight. He would do whatever he could to keep his life's work intact. His oldest son, Peter, was his legacy. That is, as long as there was something left to leave behind.

"Father. Listen to me. I know you're feeling the pressure from all this scrutiny. That's why we must make this go away. Now more than ever. It would give them an in." Peter's eyes widened. "They would want to interview the witnesses. The last thing we need is to give the entire group of disconsolates a platform. Trust me, I can handle it. I've never failed you before, have I?"

"No."

Curtis had to admit, Peter was an asset and had become a strong leader. He was amazed how well Peter was able to turn off emotion amidst circumstances like these.

Even as a child, Peter had the ability to make tough decisions without being clouded by desire, anger, or empathy. It was one of his strongest qualities, even if overzealous private school counselors were quick to label him. Sociopathic tendencies, they suggested.

Laughable.

It was ridiculous how a supposedly exclusive educational institution could put stock in such pseudo-science. Peter was loyal, organized, and strong-willed—all traits Curtis himself had fostered. Traits he and Curtis shared. And Curtis, of all people, was the opposite of a sociopath.

"Do it," Curtis said. "No mistakes."

"Of course, Father." Peter smiled. "You know me. I don't make them."

CHAPTER 5

BLAKE STOMPED THE ACCELERATOR. The rented Ford Mustang dropped a gear and bucked forward.

"Look at this place!" Haeli hung her arm out the passenger side window. Her long dark hair danced in the wind. "No wonder your folks wanted to come here."

The sentiment was mutual.

On either side of the Dunedin Causeway was blue Gulf water and even bluer sky. A smattering of small islands pocked the flat horizon.

Although accustomed to living on the water, Florida's seaside was far different from Rhode Island's. Not better or worse. But distinct.

On the Gulf, the sky seemed bigger. The water seemed clearer. It even had a different scent.

Despite all it had going for it, Florida lacked the old-world charm of the Newport area as far as Blake was concerned. Maybe he was just biased.

"This should be Honeymoon Island here." Haeli studied her phone's screen, then pointed ahead. "Seven Dunoon Place is one of those buildings, or right behind those. Take your first right onto Gateshead."

Blake followed Haeli's directions, pulling through the maze of condos along the edge of the island's bulkhead.

Funny, he thought, how different it was to what he had pictured. By the time his parents had moved there, he and his parents had stopped speaking—save for the few clandestine phone calls from his father. Blake had never visited or even Googled the address to sneak a peek at their living situation—assuming Google offered the feature at the time, which it likely hadn't.

"This is it," Haeli said.

Long teal buildings spanned the block, a parking lot separating them from the street. It was very—what was the word he was looking for? Ah, yes—Florida.

The complex was made up of several buildings. Between each was a gap, offering a glimpse of the Saint Joseph sound. Gentle waves lapped up to the wall within a few dozen feet of the dwellings. It was a nice setup, for those who liked condos.

Each unit of the three-story buildings had exterior entrances of their own, all clearly marked. The one they were looking for would be at ground level.

"That's it right there," Blake said as they passed by. Haeli twisted to look over her shoulder. He figured she was probably worried they would keep driving, right back to the airport. Until he found the empty parking space marked "Visitor" and pulled in.

"Here we are." Blake shut off the car and sank into his seat with a sigh. "Long time coming."

"I'm proud of you, Mick." She rubbed his arm and smiled. "I know it took a lot to get here and call me a broken record, but I really think you made the right decision."

"It's surreal, you know? They're right over there. After all this time, they're a few steps away. So awkward when you step back and look at it. Me just showing up like this."

"You called like four hundred times. What else could you do? And not for nothin', but it's a little awkward for me too. I'd be anxious to meet your family under *normal* circumstances."

"Come on. They're going to love you. Everyone does."

"Of course they will. 'Cause I'm going to charm the socks off them." Haeli laughed. "Now give me a kiss and get your butt out of this car."

23

Blake complied with both directives.

As if slogging through wet concrete, they ambled arm-in-arm to the door and rang the bell.

A minute passed with no response.

"Try it again," Haeli said.

Blake pushed the button, then gave a few rapid knocks.

Again, there was no response or any noise from inside.

"Maybe they're out," Haeli said.

"We can find their parking space and see if the car's gone. The spaces are all numbered."

"We can wait for a bit if you want," Haeli said.

"Who knows how long they'll be? They could be on vacation this week for all we know. I can leave another message, but that's pretty much pointless."

"Or they're here and they're ducking us," Haeli said. "Can you see inside?"

Blake shrugged, shielded his brow with a cupped hand, and pressed his face against the window. "Can't see anything."

As if she didn't believe him, Haeli pushed Blake aside and tried for herself. Just as it was for him, of course, the gaps between the closed blinds were too slight to provide a glimpse.

"No one's there," a voice said from their side.

One unit down, a short woman with a golden-brown complexion and a bright red robe stood in the doorway. Her accent hinted at Middle Eastern origins.

"Oh," Blake said. "Do you know when they'll be back?"

The woman scowled as if annoyed—or confused. "Who are you looking for?"

"Sorry." Blake reached out his hand and approached the woman. "I'm Blake. Blake Brier. My parents live here."

"*Acha*," she said. "Sweetheart, the Briers left a year and half ago."

"You mean they've moved?" Haeli asked. "Where to?"

"I don't know. They did not say. One day they were here. Then they disappeared. It is not the first time."

"What do you mean?"

"It's no business of mine, but since I am never seeing you here, I am assuming you are not close with your parents."

You're right, it's no business of yours. Blake bit his tongue.

"What I mean to say is, do you know your parents are involved in the Church?"

"Yes, I'm aware." He glanced at Haeli. Her slack jaw told him she had as many questions as he did. "The Church of Clear Intention. Are you a member?"

The woman sneered. "Never." She looked around as if to check if someone was listening. "No good intention."

"Does the Church have something to do with them moving?" Haeli asked.

"I don't know. People come and go," the woman said. "But I do not doubt it. The Church owns that place. They own most of these. I did not know this when I came here. I wish I did. I would have gone to Miami like my cousin."

The woman grabbed the bottom of her robe and turned in an apparent effort to retreat inside.

Blake stepped forward. His voice carried an unintentional urgency. "Ma'am. Sorry. Are you saying my parents didn't own their condo? That the Church owned it?"

"Yes. They told me themselves."

"So you were friends? Were you close?"

The woman dropped the fistful of fabric. "We weren't friends. We were neighbors. People like them don't have friends. I talked to them now and then, that's all. It's smart not to get involved. Like I said, no good intention."

Blake could feel his face getting warm. He wasn't upset with the woman, none of this was her fault. He was upset with himself for waiting so long. The woman's obvious disdain for all things related to the Church only solidified what he already knew—he should have tried harder from the start.

"Is there anything you can tell us that may help us find out where they went?" Haeli asked.

"No," the woman said. "But they won't be far. Their precious

Church is here in Dunedin, they will be too. Trust me."

This time, as the woman started to make her exit, Blake didn't attempt to stop her. Still, she paused in the doorway and turned around again as if summoned.

"You want my advice?" The woman continued without waiting for Blake's answer. Which, at that point, would probably have been 'no.' "I don't know what you're looking for here. But if you're trying to save them, don't waste your time. There is no way to change their minds. Any of them. My advice is, let them go sweetheart. Let them go." With that, she disappeared and slammed the door.

"Geez," Haeli said. "Interesting woman."

"Not a good sign," Blake said. "We're here one minute and we already got the doomsday speech. I told you this Church was something else."

As Blake started back to the car, Haeli peeked through the window one more time, then called after him as she tried to catch up. "There was a bit of good news. Like she said, they probably didn't go far. Let's go over to the Church and ask. I'm sure they'll be able to point us in the right direction."

Blake turned, stopping Haeli in her tracks. "Believe me. I intend to."

CHAPTER 6

FEZZ UNZIPPED THE CARRY-ON-SIZED SUITCASE, grabbed the tube of toothpaste, and tossed it to Ian.

"Thank you." Toothbrush in hand, Ian withdrew to the bathroom, still in full view of the rest of the room. He turned on the water.

"Grab a nap while you can," Fezz said, loud enough for Ian to hear over the running water and the sawing of his brush. "I hope to be back on the road this afternoon."

Ian paused his task to respond. With a mouthful of suds, he tried to enunciate each word. "I'm not tired. I'm hungry. Can we find some food?"

"Sure." Fezz smiled.

As far as kids went, Ian was pretty easy. Not that Fezz had much experience to compare to, but he couldn't imagine other kids were as resilient. For the most part, Ian never complained. Long hours, poor conditions—Ian rolled with it. If he had some basic need to be met, he said so. It was akin to traveling with his team. Quiet professionals. And God knows, in those days there were plenty of long hours and poor conditions to go around.

"You're a quiet professional, Ian," Fezz said.

Ian was busy rinsing or just ignoring him. Ian did tend to disregard anything he found nonsensical.

"We'll take a walk. I'm sure we can find something to eat around here." Fezz zipped up the bag and tucked it next to the dresser.

The bag, and just about everything in it, was a recent acquisition. After the first night on the road, they had exhausted their supply of clothing and it'd been clear they'd need a few things to get them through until they could figure out where they were headed.

Washington, Pennsylvania, had served as their first temporary destination. The accommodations were about as luxurious as the Long-horn—the front seats of Fezz's truck.

Parked in a rest area, it'd been good enough for a few hours of uncomfortable shuteye. Fezz needed to get his eyes off the road for a bit, but his primary concern had been giving Ian's frenetic brain a rest. He had a lot to process, and it had no doubt been the longest day of his young life. Still, Fezz hadn't been sure Ian slept at all.

The following morning had started off with a visit to a truck stop to pick up some toiletries and use the bathroom. The place offered coin operated showers, but truck stop showers were notoriously shady. Fezz wasn't about to put Ian in that situation.

Next, they stopped at a nearby Marshalls department store. There they'd been able to pick up the small suitcase, some clothing, socks, underwear, and a pair of sunglasses that Ian thought were "cool."

"What's that thing?" Ian emerged from the bathroom, wiping his face with a small towel. He pointed at the top of the dresser.

"What thing?" As far as Fezz could see, there was nothing on top of the pressboard chest of drawers but a television and a remote control. "The TV?"

"That's a TV? Why is it so big?"

Fezz laughed. The circa 1989 tube television had a convex screen, no more than twenty inches on the diagonal, but was about three feet deep. It never occurred to Fezz that Ian had never seen one. Even he had forgotten how bulky they were.

"Welcome to the eighties," Fezz said.

Overall, the room's decor was more seventies than eighties. A desktop phone, stucco walls, commercial carpeting. But what really stood out were the brown and gold floral bedspreads that looked like they came straight out of 1975. Fezz had no doubt they were original—a hypothesis he preferred to ban from his imagination.

The place was old, but not disgusting. It was about as good as it got for sixty-nine dollars a day. Besides, there were no better options, and it would only be home for a few hours.

"You ready?"

"Ready." Ian bounced toward the door, wearing a t-shirt, shorts, and a smile. "I'm starving."

Fezz checked that the door would lock behind them, then the two made their way outside.

A pit formed in Fezz's stomach. An uneasiness, born from Ian's composure. From his smile.

There was no way Ian had yet come to terms with his mother's murder. Ian was a house of cards, waiting for a strong breeze. Fezz could feel it. His only solace was that he would be there to pick up the pieces after Ian's collapse. To reorganize the deck, so to speak.

In the same parking lot was a Mexican Restaurant that was closed until later in the afternoon. Across the street off the main road was a feed and tackle store. Helpful, if Ian was a horse.

Heading north, they saw a sign for "Byer's General Store" across from the Sinclair gas station. "Let's try that," Fezz said. "A general store has to have something."

Past the shared bank branch and Motor Vehicle Department building, they found the larger-than-expected red barn-like building, set back from the road. Further north, there was nothing but open land. Aside from wherever Ernie's shop was, Fezz figured they'd just surveyed the entirety of Byers' commercial district.

"Look." Ian pointed at the sign announcing "Subs. Pizza. Deli."

"We've come to the right place," Fezz said.

"I want roast beef and cheese and mustard. And potato chips."

Blake's favorite. Ian was a creature of habit. And Blake had convinced him the only way to eat a roast beef sandwich was with potato chips inside. Comfort food, Fezz figured. Ian deserved some comfort and, truth be told, a little bit of home sounded good to him, too.

"Look at that girl," Ian said as they approached the main entrance. "She's my age."

Sitting on the edge of a picnic table to the right of the main doors was a cute young girl with light brown shoulder-length hair, wearing a yellowing white tank top and cutoff jeans. Her face was crusted with dirt, and her hair was a mess. She looked pathetic. Which, Fezz assumed, was the point. A cardboard sign, leaning against the base by her feet, read simply, "Hungry."

"That's one thing you have in common. You're both starving." Fezz ushered Ian inside.

"That's not funny," Ian said.

"You're right," Fezz admitted. "It's not funny. Just like it's not funny how that girl's parents or guardians, or whoever, dress her up and send her out to beg for money. Disgusting, really. Everyone's got a racket, I get it, but she's a kid." Fezz looked around. "Wow. This is a legit grocery store."

By the name and everything else they'd seen so far, Fezz expected to find a strange assortment of food items mixed in with hardware, trinkets, and possibly a healthy selection of guns and ammo. Instead, they found a Winn Dixie.

At the deli counter, they took a number, even though there was only one person ahead of them. A pudgy older man worked behind the counter, wearing a white coat smeared with blood. He looked like the demented doctor character in an independent horror flick.

"Fezz, I was thinking about what you said in the truck yesterday."

"Which thing?"

"About me going to school."

"Okay. Are you nervous?"

"I don't think I need to go to school." Ian hesitated, avoiding Fezz's gaze before he continued. "If we went home, Griff said he would teach me everything he knows. And Blake too. I could be just like Mom."

At the mention of the friends they'd left behind, Fezz's heart sank to his stomach. He steeled himself to answer the young man beside him. "We're not going back, Ian. I told you already. You need to be around other kids your age. You need a real life, a teenage life. If your Mom wanted you to be like her, she would have taught you herself. It's the opposite of what she wanted for you."

"But she's not here, is she?"

Fezz wanted to bark back at him, but there was nothing to say. No words to combat the sad statement. She wasn't there, that much was true. It was why he had to hold fast in her stead. Ian's warped logic be damned.

"Next," the man in the white coat said.

"Two roast beef subs," Fezz replied.

"Twelve or sixteen-inch?"

"Sixteen," Ian said. "And can I have two?"

"That's a big sandwich. You sure you can eat two?"

"I'm really hungry."

"Fine." Fezz picked up three bags of chips from the rack in front of the counter. "Make it three roast beef. American cheese."

"Comin' up."

Fezz took a breath and put his hand on Ian's shoulder. "I know you miss everyone. I do too. But you have to trust me that I know what is best. I'm looking out for you, and you might disagree with me at times, but you have to know that everything I'm doing is for you."

"For me, or for my Mom?"

Ouch.

The kid wasn't wrong. Some of it was for Ima. Fezz was partly to blame for what had happened to her, after all. So there was some guilt involved, but that wasn't the whole story, was it? One thing was for sure, Ian's intuition was uncanny. And somewhat annoying.

"Do me a favor," Fezz said. "Give it some time. See what comes. You might feel differently in a few months. Deal?"

Ian shrugged.

They waited in silence for their order.

"Here ya go, three roast beef." The man handed over the sandwiches and started cleaning his station.

Fezz paid after first having an unusual conversation with the woman at the register about her ex-boyfriend's new girlfriend Lainey, who she described as a "crack whore, tweaker bitch."

Grabbing his two sandwiches, Ian scurried toward the exit, again leaving Fezz to play catch up.

Outside, Ian hooked left. Fezz watched as Ian handed one of the two sandwiches to the young girl at the picnic table. Her eyes lit up.

"Thank you," the girl said. Her voice was sweet and carried a convincing air of appreciation.

"I'm Ian."

She smiled as if struggling to stop herself. "I'm Jodi."

"Are you homeless?"

"Ian," Fezz interrupted. "Come on, let's leave her alone."

For a moment, Ian stood silent, looking at Jodi. Jodi seemed to stare back, directly into his eyes, as if they were each caught in a tractor beam. Jodi's smile dropped away, and the sadness returned.

"Bye." Ian said.

Jodi raised her hand in a motionless wave. "Bye."

As Ian joined Fezz and started walking away, Fezz put his hand on Ian's shoulder. "That was very kind."

Ian looked over his shoulder and sighed. "She's kind too. I can tell."

Fezz glanced back. Jodi was hunched over the table, devouring the sandwich like a wild animal.

"Hungry," indeed.

CHAPTER 7

PETER HAMMOND SAT in his car, his eyes closed. Parked behind an unoccupied building on North Occident Street in Tampa, Peter not only soaked in the moment of seclusion, but the raw power radiating from within him. He visualized his aura, green and glowing, as it enveloped the car, the lot, the building. It extended to the center of the earth and the far reaches of the atmosphere.

Out loud, he reaffirmed his faith. "I am the master of my own mind. The creator of my world."

To give credit where credit was due, it was his father who'd taught him life's most important lessons. The simple secrets that most people were too dull to comprehend.

Mindfulness and projection.

"The universe can't give you what you want unless you ask for it," his father would say.

Wherever he was, Peter claimed his little bit of the world for himself. The master of his reach, as the affirmation went.

This moment was only another small test. A foregone trial of his confidence and conviction. One that wouldn't even cause him to break a sweat.

For most people, he imagined, waiting in broad daylight for a cop with a dead body in their trunk would qualify as a stressful day. But not for Peter. He had learned to trust the Universe. To accept its protection.

That's not to say he hadn't faltered in the past. The first time, there had been some trepidation. But that was before he'd broken through the final barrier. Before he achieved what the Church called "transcendent awareness."

Members often asked the question, "How will I know if I achieve it?" Peter himself could remember asking the same question of his father as a child.

"You will just know," was always the answer. And the obvious one. Logic said that someone with ultimate awareness would not also be confused about their own state of enlightenment. Conversely, someone who needed to ask that question—yeah, not quite there yet.

Peter's final triumph came only a few months prior. A reward for a lifetime of hard work and reflection, delivered by the universe in the form of an online newspaper article. Happening across a fluff piece on the recent death of a Hall of Fame baseball pitcher named Gaylord Perry, Peter had his epiphany.

The article outlined Perry's many accomplishments and made an effective case that the late pitcher was one of the best of all time. Only Peter had never heard of him. No one he knew was talking about him. Other than the one obscure article, no one was paying him any reverence.

Here was a man who had reached the top of his profession, Peter'd thought at the time. He had achieved ultimate success and yet the world had forgotten him. Disregarded him as soon as he was no longer relevant.

It was that notion that got Peter thinking. Awareness is understanding that nothing you do matters to anyone else but you. The world is you. The universe is you. And only you. Everything else revolves around the individual. A matter of perception.

With this revelation came another. His father, the Sage, the great Guru himself, hadn't yet figured it out. Of all the talk, the preaching and patting himself on the back, it was just that—talk.

Awareness meant seeing things how they really were. The sad

reality was, his father was weak. The Church needed Peter to survive. To truly thrive. He was sure of it. And he would do whatever was necessary to make that happen.

Preceded by the telltale whine of the motor, an old Ford Crown Victoria rounded the corner, disrupting Peter's meditation.

It was who Peter expected. Detective Grady Larson.

A longtime member of the Church, Larson had proven himself loyal by answering the call to service on more than one occasion. Although he looked like a chronic alcoholic, his disheveled appearance was deceiving. Larson was as sharp as he was dedicated. No, he would never be able to get out of his own way enough to reach transcendent awareness, but that didn't mean he wasn't useful.

Both men stepped out of their cars at the same time.

"What happened now?" Larson asked.

"Another untimely demise," Peter answered.

"But how?"

"How should I know?" Peter popped the trunk and motioned for Larson to join him at the back of the car. "Heart attack, stroke. Why don't you ask him?"

Larson peered inside. "Shit. Garrett?"

Peter nodded.

"Is that Karma or what?" Larson handed Peter a pair of rubber gloves and commenced in putting on his own pair.

"That's exactly what it was. Karma."

A few weeks prior, Garrett Brody had gotten ahold of a phone to contact someone at the Sheriff's Department. He'd made claims of being held against his will, of being abused. Larson had stepped in to squash any possible investigation by making Brody out to be a crackpot with a history of delusions. The deputies had taken Larson's word and had trusted him to handle it.

What upset Peter was not that Brody had called the police, nor that he'd told them he was being held—that part was true. It was that he'd claimed abuse. To Peter, it was disheartening that a member could become so jaded and short-sighted as to not appreciate the efforts of so many.

"We tried our best to help him," Peter said.

"You can only do so much." Larson shook his head over Brody's corpse. "Still, I think you lucked out on this one. Not to disrespect the dead, but he was going to keep trying until he got someone to listen. Someone would have eventually paid attention to him." He looked back at Peter, eyebrows raised. "You get that, right?"

"I do. That's precisely why it's important to maintain strict control of the disconsolates. They've been corrupted and they're not thinking clearly. It is imperative they remain isolated from the naysayers until they complete the program. Their salvation depends on it. I remind you of this because when you rise to the echelon, you will have their well-being in your hands."

"Of course, I understand." Larson reached in and grabbed hold of Brody's legs. "Help me lift him."

Peter took the arms, and the two hobbled toward the building. "Shouldn't we just dump him in the glades? Let the gators handle it?"

"Na. Don't want one of those boy scouts from the county getting hold of this. They'll make it their mission. Nothing better to do. This way I can jump the case. Make sure it doesn't go anywhere."

When Larson stopped walking, Peter let go. Brody's body hit the ground with a thud.

"Careful." Larson slowly lowered Brody's legs. "There can't be any post mortem damage. It would be impossible to explain if he was here by himself."

"My fault." Peter stepped back and wiped off his shirt and thighs as if Brody had left some invisible film on him. "Do you have the stuff?"

"I do. But first we need to pull up his shirt and pull down his pants."

"Why? It's supposed to look like an overdose, not a rape."

Larson laughed. "We need to look for lividity. Where the blood pooled after he died. Was he on his stomach? His side? If we don't position him exactly as he was, the lividity won't match, and it'll be obvious he was moved."

"Ah. That's why you're here, Detective."

"Yes it is," Larson said. "But this really should be the last time. I get why you don't want this blowing back on the church, and I'm happy I've been of help, but we're pushing our luck here. We're running the risk of getting caught. I know we didn't kill the guy, but it'd be a hell of a time trying to explain, ya know what I mean?"

"Let's just hope there isn't a next time," Peter said.

Larson positioned Brody with care, making slight adjustments as he went.

"You can just call the police. It might be a pain in the ass for a bit, but it is what it is, right? People die. Even at church." Larson surveyed the finished product. "Now for the final touch."

Watching Larson work was a joy. He had real potential in the organization. The ability to execute without emotion—it was a rare skill, for sure.

"A touch of magic pixie dust." Larson took a bag of white powder from his pocket, dipped his gloved finger inside, and then shoved his finger inside of Brody's nostrils. He let a little powder fall onto his lip, then dropped the bag where Brody would have been sitting before falling over. "Opiate overdose. It's an epidemic."

"Awful, isn't it. As I was driving through this shitty town to get over here, I couldn't believe the squalor. These junkies are right out in the open. The homeless, the poor, all worthless. That's what sets us apart from them, Grady. Taking control of our own destinies. It just solidifies the importance of our mission."

Larson removed his gloves and wrapped them around themselves. "You hit the nail on the head. They've forfeited control to the drugs. The people out here are being ravaged by this stuff. If only we could put them in your remediation program, that would be something."

"Remediation is for those who have the drive but have lost their way. These people are on their own path. And it doesn't end well.

"Sad but true," Larson said. "People are dying every day. That's the whole reason this works. There are so many of these overdoses, we don't even order a tox screen anymore. No point, the case would already be closed by the time it got back. On to the next one."

"And if they did the screening?"

"Then there'd be questions," Larson said. "But for a medical like this, it still wouldn't go anywhere. It would just be assumed he croaked before he was able to ingest it, I guess." Larson headed for his car.

"Your help is much appreciated. You exemplify the pillars, brother."

"Thanks. Will I see you at the seminar next week?"

"Of course."

"Great." Larson got in his still running car and rolled down the window. "I wouldn't stick around here much longer if I were you."

"Don't worry," Peter said. "The Universe has my back."

CHAPTER 8

"IS THIS A CHURCH OR A FORT?" Haeli gawked at the enormous concrete wall spanning a half mile stretch of Orange Street along the eastern edge of an adjacent bike trail. Above the partition poked a bevy of tinted windows and tall palm trees. "It looks like a freakin' embassy."

On the left, the driveway of a small marina mirrored the driveway to the compound on the right. Although flanked by huge iron gates, the entrance remained wide open. To Haeli's point, it did resemble an embassy. In a weird way, it was one. A foreign consulate, where the prevailing rules of common sense didn't seem to apply. Based on every-thing Blake knew about its doctrines and practices, it might as well have been its own country.

Blake pulled in and parked in one of the spaces encircling a central fountain. Beautiful grounds, impressive structure—at least what they could see of it. In either direction, the modern glass and steel complex disappeared into the distant bloom of palms and maples.

From the overhead google view, Blake and Haeli had determined the compound consisted of several separate buildings, joined by covered walkways or pedestrian bridges. He'd known it was large, but now, seeing the multistory structure in person, Blake was sure it was tens of thousands of square feet.

"Don't forget this." Haeli reached into the back seat to retrieve the document Blake had brought along. On it were photographs of his parents, albeit younger versions of them, and their identifying information—name, dates of birth, biometric data.

Haeli had poked fun at him when he'd printed it out, saying that they weren't lost kittens. She may have been right, but Blake wasn't taking any chances. Especially now that he learned they had disappeared from their condo. He would show it to anyone and everyone who might be able to point him in the right direction.

Blake stepped out. Haeli didn't.

"You coming?"

"You go." Haeli said. "I'll be right behind you. When I come in, act as if you don't know me."

Divide and conquer.

"Gotcha." Blake closed the door and trotted to the lavish main lobby, dossier in hand.

Inside, he was greeted by an attractive woman, sitting behind a massive circular desk. "Welcome to the Church of Clear Intention. My name is Anastasia, how can I help you?"

Anastasia's accent was immediately recognizable. Blake sometimes heard it in his sleep. Anastasia was Russian.

"I hope you can." Blake slapped the paper on the desk, then scanned the expansive room. In each of the two far corners, along the same wall as the front doors, stood a man. One larger than the other, both wore identical polo shirts that stretched against their chests and arms. "I'm trying to contact two of your members." He slid the paper toward Anastasia. "I'm family."

Anastasia smiled, took the paper, and turned toward her computer screen.

"I understand you have residential buildings on the premises, is that correct?"

"It is." Anastasia kept her attention on the screen as she tapped the keyboard. "Some of our more involved members prefer to visit for extended periods of time. Do you mind if I ask your name?"

"My name is Blake."

"Brier?"

"So you're familiar with them?"

Anastasia gave a deadpan expression and held up the document. Even from a distance, the large font made the name Brier legible.

"Ah, of course. If it helps, I believe they're currently staying here."

Of course, Blake had no reason to believe that. But it was a plausible theory. And if it were true, it was better that Anastasia thought he had more intel than he actually did.

"That's not possible," Anastasia said. "I know everyone who resides with us, and I do not recognize these people. I have no record of these names in my system. I'm sorry, I think you're in the wrong place."

Blake laughed. Both out of frustration and the absurdity of the statement. "They have been members for thirty years. Don't tell me they're not in your system."

Out of the corner of his eye, Blake caught movement. The security guards had moved from their positions and began squeezing in tighter.

"Easy boys, just —" As Blake spun around to address them, he came face-to-face with Haeli. She caught him by surprise.

Haeli grinned. "Hi there."

"Sorry, Ma'am," Blake said. "I'll just be another minute."

"No worries," Haeli said. "I'm just curious. Heard so much about this place. Are you a member?"

"I'm not." Blake said.

"Miss, I can help you?" Anastasia asked, side-eyeing Blake. "Mister Brier was just leaving."

"No, he wasn't," Blake said.

"That's okay, I'll just wait over here." Haeli moved off to the sitting area under an elaborate low-hanging chandelier.

"Look, Anastasia. I'm not leaving here until I get some answers. Call whoever you have to call to get me someone who can help."

"I really do apologize, Mister Brier, but we cannot have you upsetting arriving guests. Like I said, I think you are mistaken. There is nothing I can do for you. Now I'll have to ask you to please leave."

With a slight jerk of her head, the two security guards pounced, each grabbing one of Blake's arms. "Let's go," one of them said.

For a second, Blake tensed, preparing to lash out. A reflex. One that he had to make a concerted effort to override. He wanted to cause a stir. Shake the tree to see what would fall out. Not to get in a fight. Besides, this was a battle he'd probably lose.

"Fine. I'm going." He raised his hands.

The guards let go and followed Blake to the door.

From behind, Blake could hear the Russian accent. "Sorry for the wait. Come, let me get you some materials. We have a lot to offer—"

———

"I THOUGHT YOU LEFT ME." Haeli jumped into the passenger seat, gripping a stack of brochures, and slumped down in her seat.

"I figured you'd find me." After getting thrown out, Blake knew they'd be watching him. He pulled out, circled the block for a few minutes, then returned to the marina parking lot across the street from the compound. "What'd you find out?"

Haeli handed Blake one of the tri-fold promotional pamphlets. "There's a free seminar called 'Getting In Touch With Your Intuition,' if you're interested."

Blake grimaced.

Haeli giggled. "These people are a different breed. Anastasia asked me what size my waist is. What kind of question is that?"

Blake rolled his eyes, then stared ahead and sighed. "Well, that was a total fail," Blake said.

"Not entirely."

"How do you figure?"

"When you left, our favorite Russian ambassador got a phone call. It was about you. She seemed nervous. She told them you were there looking for your folks and that she didn't tell you anything. Promised to call the person if you came back." Haeli paused and chewed at the inside of her lip. "I think they're in there. Those people are hiding something."

There was no doubt they were hiding something. The question was, what? And why?

"Let's go get settled at the hotel," Blake said. "We might be here a little while."

CHAPTER 9

GIFT SHOP, hair salon, post office. The few shops Fezz passed during his walk into town could have been found in Newport, RI, or anywhere else. But here, everything seemed foreign. At first blush, the Kazakhstan steppe came to mind.

With wide open expanses of near-flat terrain, dusty roads, and weak collections of corrugated steel buildings and prefab homes, the place was more reminiscent of an outpost than a town. A modern-day Dodge —without the brothels, gambling halls, or saloons. Then again, he'd only just arrived.

A half mile down the main street, he found what he was looking for. Amidst a backdrop of silos and power lines, was Campbell Automotive. A boxy steel building with two garage bays, it fit the town's prescribed style. Likewise, the dirt yard was decorated with several broken-down cars in various stages of disassembly, and there were two large Harley Davidson motorcycles parked in front of the front door. So close, in fact, they made it difficult for Fezz to squeeze by.

Fezz swung the glass door open, jingling the attached sleigh bells. "Knock, knock. Ernie?"

It took a moment for Fezz to process the scene in front of him. Behind the cluttered counter and in the corner was Ernie, his bright smile hidden behind tense lips. A handful of his flannel shirt was balled up in the fist of a greasy-looking man with a ponytail, wearing a black leather vest. The man's arms were covered in poorly drawn tattoos.

Behind him was another biker, a foot shorter, who stared back at Fezz. Frozen, as if he had gotten caught with his hand in a cookie jar. Fezz figured that was precisely the case.

If anyone knew a shakedown when he saw it, it was Fezz. He often served as the intimidation factor, only he was used to extracting information instead of money. Something told him these guys were more interested in the latter.

"Ray, I'm busy right now." Ernie spoke with insistence, but his tone carried a message of defeat. "Come back in a bit. We'll get you squared away then."

Fezz understood. Though unintentionally, he had injected himself into an already volatile situation. Extortion doesn't just happen once. It's an ongoing deal. And Ernie was no doubt used to it.

"Give 'em what they want and they'll leave" was most likely Ernie's tactic. And not a bad one, when you're outnumbered.

But Ernie wasn't alone. Not this time.

"Why don't you let go of him?" Fezz eyed the man gripping Ernie's shirt.

Both men stood speechless. The nerve of him. The gall.

Without letting go, the big man in the vest finally spoke. "Who the hell are you?"

Fezz's eyes narrowed. "I'm Ray. That's my buddy Ernie. And you're —wasting my time."

The big man let go with a push, sending Ernie staggering back into the wall. While Ernie straightened his shirt, the big man made a show of walking along the shelving units, running his hand over the various car parts. "I don't know you, Ray. You from out of town? That would explain why you think you can come in here and talk to us like that."

"He's just a customer, Snake." Ernie said. "He's got nothing to do with this."

"He does now." Snake picked up what looked like a shock absorber and bounced it in his hand as if testing its weight. He spoke with a condescending confidence. "But we're civilized men, right? Reasonable men." Snake approached, tapping the metal tube against his other hand. "You can keep your mouth shut, leave now, and forget about this little conversation. Or—"

The shorter man came around the counter, his chest puffed up. He stood to Fezz's side.

Fezz gave it a beat, mostly to see if Snake was going to finish his sentence. The guy was a walking parody, and pretty entertaining. But since it appeared Snake was all out of choice nuggets, Fezz took his turn to speak.

"Look, gentlemen." Fezz raised his hands to chest level. "I'm not going to lie. There was a time where I would have taken that hunk of metal and shoved it down your throat."

Snake's lips pursed and his eyes widened. Fezz held up one finger.

"But," he continued, "I'm not looking for a fight today. How about we all leave and let this man conduct his business how he sees fit?"

"That's not how this works," the shorter man chimed in.

"I know, I know. I get it. Normally, I'd agree with you. But listen guys, I've had a hell of a week. My truck broke down, I lost an amazing woman, and I don't even know what I'm doing out here. I can't catch a goddamn break and the last thing I wanted was trouble. Not with you, the law, the—" Fezz paused. "Aw, screw it."

Lunging to his left, Fezz caught the shorter man in the nose with his elbow. He yelped and fell backward.

To the right, Fezz dodged the metal pipe he knew would be coming. He grabbed it with his left hand and swung it over Snake's head, spinning him away and forcing him to let go.

Fezz reached over Snake's shoulder and gripped the other end of the pipe, driving it into his throat lengthwise. Snake's back pinned against Fezz's abdomen, Fezz applied more pressure to Snake's neck.

The smaller man got up and lunged forward. Fezz held his grip and kicked the rushing man in the left thigh, knocking him off balance and sending him to the ground.

Gagging, Snake reached into his waistband and pulled out a pistol.

Before he could point it in Fezz's direction, Fezz let go of one side of the pipe and swung hard at Snake's gun hand.

The crack of small bones preceded the sound of the pistol clattering on the floor. Fezz kicked the gun toward the counter. It laid spinning on its side.

With one meaty hand covering Snake's face and the other behind his head, Fezz dragged the man toward the door and threw him with all his might.

Snake's momentum pushed the door open and sent him crashing into the two bikes, knocking them over. Snake landed on top of one with a groan.

The smaller man lunged again. This time, instead of coming at Fezz, he pushed through the door to join his buddy outside.

Fezz picked up the pistol, released the magazine, cycled the round out of the chamber, and locked back the slide. He opened the door and threw the empty gun at the smaller man—who was attempting to pick up his bike—and struck him in the ear. The man shrieked and cupped the side of his head with his hand.

Fezz was going to say something clever. To put a finer point on it. But there was no need. The big bad bikers were done. He could see that, and he had no desire to waste any more energy on them.

"You okay?" Fezz asked.

Ernie nodded. He rolled his chair out from under the counter and sat. "What'd you go and do that for?"

Outside, the Harley motors roared to life and tires squealed.

"That's why." Fezz motioned toward the sound of the thugs fleeing.

"I'll admit, it was incredible to watch, but it's only going to make things worse. I'm going to have to pay for that."

Ernie was right. Fezz had just stirred up a hornet's nest. There were probably more where those two came from and none of them would be happy. Fezz knew he should have walked away. He had every intention to. But he just couldn't help himself. Old habits, as they say.

"I'm sorry, Ernie. My big dumb ass should have stayed out of it. If I could learn to mind my own—"

"No, no, no." Ernie smiled. "Don't beat yourself up about it. I'm being dramatic. I'll be fine. Really. Hey, the good news is I was able to take a look at your truck. Easy fix."

"That is good news."

"The bad news is I don't have the parts. They're on order, but I won't have them 'til tomorrow. I hope."

"Looks like we're staying the night. I'll check in tomorrow."

"Sounds good. Try to keep out of trouble will ya?"

"I'll try my best. Listen, Ernie, you have my number. If these guys show up again today or tomorrow, call me."

Ernie laughed. "Not a chance."

CHAPTER 10

CURTIS HAMMOND DOUBLE-CLICKED, expanding the overhead feed of the lobby to full screen. From the comfort of his office, he watched the replay unfold with full audio.

It wasn't a shock to find Blake Brier in his lobby. This day was inevitable. Only Curtis had thought it would have happened much sooner.

From what he could remember, Blake was a scrappy kid. Even back then, he'd been a pain in the ass. Now, a grown man, he looked downright dangerous. Not necessarily because of his size, or physical presence. It was the look of determination in his eyes. In his voice.

Curtis knew a little bit about Blake's background, in a general sense. He didn't strike Curtis as someone who would walk away without a fight.

But as fascinating as Blake Brier may have been, he wasn't the reason Curtis had watched the video clip three times already. That honor belonged to the woman who came in after Blake.

As soon as Curtis saw her, he was stricken. Smitten, even. She was gorgeous. And she had a dangerous, exotic quality all her own. A dead ringer for Gal Gadot, in his opinion, Curtis had to zoom in to be sure it wasn't the actress.

In the beginning, Curtis hadn't been very discerning about the women he brought into the fold. None of them dogs, willingness was still their primary virtue. Then, as the willing became more plentiful, Curtis began to curate. Often to his ever-changing tastes. It was the benefit of polygamy, he thought. Variety.

In general, it was a numbers game. Like in his youth, the more shots you took, the more chance of landing a date. It was statistics.

Most of his friends were too worried about rejection to put themselves out there. But the way Curtis always looked at it, nineteen rejections for one taker weren't bad odds. So long as you were willing to play twenty times.

It was the same in business. And above all else, business was what he was in. Though currently, his mind was clouded by one thought. It had to be purged if he were to regain balance and there was only one way to do it. He had to take his shot.

Curtis picked up the receiver and pressed the button for the reception desk. "Anastasia, can you come up here for a minute? Have Bruce take over."

Anastasia arrived after one more loop through the video.

"Come in," Curtis said. "I have a quick question."

"About Mister Brier?"

"No. You handled that perfectly. It's about the woman who came in afterward."

"Ah, yes." Anastasia smiled. "You like her?"

Curtis chuckled. "Yes."

Anastasia understood his interest, he figured. She had been around a while, and she didn't seem to mind dishing the dirt. The funny thing was, Anastasia had no interest in being a member nor in Curtis, as far as he could tell. They had never been involved, sexually or otherwise. He had no knowledge of her personal life, and he made it a point not to pry. Of course, as was usually the case when it came to any woman who wasn't interested in him, he suspected her to be gay.

"What did she want?" Curtis asked.

"She's interested in joining. Her name is Adrianna. She said she was intrigued after meeting a few members at an event. I gave her all the information and asked if she wanted to set up a tour. She said maybe later."

"Did you get her number?" Curtis asked.

"Of course. I wrote it down in the book. Do you want me to go get it?"

"That's okay. Is Evie in the building?"

"Yes, I believe so."

"Let her know I need to see her."

"Yes, sir." Anastasia turned to leave. High heels clacking, her white flared skirt bounced up her thigh. Curtis watched until she was out of sight.

Curtis could have called this Adrianna himself, but he had learned that having a woman reach out was much more effective. And there was no one better than his right hand woman, Evie. Although she was one of the wives, and mother to one of his children, Evie had become so much more.

While it was true that the "marriages" weren't legally recognized by the state, internally they were every bit as binding. A symbolic commitment for life that Curtis took seriously.

As unusual as it was, he and Evie no longer shared an intimate relationship—the same age as Curtis, she was way too old for him. Instead, their ties transcended the physical.

Den Mother was her official title, and it was the most important job of all. As the de facto leader of his harem, Evie was the go-to person for all the wives and children in the residence. She ran the show, and she ran it well. What was more important, she was a devotee. A true believer in the cause. Just like their son would be.

"You wanted to see me?" Evie popped her head in. Her bubbly disposition indicated that she was in a good mood. *Perfect.*

"I need your help with something."

"Is it about the wives?"

"It could be. Eventually."

Evie shot him a disapproving look. He knew it well, just as well as he knew she wasn't actually upset. If she were, he would have steered clear. For a woman of such small stature and advanced age, she could be terrifying. If Curtis thought about it, she was the closest he had to an actual wife.

"Who is she?" Evie smirked.

"Her name is Adrianna. Trust me, the girls would like her. Did you ever see Wonder Woman?"

"Linda Carter?"

"Not that one. The new one with the—never mind. Anastasia has the info. Can you do me a favor and get her in here for a tour? I'll handle it myself."

"I'll take care of it," Evie said, then turned to leave the room.

"Evie, don't take no for an answer okay? This one is special."

"Wow. I haven't heard you say that, since Dottie."

"You know how I get, Eve. Can't get her out of my head."

"I'll let you know what happens." Her patronizing sneer faded. "Are you all set for the ceremony tomorrow tonight? Do you need anything?"

"Is that really tomorrow?"

"It is. The girls have been preparing all day. I'll handle setting up this appointment, then I'm heading back to the residence. Cathleen asked for a sit down, and I want to nip any new drama in the bud."

Evie was in a hurry, like she always was. Between her personal growth and her duties, she never stopped moving. She had been on her way back out, inch by inch, since she'd stepped in. In another second, she'd be long gone. He decided to speak fast, while she was still in earshot.

"Thanks Evie. And don't tell the others about this yet. I want it to be a surprise."

CHAPTER 11

"HOW CUTE IS THIS?" Haeli exclaimed as she and Blake passed from the arched portico into the main lobby of the Fenway Hotel. "Did you see that rooftop bar?"

If Blake were being honest, it irked him a bit that Haeli was treating this like a vacation. Yes, the hotel was nice. In fact, it was very nice. But what mattered was that they were no closer to achieving their goal.

Normally, Blake would have been interested in the finer details. A historic building, the Fenway, was one of the original bastions of the jazz era and served as the country's first radio station. As a fan of jazz, the significance of the place wasn't lost on him. He just had a hard time caring right now.

"Cheer up." Haeli squeezed Blake around the waist. "We'll track them down. Heck, we can stay here as long as we need."

Blake tried to hide his grimace.

The interior was decorated with jazz relics with a modern-art twist, or the other way around. Either way, it was unique and inviting. If they did have to hunker down, there were worse places to do it.

"Should we have brought our bags?" Haeli stuck next to Blake as they approached the counter.

Blake shook his head. "The valet said they'd have them sent to the room."

"Good afternoon and welcome." The bleached blonde's silk scarf and blue blazer made her look like a flight attendant.

"Hi, we have a reservation," Blake said. "Brier."

"Ah, yes. Classic King with water view?"

"That's us."

"Very well. Do you want to use the card on file for incidentals?"

"That's fine."

The woman provided key cards and pointed them in the direction of their room.

"Hey, one quick thing," Blake said. "Do you know anything about the Church of Clear Intention?"

"I know of it. Everyone does." She looked at him curiously. "Why?"

"Just a shot in the dark, but—" Blake took the paper from his back pocket and unfolded it. "Have you seen these two? Have they been guests here?"

"No, I don't think so." The woman squinted. Her eyes flittered up and down as if sizing him up. No doubt trying to decide what his motives might be. "I can get the manager for you."

"That's okay," Haeli said. "We were just wondering. Thank you. We'll be heading to our room now." She tugged on Blake's arm.

Blake waited until they were out of earshot. "What?"

"I don't think we should be throwing that name out everywhere we go. People are going to think we're lunatics."

"Since when do you care what people think?"

"I'm just saying, it draws attention. We might want to keep a low profile, especially after today." Haeli swiped her key and pushed the door open. "Besides, if she was connected, do you think she'd tell you anything?"

Blake looked around the room. He had to admit, he was pleased. The furnishings were perfect, from the nightstands made to look like old trunks, to the Spanish tile in the bathroom. But the best part was the beautiful view of the lawn and ocean beyond.

"You win," Blake said. "Let's get cleaned up. Have a drink. A bite to eat. And figure out where we go next."

Haeli kicked off her shoes, tossed her handbag on the nightstand,

and hopped onto the bed. She turned to her side and supported her head in one hand while patting the comforter with the other. "Let's not get cleaned up just yet. I think you need something to take your mind off all this."

Blake rested his knee on the edge of the bed, leaned in, and kissed her. With a giggle, she wrapped her arms around him and pulled him in. There was no doubt she had a knack for taking his mind off everything else.

On the nightstand, Haeli's purse vibrated.

Blake sat up. "Is that—?" Haeli's phone was a burner. A throwaway number they had purchased for the trip. Unless it was a random cold call, there was only one thing it could be. "Pick it up."

Haeli fished out the phone and answered. "Hello? Yes, this is she." Haeli looked at Blake and nodded.

He mouthed the word, "Speaker."

"Hold on." Haeli put the phone on the bed and pressed the speaker button. "Okay, I'm here."

"Can you hear me? I'm calling from the Church of Clear Intention. I underst— you were interested — getting some — —ormation about what we have to off—."

The woman's voice was cutting in and out. With one bar of service, it was no wonder. Either they just found the one flaw with the hotel, or poor service came with a rinky-dink prepaid plan.

"I'm sorry. I'm having a little trouble hearing you." Haeli grabbed the phone, jumped off the bed, and moved to the window. "Can you hear me?"

"I'm just calling to extend an invitation. Mister Hammond has ask — me to extend the —rtunity for a f— private tour. I'm s— you would find it —rmative and inspiring."

Haeli gave Blake a goofy face and winked. "Oh, *the* Mister Hammond? Will I get a chance to meet him?" She looked back at Blake, scrunched her lips, and shrugged.

"If you'd like, I might be able to arrange that. I'll see what I can do."

"Okay." Haeli said. "When?"

"Say —morrow morn—? Is that good? Eight o'clock?"

"Eight o'clock. I'll be there. Thank you for the invite."

The phone disconnected.

"I guess I made an impression," Haeli said.

"You always make an impression."

"At least we're back in business. See, I told you. Low profile."

Blake motioned for Haeli to rejoin him on the bed. "Now all you have to do is find out where in that compound they're staying, and how we can get to them. Easy peasy."

Haeli put her palm on Blake's cheek. Her fingers brushed his ear. "That's for tomorrow." She leaned in close. Her warm breath filled his lungs and her lips hovered over his. "Now where were we?"

CHAPTER 12

ONE CHANNEL. 7.1, ABC. That was all Ian got. After Fezz sat him down and handed him the remote, he hadn't even left the room before Ian was bored with it.

To the onlooker, it might have seemed like he was riveted by the episode of General Hospital. But staring into space, he'd forgotten it was still on. His thoughts were permeated with the young girl he had met outside the grocery store.

Jodi.

A new sensation for him, he couldn't understand why his stomach felt wobbly when he thought of her. Was there something unusual about her? Was she some kind of witch?

Or maybe the sandwich just didn't sit right.

Still, the only thing he could think of was seeing her again. Getting another chance to say more than *hi* and *bye*. Even if he was able to work up the courage to go back, Fezz had told him to stay put.

But why? He was old enough to watch out for himself. He had killed a man.

The problem was, if he left and Fezz found out, there was a good chance he'd be the one getting murdered. On the other hand, the store was close by. He could go and come back before Fezz returned. For sure.

Ian stood up and sat down five times before he flipped the switch in his brain and committed. He was going. And he'd have to make it quick.

Wasting no time, he bolted outside. As soon as the door clicked shut behind him, he realized he'd made a mistake. He didn't have the key.

It didn't matter, he thought as he jogged. He could ask the people at the desk. Or he could wait outside the room and just tell Fezz that he stepped outside for a second and got locked out.

As he reached the big red building, he headed straight for the picnic table. Jodi wasn't there.

He checked the other side.

She was nowhere to be found. He had waited too long.

Overcome by emotion, Ian felt his eyes welling. Why was he so affected? What was wrong with him?

Staring out across the street, he caught a glimpse of someone walking. Someone with dirty blonde hair, a yellowing tank top, and jean shorts.

It's her.

Ian sprinted toward the street. "Jodi, wait."

But Jodi disappeared behind the building.

Ian did his best to catch up, but when he rounded the station, he couldn't see her.

There was only one place she could have gone. Through a missing piece of a chain link fence, and into the trailer park beyond it.

Finding himself in the backyard of one of the trailers, he cut straight through to the street. Remnants of asphalt implied the road was once paved, but it had since disintegrated into dirt.

There were several dozen trailers, maybe even more. All of them looked like they were about to fall down. Rusted cars, old furniture, and garbage littered the ground.

Out of the corner of his eye, he caught a glimpse of Jodi cutting through another one of the miniature properties.

Ian ran as fast as he could. If he lost sight of her again, he'd never find her in there.

CLEAR

As he snaked between two old station wagons, sinking into the mud driveway, and into the backyard, he was faced with a stockade fence. It was leaning and missing pieces, but it was otherwise solid. With one exception. At one edge, there was a small hole a small person could fit through.

Did she sneak through?

A tugging around his collar shifted his attention to the large woman whose grip was so forceful, his feet almost left the ground.

"What're you doin' on my property, you little rat?" She twisted him around to face her.

The woman's eyes were beady, and her skin was a splotchy red. She had to weigh at least three hundred pounds.

"Let go of me." Ian squirmed.

From over his shoulder, an object whizzed past him and at the woman's upper abdomen. The stone bounced off one of her huge sagging breasts and pinged against a metal drum full of burnt logs.

She let go and turned to the source. "You little bitch."

Through the hole in the fence, Jodi waved and yelled to Ian. "This way. Run."

Ian took two steps, then dove. He hit the ground and scurried through the hole on all fours.

Jodi was already several feet in front of him. She stopped running and turned. "Come on, hurry."

Through an obstacle course of trash, Jodi and Ian zigzagged through the park. She led him into a dilapidated trailer at the far side.

Ian hadn't looked back, but he knew there was no physical way the woman could have followed them.

Out of breath, the two of them sat on a cushioned bench. The trailer was clearly abandoned, but there were books everywhere. Hundreds of them.

"That was close." Jodi giggled. "You don't want to let Darlene get a hold of you. She'd probably cook you for dinner."

"Thanks for the help," Ian said. "I went back to the store to find you, but you—well, you know."

59

"You came to find me?"

Ian could feel the blood rushing to his cheeks. He didn't know what to say. "I mean, I just wanted to say hey."

"Hey," she said.

There was something pure about her face. Her gentle expression. It made Ian want to reach out and touch her cheek. To absorb some of whatever it was.

Of course, he didn't. "How old are you?"

"Thirteen."

"Cool." Ian's skin flushed again. "How'd you find this place? It's kinda gross but also kinda cool. Look at all these books. Do you think somebody actually lived here?"

"It's not that bad," Jodi huffed. Her mouth drew downward. "I bet your place isn't so great."

Ian's brain whirled. For someone with a high IQ, he was such an idiot. It was her place. She lived there. "I'm sorry, I meant—" There was no reversing it. The best he could do was change the subject. "So, are they your books? Or your parents'?"

Jodi still looked dejected.

"I'm sorry if I made you feel bad. I like it. It's great."

"They're mine." Jodi said. "The books. I ain't got no parents."

"Oh. I'm sorry. Who do you stay with?"

"I don't stay with nobody. This is mine."

"Really. By yourself?"

"So?"

"I'm just surprised, that's all. It must be hard."

Jodi put her palms on her lap and kept her eyes trained at her knees.

"I'm, s-s-staying at the motel," Ian stuttered. "I have to get back to my—um–Dad. If he'll let us stay overnight, can I come back and see you tomorrow?"

"If you want to."

"I do."

Jodi smiled. "Okay."

Ian stood and dried his sweaty hands on his shorts. He didn't know whether to offer a handshake or what, so he did nothing but turn and leave.

Jodi appeared in the open door. "Don't go near Darlene."

CHAPTER 13

HAELI ARRIVED in the lobby with two minutes to spare.

She had given herself ten minutes to walk from where she'd parked, several blocks away. It was just far enough.

At the front desk, Anastasia was already at her post. She had her hair tied back and was wearing a sheer blouse, encrusted with crystals. Swarovski, Haeli guessed.

Anastasia greeted Haeli with her trademark saccharine smile. "Welcome back, Adrianna. Mister Hammond will be right with you."

Picking up her phone, she said two words at the most, and hung it up again. "You can go in." She pointed at a set of frosted double doors. "Right that way. Mister Hammond will meet you there."

Haeli thanked her and followed the directions. As she approached the doors, a red light near the handle turned green.

Access control.

It was Haeli's mission to note as many security details as she could remember. There were three cameras in the lobby, one outside the door and at least two in the parking lot. It was a wonder they didn't pick up on the fact that she had gotten out of Blake's car the day before. Then again, the interesting parts happened after Blake was already inside.

In addition to the cameras, there were two guards posted in the lobby—a different two than there'd been the previous day. Outside, another drove around in a white Ford Fiesta.

Behind the secured doors was another long, narrow common area. This one featured art, more plush couches and chairs, and a whole line of ornate chandeliers on the ceiling. Doors lined either side, spaced every twenty feet or so.

Ahead, a man approached. She recognized him immediately.

Very much like his picture, Curtis was tall and handsome. The distinguished gray, the confident posture. He was fit, but not big. Overall, he screamed, "cocky."

"Adrianna, I presume."

"You must be Mister Hammond." She offered her hand.

He reciprocated, and with his thumb, caressed the back of her hand. "Please, call me Curtis."

Haeli did her best to hide her disgust. It had only been ten seconds and she already felt like she needed a shower.

CURTIS HAMMOND PACED in the small office off the lobby. In a moment, she'd be there. In his presence. Or he in hers, rather.

He buttoned his jacket.

Too much?

While wanting to impress, he didn't want to seem stuffy or unapproachable.

Definitely too much.

He pulled the jacket off and laid it on the vacant desk.

Better.

But if he were to appear casual—a real working man's man—he'd need to go all the way.

Outside the office, the sound of the door clicking open echoed through the empty chamber. As fast as he could, he ripped off his tie, unbuttoned his sleeves, and rolled them up to his elbows. Composing himself, he stepped out.

Ahead, a striking woman approached. He recognized her immediately.

Very much like in the video, she was slim and beautiful. The dark features, the sexy walk. She was fit, but petite. Overall, she screamed, "perfect."

"Adrianna, I presume."

"You must be Mister Hammond."

He touched her hand. Her skin was soft and supple. "Please, call me Curtis."

There was a slight coy smile, Curtis was sure of it. It had only been ten seconds and he was already in love.

"Come, let me show you around. I can answer any questions you have." Curtis started through the chamber. He kept the pace slow, so as not to interfere with any conversation.

"Thank you for inviting me," she said. "I didn't expect you to—I mean, I've heard so much about you. I thought you must be really busy. Do you always do this?"

"I try to. It's important to me to connect with the members, and potential members. I want people to know that I'm just like them. We're all the same. That's the whole basis of our mission here."

"So what do you have, like mass or something?"

Curtis chuckled. Adrianna was a bit of a ditz, it seemed. And that was alright with him. More than alright.

"No. Nothing like that. We have sessions. Sometimes in groups, sometimes one-on-one. The goal is unlocking your potential. The human brain is powerful. Mysterious. It is capable of more than most people are aware. It's our link to everything. We're connected to it, and it to us. But I'm getting ahead of myself."

Adrianna seemed to be having a favorable reaction, but he didn't want to lay it on too thick. He hadn't yet gotten a sense of what she was looking for. Everyone had a hook. That thing that makes them say, "I can see myself caring about this." Adrianna's was yet to be determined.

"Let me ask you this," Curtis said. "Do you ever feel like the world is preventing you from achieving your goals? As though, if you could only catch a break, you'd be doing so much more?"

"Sure. Like, if I could have just gotten that job I wanted, or if I could have just met the right guy."

She's single. Check.

"Exactly. What if I told you that I could teach you how to ensure you always did get that job or that raise or that goal? What if I told you you could have the perfect relationship, with all of your needs and desires fulfilled?"

"I'd say sign me up."

He smirked. "I thought you might."

Adrianna didn't know it yet, but he *was* that perfect relationship. In time, she would be his. He could feel it in his gut.

Over the next hour or two, he'd get far enough into her head to start tinkering. Little by little. But for now, he would try to focus. To deliver a legitimate tour. A professional pitch for the organization. It was a difficult proposition when the only thing he could think about was getting her into his bed.

"This area is where most of our classrooms are. There are seminars throughout the week. We have thousands of members, both locally and around the country. Some visit every so often, others are on a more serious path."

"Is it true that people actually live here?"

"It is. We have several residential wings, including our celebrity retreat. Although I can't say who has a suite here, I'm sure you've heard a few of the names in the media."

"Can we see?"

"We can't go inside," Curtis said. "Our guests' privacy is of the utmost importance, you understand. But I can show you our mediation rooms, our fitness center. We have three restaurants on site. This building is like the Pentagon, in a way."

"Pentagon. Like devil worshiping?"

Ditzy might be an understatement.

"No. Not pentagram." He chuckled. "The Pentagon is a building. And like that building, here, the more involved you are and the more progress you make, the further into the compound you can go. That is to say, the more exclusive it becomes. Come, I'll show you."

Curtis started to walk but realized she hadn't moved. Instead, she was looking up at the ceiling. By instinct, he looked up as well. "Are you okay?"

"Sorry. I was just thinking, you have a lot of cameras."

"Like I said, we take our members' safety and security as seriously as their privacy. More importantly, we look after their mental well-being. Look out this window—"

Placing his hand on her back, Curtis guided Adrianna toward the glass. He let it linger there, long enough to feel the ripples of hard muscle along her spine. It gave him chills. "This is our eternity garden. It's a place for our members to unwind. To be at one with nature. Of course, it's only for level threes."

"There are levels?" she asked, her eyes bright and wide. "How long does it take to get to level three?"

"It depends how much work you put in. A few months. A year. Of course, there are ways to skip ahead. My wives, for example, have full access to everything. I trust them all very much."

"So it's true what they say? You have more than one wife?"

"I have many. Does that shock you?"

The moment of truth.

Adrianna thought for a moment. "No. I think that's very progressive. I'm not much for monogamy myself."

Curtis struggled to maintain his composure. "Exactly. What law of nature says I can't love them all equally? And I must say, I'm known to spoil them all equally as well. They want for nothing. The best food, the highest quality jewels, whatever they want. And many of the women enjoy each other. Sexually, I mean. It's a very free environment."

Curtis glanced back to gauge her reaction. If she was into it, it would be written on her face. Instead, her attention was on her phone. "Are you texting?"

"Sorry. Yes. My mom. In Boca. She hits me up a hundred times a day. I swear the woman can't do anything by herself."

Damn it, Anastasia.

"I'm sorry you weren't told. We don't allow cell phones here. Anastasia should have collected it at the desk. We try to promote mindfulness within these walls. This type of technology is detrimental to that goal."

"No problem, I'll put it away. Mom will survive for an hour." She laughed as she stuck the device back in her purse. "This place is amazing. What's next? I want to see it all."

"We will. And I can show you my own residence. Even introduce you to my wives, if you want. Come, follow me."

Curtis walked on. His mark followed. So far, so good, he thought. The more time he had with her, the better. He'd clear the rest of the day if he had to. "What do you think so far? Is there anything specific you want to know?"

"Hmm." She thought for a moment. "Tell me more about the jewels."

CHAPTER 14

"FOUR EGGS, over easy. Bacon. Rye toast." Blake closed the menu and handed it back to the waiter.

"You're easy," the waiter said.

Blake took out his phone, punched in Haeli's new number and texted. "How's it going?" Then he waited.

The patio was bustling, and no wonder. The weather was perfect. Seventy-nine degrees. Clear and sunny.

At the table next to him was a fifty-something year old man with shoulder-length hair. It was hard to tell through the sunglasses, but from the way his head bobbed down and jerked back up every few minutes, it looked like he was struggling to stay awake.

On either side of him were two blondes wearing tight black mini dresses. At 8:15 in the morning, Blake guessed the clothing was from the night before. One of the women ran her fingertips around the man's back as if tracing a secret message.

"Rough night?" Blake asked.

The man twisted his head. "You don't know the half of it, mate."

Blake laughed and checked his phone again. Nothing.

"Cindy here kept me up past my bedtime," the man added in a gravelly tone.

"Shirley," one of the blondes said.

If this guy wasn't a washed-up rock star, he should have been. He would have given David Coverdale a run for his money.

"Right. Shirley." He pulled his sunglasses down and looked at Blake. His eyes were puffy and bloodshot. "I did enough blow and smack to kill a horse. It was a fuckin' blast. Cindy here had to hit me with the Narcan. Brought me back to life. Shit you not. That's why I keep a supply. Ya never know."

And thus, an illustration of the danger of striking up a conversation with a stranger. Blake reminded himself to keep his snarky comments to himself in the future. "Congratulations, I think. Sounds like a heck of a time."

"You should come party with us," Shirley said. "Shouldn't he?" She directed her question to Coverdale, who seemed to be engaged in another catnap.

Blake's phone buzzed.

Haeli.

He read, blocking out the freakshow beside him.

"With Hammond," she wrote. "Heavy security. Lots of cameras. All wireless. ALL WIRELESS. Call Griff. Get the Wi-Fi thing he was going on about. I'll keep you posted."

Wi-Fi thing.

A Piranha Wi-Fi Interceptor. And Blake knew exactly where she was going with it. With the flick of a switch, they could have eyes on the inside.

The problem was, the device they'd need wasn't easy to come by. When they worked for the Agency, it wouldn't have been a problem. But they no longer had that kind of access. Luckily, they all knew a few unscrupulous characters who did.

If this idea was going to work, he'd have to get the ball rolling as soon as possible. It was guaranteed to take some time. He'd make the call, but not here. He wouldn't be waiting around for breakfast. Anyway, he'd lost his appetite around the present company.

Blake stood, fished two twenties from his pocket, and dropped them on the table. "If you want some eggs, they're on me. Looks like you can use them."

"Right mate, thanks." He lowered his glasses again. "If you want to party later, stop by. Room 315. Change your life. Trust me."

The best response Blake could give, was none at all.

CHAPTER 15

FEZZ YAWNED and stretched his limbs.

Surprisingly, the bed was big enough that only his toes hung off the end. As motel beds went, he'd call that a win.

Ian was already in the bathroom.

"Everything good, bud?"

"Good," Ian called back through the thin door.

The previous night had been enjoyable. They ordered Mexican food and played cards until about nine o'clock, when they both hit the wall. Fezz conked out fast and slept through the night. He hoped Ian had done the same.

Rested, yes. But the gurgling in Fezz's stomach suggested he was about to have a different problem. Probably the same reason Ian was already camped out in the bathroom. Mexican food may have been a bad idea, but it was worth it.

"I'll have to get in there at some point," Fezz said. "No pressure."

"Almost done."

Fezz was surprised how well Ian had taken the news that they would have to stay overnight. Excited, even.

He was planning to get Ian off the road and settled in somewhere sooner than later. But it turned out to be a good thing. A chance to relax. Decompress. And spend a little quiet time with each other.

While he had hoped that they'd talk more about Ima, he wanted to wait for Ian to broach the subject first. When he was ready.

The toilet flushed, the sink ran, and Ian emerged, already dressed.

"I have to tell you something," Ian said.

"Okay." Fezz sat up in his bed.

Ian sat on the edge of the other. "I did something I wasn't supposed to. And I wasn't going to tell you." Clasping his hands, the veins in his neck popped out on either side.

Fezz couldn't begin to guess what Ian could have done that would suddenly have tied him in knots. "Well, you're telling me now, right? I'm listening."

"You know how you told me not to leave the room yesterday?"

It was obvious where this was going. Fezz let him continue anyway.

"Well, I did leave. I went back to the store to see Jodi. Only she had already left."

Fezz took a breath. Even though he knew Ian wasn't capable of doing anything awful, he was relieved to know he didn't rob a bank or steal a car or something.

"That's too bad," Fezz said. "She must have moved on."

"No. I saw her across the street, so I followed her."

"Followed her?"

"She went into this trailer park and there was a mean woman and we went to where she lived and she had a whole bunch of books and—"

"Wait." Fezz swung his legs off the bed. "You went into that trailer park across the street without me? What were you thinking?"

"I just wanted to talk to her."

"Ian. What is the deal with this girl? Why are you so fixated on her?"

As soon as the words came out of his mouth, Fezz knew it was a dumb question. Ian was a teenage boy. Jodi was a teenage girl. Enough said.

"The thing is, she doesn't have any parents. I mean she doesn't have anybody. She's alone, and she's got no money. And we could help her."

"What do you propose we do to help her? Give her money? Sure, no problem. Will that fix it? How about we adopt her? Take her on the road like a traveling circus."

"I don't know. I guess we can't really help her but we can do something nice. Can we take her out to eat? Like sit down and order food? Please?"

Taking the poor girl out to eat, while a nice gesture, wasn't exactly something the girl needed. Fezz assumed the idea had more to do with him than her. Either way, it wouldn't hurt him to throw Ian a bone. And the girl could use a few calories.

"If we're still here and she wants to come with us. We'll take her. Okay? Once." Fezz sighed. "But there's a good chance the parts will be in today. If he can get it fixed, we won't be staying tonight."

"We can go early tonight. Please."

"You don't even know if she wants to."

"She wants to. We can go together and ask her. Say yes. Please say yes."

"I already said yes, Ian. We'll ask her."

"Thank you, thank you." Ian lunged at Fezz and hugged him around the neck.

Fezz wasn't aiming to bribe Ian for his affection, but he'd take the payout, anyway.

"And don't be mean to her," Ian said.

"Of course not. But she is filthy. I mean, where are we going to take her looking like that? I don't even know if there are any restaurants in this town other than that Mexican place. I don't think either of us can handle another round of refried beans."

"It doesn't matter. Anywhere is fine. You're really going to like her."

"I'm sure I will. But buddy, don't get too attached. It'll just make it harder to leave."

"It's not like we have somewhere to go," Ian said. "Not really. We just picked a place on a map because it had big trees. We could go anywhere. Even here."

"Look around you, Ian. There's nothing for us here. This place isn't in the plan. It's a pit stop."

"What if my Mom were here?"

"Ian."

"No. Really. I know you liked her. Maybe loved her, I don't know. If she were here, would you go?"

"She's not here."

"But don't you wish she was?"

"Of course I do. And I know you do, too. Your mom was amazing. You, me, we'll both miss her forever. No matter where we go. But what does that have to do with anything?"

"You don't understand. You don't understand anything." Tears began to fill Ian's eyes. Maybe for the first time ever. "We can't go home. And we can't stay here. I just want my mom."

Ian broke down. Fezz grabbed him and held him tight, letting the boy sob into his shoulder.

They were on a journey together. In more ways than one. And Ian had just taken the first step.

CHAPTER 16

CURTIS'S TEMPLES THROBBED. The dull pain burrowed deep into his brain.

He eyed the bottle of rye among the various spirits by the window of his office. Never a big drinker, the selection was only there for the occasional guest. But if there was ever an occasion to start, this might have been it.

Instead, he popped two Advil and guzzled a bottle of spring water.

Alcohol was never a true temptation. Often needing to rely on his wits, he made avoiding it a priority. In fact, he rejected all the usual vices—all except one.

The problem was—that *one* was getting worse.

His mind was clouded. His nerves were raw. Sure, some of it had to do with anticipation—not knowing what Adrianna would do, how she felt, if she would return. But that wasn't the whole picture.

Something was off. Something inside of him. All his life he had devoted his entire being to building the Church. Turning an idea into an empire. But now, even if he dug deep, he couldn't seem to find that same drive. It was as if apathy were an untreatable virus by which he was infected.

Right now, his obsessive mind was consumed with Adrianna. But he knew it had nothing to do with her. Tomorrow, there might be someone else. Or, he'd succeed in adding her to his collection, only to lose interest after a few months.

He was sick. Probably always had been. He had just been too busy to notice. Too ignorant to pay attention. Or too proud to admit it. Which, in his opinion, may not have been such a bad thing.

The outside world acted like pride was the worst of sins—no doubt due to the doctrines of the so-called old religions. But he *was* proud. Proud of what he had accomplished. When he looked back at his twenty-five-year old self, working as a finance manager for a local car dealership in Upstate New York, he could never have imagined where he would end up.

It was funny how the Universe worked, he thought. How a single insignificant moment could change the course of not just one life, but thousands.

For Curtis, that moment came courtesy of Lindsey McGough.

Set up on a date by a mutual friend, it'd been Lindsey's idea to attend an open mic night, put on by the Schenectady Community Theater. Lindsey had begged him to get up on stage. Maybe he'd wanted to impress her, or just hadn't wanted to back down from a challenge, but either way he ended up throwing his name into the hat.

The trouble was, he'd had no talents. He couldn't sing or play an instrument like some of the other participants. He didn't even know a poem he could recite, like the old beatnik right before him. Instead, he'd decided to tell a story. One he'd had to make up on the spot.

What had started out as an unimaginative tale about a car salesman who set out to unlock the meaning of life, turned into an inspiring fable, laced with rantings about greed, ethics, and religion. He'd surprised himself by how effortlessly it all poured out.

Stranger yet was how the crowd had responded. He could see it on their faces—a mixture of confusion and intense focus. They'd hung on his every word.

Though not quite good enough to garner a second date with Lindsey, it had seemed, he'd come away with something much more valuable—the knowledge that he not only had a knack for public speaking, but a calling.

And that was it. The very beginning.

It hadn't been the big break—that would come years later, in February 1998, when he'd made an appearance on the televised TED talk event. That performance had been the true catalyst, launching him to a moderate celebrity status and gaining him his first followers. The milestone that had allowed him to leave his day job and never look back.

The Universe had delivered. But it wasn't all kismet. There had been a lot of hard work involved to get off the ground. Organizing the thoughts and opinions that had flowed out of him that night in Schenectady into a polished speech he could take on the road.

In time, with the help of an over-exaggerated resume, he'd started booking bigger and bigger gigs. Corporate training events, conferences, anything that paid.

"You are better than yourself," he'd called his program, which focused on techniques for improving self-confidence, self-awareness, and personal growth.

By the time he'd landed the TED talk, he had honed the material into something so comprehensive, he'd almost started to believe it himself.

It'd been a boon. And it was lucrative. But the universe had more in store for him. Much more.

As his small, devoted following began to grow, he'd started offering private sessions and developing a track to prepare others to teach his methods. Those close to him had brought friends, who'd brought even more. Some came and went, but others had remained devoted, hungry to be more involved and gain his attention.

The burgeoning inner circle had treated him as if he were a guru. Something more than human. A God or deity, in a way. It'd stroked his ego for sure, but it'd also set the tone with newcomers. It'd had a snow-ball effect, almost out of his control.

The influx of cash and people had sparked the idea that would truly change his life forever. Purchasing a piece of farm property in Kingsbury, he'd incorporated his fledgling company, The Church of Clear Intention. Its cornerstone had been putting a premium on spirituality without dogma and focusing on the individual nourishing their soul through reason and positive action. An anti-religion religion, per se.

Calling it a church had just been a dig at the establishment, but an imperative step toward his ultimate goal. Tax exemption. Curtis had been nothing, if not pragmatic.

To that end, he'd converted one of the several buildings on the rural property into a gathering place where they would hold group sessions. Several of the more devoted proteges had lived in the four- bedroom farmhouse.

Somewhat socially awkward at the time, Curtis had enjoyed the attention and trust he'd received from his female followers. He couldn't say it was intentional, at least not at first, but he began grooming some of the women, tailoring the ideology to suit his desires. Polygamy. Hedonism. Whatever he could get away with.

Over time, his inhibitions faded and his sexual appetite grew. He'd enlisted as many women as he could, hoping to coax them into joining his harem.

Some kept their distance, some left completely. But some were all in.

These women seemed to fall into two important categories—those with aspirations, and those devoted to the so-called, "mission." Young Evie had fallen into both.

It was why he'd kept her close all these years. Now, more than ever, he relied on her. She had a drive he didn't. She had the guts to call him out when his compulsions began to spiral. But now, he wasn't sure even she could help him.

Curtis rubbed his temples and swiveled his jaw. The pressure seemed to be subsiding.

He touched the mouse, bringing his computer to life.

On the screen was a freeze-framed image of Adrianna, passing through the covered walkway from the admin building to the members' lounge. The soft side light accentuated her curves and highlighted her eyes.

"What are you thinking, Adrianna?" he mused.

As a practical matter, he needed to know about this woman. Where did she come from? What was her story? Where was she walking to? Did she live close?

She'd said she lived in downtown Tampa and he had no real reason not to believe her. But with all the recent attention, it was no time to get lax. He could have Evie do a workup on her. She'd done them before. He could have his guys follow her, as they had done that a million times.

Whatever needed to be done, it needed to be done fast. He could barely contain himself.

The phone rang, shaking him out of his obsession.

Anastasia.

He answered. "What is it?"

"There's a woman on the phone for you. It's not Adrianna. Her name is Sarah. Says it's urgent."

Curtis sighed. "Put her through."

Sarah was a member in good standing. In normal circumstances, someone Curtis wouldn't have known from Adam. But he had taken a fancy to her after seeing her at one of the open seminars. He'd wined and dined her—the usual protocol—and, after a few weeks, proposed. She'd turned him down flat. Ghosted him for over a month.

She'd taken a job as a waitress at the diner down the street, he was told, and stopped coming to her sessions.

Then, out of the blue, she'd shown back up, professing her love and trying to accept the proposal. She'd rejoined, saying she was devoting herself to the Church.

By then, of course, he'd lost interest. The relationship had left a bad taste in his mouth and there were better, newer prospects to pursue.

Since then, she'd called at least a dozen times with gossip or to rat someone out. Curtis knew what she was trying to do, and it wasn't going to work. But he'd gladly take the information.

"Hello Sarah. Who's M-F-ing me this time?"

"Sage, this is bad. I mean really bad."

"Calm down. What happened?"

"I'm at work. There's a bunch of guys here. Agents. Like FBI or something."

"Sarah, are you in trouble?"

"No. First, a couple guys came in and they got a big table. Then more showed up. It looked like they were meeting, like they're getting ready for something. So, you know me, I can't help it—I pretended like I was filling a bunch of napkin holders so I could hear what they were saying. Curtis, I think they're going to the Church."

"What do you mean they're going to the Church? Sarah, what did they say?"

"They were talking about a search warrant. I'm out back, but I think they're getting ready to leave. I don't think you have much time."

Curtis's pulse quickened. The IRS had been harassing him, that was nothing new. But were they really ratcheting it up to this level?

"Sarah, listen to me. Are you absolutely sure?"

"I'm sure, Sage. Please, please, please. Get out of there now."

Curtis hung up the phone. If they were coming, let 'em. This was his domain. He was the Sage. And he wasn't going anywhere.

CHAPTER 17

HAELI BURST IN. "I swear to God, you couldn't pay me to see that guy ever again."

Blake remained reclined, his butt on a chair and his feet up on the bed. He gave Haeli a questioning look. "That bad, huh?"

"The guy's a creep. And he kept touching me." She shivered. "He's lucky I didn't break his fingers."

"Yes, he is," Blake swung his feet off onto the floor. "Successful though, I'm assuming?"

"If the goal was getting herpes, then maybe."

"I'm serious. What else did you find out?"

Haeli threw her handbag on the bed and flopped down next to it. "I told you about the cameras, they're everywhere. They have access control, key fobs, and cards. I think I found the data closet, or one of them."

"How about entrances and exits?"

"There's a ton of them. When we were outside, on the grounds behind the main buildings, I could see plenty of doors, but they all opened out. No handles or anything on the outside. The whole place is fenced in. It's like being in a prison yard—with flower gardens."

"How about the residences? Were you able to get in?"

"Just the common areas. The place is huge. You'd need a map just to know where everything is." She scrunched her nose. "Unfortunately, I did get to see Hammond's personal residence. He introduced me to a few of his slaves—I mean, wives."

Blake laughed. "You play your cards right, you could be one of them."

"You're not kiddin'. I was a little worried he was going to lock me in there and I'd have to live out my days in a cage in the basement. No joke, the place feels like a Venus fly trap. He kept dropping hints, like I was going to say 'Sure, I'll join your little cult harem.'"

"What did you say? I mean, how'd you leave it?"

"I didn't say anything. Just played dumb like I wasn't picking up the advances. Told him I was really interested in learning more. Threw a bunch of compliments at him. He seemed to eat that up. Other than that, I just tried to see as much of the place as possible without getting molested."

Blake got up, then leaned over Haeli and kissed her on the head. "Thank you for doing that." He sat down next to her. "Now, start from the beginning and tell me everything he said."

"First we have to call Griff. You know what I was saying in my text, about the Wi-Fi? I was thinking, because there were so many wireless cameras, we could—"

"It's in the works." Blake said. "I spoke with Griff and Khat. Khat has a contact in Miami that can get us a unit. It's called a Piranha. It's actually made by a couple of your brethren."

"Of course it is." Haeli rolled her eyes.

"The Israelis don't mess around when it comes to cyber warfare, that's for sure. I've used one of these units before, they're impressive. Well over a quarter mile range if you use an external amplifier. But I'm not sure we'll be able to get the amp."

"How does it work?"

"Lets us connect to multiple devices at once, around fifty I think, and exploit vulnerabilities in the Wi-Fi to intercept the data. And once it's set up, we can access it remotely, so we're not stuck wherever. The only thing will be finding a place to hide it where it'll be close enough and not be disturbed. Or stolen. We *are* going to have to return the thing."

"So, what do we do in the meantime?"

Blake grabbed his phone from his pocket. "Wait for Khat to text me the meeting location. It'll be somewhere local. The contact's driving the unit up from Miami. Khat says it should be around sixteen hundred hours, but I'm waiting on a definite."

"Sixteen hundred? Today?"

"Today."

"Wow. That was easier than I thought."

"Easy, maybe. But it's going to cost. Big time. I have Griff wiring me the cash."

"Khat always comes through," Haeli said. "Never fails. Griff, too. How are they, anyway?"

"They seem fine. There's been some news on Fezz."

Haeli sat up. "They talked to him?"

"No. But they got a hit on Fezz's plate. A trooper in Colorado ran it."

"Are they going out to find him?"

"It'd be pointless. If he was tagged on the highway, he's probably long gone by now. But Griff's also tapped into the toll systems, so if he hits a city, and the plate reader scans him, we'll know about it. Anyway, Kook's still out in Cali so if anything, he'd be the closest."

"To be honest, the way Khat's been taking it, I'm surprised he's not already in the car."

"Probably wants to be. But he knows it would only make things worse. We need to give Fezz his space. Ian's safe with him." Blake paused. "I know Fezz, he'll come around. It'll just be nice to know where he ends up. In case he runs into any trouble."

"You mean in case trouble runs into him?"

Blake chuckled. "Exactly."

CHAPTER 18

FEZZ STEPPED over a pile of painted one-by-fours. Nails stuck out in all directions. "Watch your step, bud."

Ian tiptoed around. "I think it's right over here."

After checking the General Store, Ian convinced Fezz to go with him to Jodi's place. Seeing the trailer park up close only made Fezz angrier that Ian had ventured in there without him. Not that Ian wasn't as capable as any other young man, but their situation wasn't typical. Neither of them technically existed and because of that, handling any issues that arose would require a certain experience.

Above all else, they needed to avoid the system. Their credentials were strong, as long as no one asked too many questions. But Fezz needed to keep Ian close, just in case.

"That's it there." Ian pointed.

Fezz's mouth hung open. Deep in three-foot-tall weeds, the trailer was covered in moss and missing pieces of its outer paneling. To Fezz, it looked like a piece of cardboard left out in the rain. He couldn't believe the roof would do anything to stop the elements, if there was any roof at all.

"She lives here? In this?"

Ian nodded. "That's what she said. Let's see if she's there." He ran up to the door and knocked.

Nearby, a man sat in a lawn chair drinking a beer. There were two sickly dogs tied to one of the arms. He didn't seem to pay any mind to him and Ian.

The door opened and Jodi, wearing the same shirt and jeans, appeared. The look on her face was one of horror.

"What did you do?" Jodi yelped.

"What?" Ian looked at Fezz and then back at the petrified girl.

"Why did you bring someone here? I told you it was our secret."

Ian put out his hands as if he thought she would faint and planned to catch her. "It's okay. This is Fe—my Dad. Ray. He won't hurt you."

"I should never have let you come here."

Fezz interjected. "Hey now, take it easy. Ian's just trying to help. I'm not going to tell anyone, okay? No one is going to hurt you. We just wanted to talk to you for a minute, is that alright?"

Jodi paused, then bowed her head.

Ian looked at Fezz as if to say, "What now?"

Fezz jerked his chin toward Jodi as if to say, "Talk to her." But Ian wasn't picking up what he was throwing down.

"Can we come in?" Fezz asked. "It's okay if you don't want us to."

Jodi backed up a step and motioned them in.

Ian stepped in first. "I'm sorry. I didn't think you'd be upset."

"It's okay." The words weren't convincing. Not the way she said them.

"Wow, Jodi," Fezz said. "Have you read all of these books?"

Jodi nodded.

"That's incredible."

"I told you she's really smart," Ian added.

"Which one's your favorite?" Fezz asked.

With no change in her slack expression, Jodi reached for a book and handed it to Fezz.

"*Little Women*. That's a good one."

Jodi cracked a slight smile.

Of course, Fezz had never read it. But something told him she wasn't about to start grilling him on the finer parts of the plot. "Ian tells me you're all alone here. No parents or grandparents. No one?"

She shook her head.

"Give me something," Fezz chuckled. "Am I that scary?"

Another head shake. This time in the vertical direction.

"Do you have a last name?"

Fezz expected another gesture. Likely a negative one. But instead, he got a verbal answer.

"Foster."

"Jodie Foster?"

"Yes."

Fezz laughed. "Taxi Driver. Contact."

The blank stare told him she had no idea what he was talking about.

"*Silence of the Lambs*?"

She perked up.

"You know it?"

"Yes." She rooted around in a pile of books, filling a gap between two counters, which Fezz guessed once held an oven or stove. She handed him a book. "*Silence of the Lambs*, written by Thomas Harris. It was published in 1988. It's the sequel to another book by him called *Red Dragon*. That one was in 1981. Why do you ask?"

Christ. She's Ian's clone.

"Never mind." Fezz said.

"I told you—"

"Yeah, I get it Ian. She's really smart. You guys are two peas in a pod."

"Can we tell her?" Ian asked.

Fezz nodded.

"We want to invite you to dinner," Ian said. "Mexican."

"Hope you like Mexican," Fezz said. "Turns out it's the only place nearby and we're a little light on transportation."

Jodi bowed her head again.

"Will you come?" Ian asked.

"I don't know."

"We understand if you don't want to. It's a hassle and all. Naturally, you'd need to get cleaned up." Fezz grinned and pulled a key from his pocket, dangling it in front of her. "That's why I got you a room at the motel. You could have a bath, and of course, you might as well spend the night. Get a good night's sleep, right? But, if you'd rather not—"

"My own room?"

"Your own room. Take it. Even if you decide not to come to dinner. The room's yours."

Reluctantly, she took the key.

"So, does that mean you'll come to dinner?" Ian asked.

"Let her think about it," Fezz said. "Our room is right next door to yours. If you change your mind, just knock."

"I'll go," Jodi blurted.

"Yes!" Ian pumped his fist.

Fezz laughed. "Well, we're happy to have you. Want to walk back with us?"

"Ok." Without taking anything, she headed outside and waited for them to follow.

When you have nothing, Fezz thought, there's nothing you need. Nothing to forget. She was a free spirit, and it showed.

"I'm glad you said yes," Ian said.

"Me too."

"Maybe you can show us the best way out of here," Fezz said.

Ahead, a large woman wearing pink spandex leggings and an over-sized t-shirt stomped toward them.

What's this now?

"Darlene," Jodi said. "We should run."

"You little shits!" Darlene yelled.

"Stay put." Fezz stepped out in front, putting himself between the kids and the charging bull. "What seems to be the problem?"

"The problem is that these little brats were on my property." She leaned to the side, eyed Jodi and pointed. "That one threw a rock at me. Yeah, I'm talking to you honey, you think I wouldn't catch you two?"

"Hold on, hold on." Fezz smiled. "I'm sure it was an accident."

"It was no accident."

"And I'm sure a lovely young woman such as yourself would be willing to forgive. I could see it in your eyes as soon as you walked over here. But I think they owe you a big apology, don't you?"

"Yes, I do."

"Kids, tell Miss—"

"Darlene."

"Tell Miss Darlene how sorry you are."

"We're sorry." Ian said.

"Yeah, we shouldn't have been playing around near your place," Jodi added.

"See. They feel horrible." Fezz put his hand on Darlene's shoulder. "It's been nice to meet you, I should get these kids out of your hair."

"You got a name?" Darlene contorted her face into something Fezz assumed was supposed to be a smile.

"Ray."

"You married?"

"Yep. Happily. But if I weren't, I might just have been knockin' on your door."

Darlene blushed.

"Well, you know where to find me if you change your mind, handsome."

"Okay kids, Let's go!"

CHAPTER 19

JIM SHOVED the gritty mop into the plastic jaws and leaned on the lever. Brown water ran into the bucket.

As penance, each member deemed in need of rehabilitation was given an assignment. Jim might have gotten the worst of them.

Scrubbing toilets was as menial and dirty a task as anything else he could think of. Especially considering his former position. While he may have once been a star, he was now one of the rejects. The disconsolates, they called them—which just meant the people they had a hard time controlling.

Jim was dead center of that category. He was done being controlled. Done being taken advantage of.

Given enough time, he knew he could find a way out. All he needed was the tiniest window to exploit and maybe a little help from one or two of the others. A few seconds head start, where no one was paying attention, was all it would take.

Once out in the public, there would be onlookers. Witnesses. He could make a scene. Shield himself with the masses. But escaping wasn't an option. Not without his wife. He wouldn't leave her there. Not even for a minute.

There was a time when he'd roamed freely around town. They both had. Living in a cute condo on the water with the love of his life, he'd never dreamed he'd be sleeping in a bunk under Fred and mopping toilet water on a daily basis.

Of course, he should have known. He'd seen it happen to many. Had even offered suggestions on how to better secure the holding quarters.

At the time, he'd believed it was the right thing to do. The theory had made sense—keep the subjects secluded from the outside world long enough to deprogram them of the ideas implanted by the misanthropes. Once they realized the error of their ways, they'd be reintegrated.

And they *were* reintegrated. Sometimes. He'd seen it happen, though not as much of late. With each generation, it seemed people were catching on quicker. Turning their backs on the Church.

If only he had done so sooner.

For the lower-level members, there was not much likelihood of being sentenced to remediation. They didn't know enough to pose a problem. Instead, they'd be released from membership and allowed to pick up their lives where they'd left off. But for those who were brought into the inner sanctum, who had earned trust and learned secrets, it was a whole different story.

Now, he had come to a crossroads. Needed to commit to a decision that had already been made for him. He would play the part. Take his punishment. Then, when the time was right, profess his loyalty. It was the only way he could gain enough freedom and access to plan a proper escape. For both of them.

Now, however, his only goal was to finish the women's room so he could move on.

Jim opened the last stall at the end and dragged his cart inside. He'd start there and work his way down the row.

Grabbing a toilet brush and bottle of cleaner from the cart, he squirted the blue liquid into the bowl and up under the rim.

Outside the stall, the door to the bathroom crashed open.

Taken aback, Jim was about to say something. "Cleaning in here," or something to let the poor woman know there was a man inside, but the woman dashed into the stall next to him before he had time to speak.

Figuring it was an emergency, and to save her the embarrassment, he decided to just leave and come back after she left. Before he could take a step, two arms and the top of a head appeared above the stall. It wasn't a woman at all.

Jim crouched down low. He watched the man—who must have been standing on the toilet seat—move one of the drop-ceiling tiles to the side, then shove a stack of file folders through the gap and rest them on top of another tile.

Holding his breath, Jim pressed his back against the partition and closed his eyes. If he could avoid being seen, he had a chance to find out what was going on.

A moment later, the man's feet hit the tile floor, and he scurried out into the hallway. As the mystery man opened the door, Jim could hear a commotion outside.

When the room returned to silence, Jim emerged.

He checked each stall.

Alone.

One wobbly step at a time, he climbed onto the toilet, straddling the bowl on either side of the seat. He steadied himself, then pushed on the ceiling tile and retrieved the stack of documents from their short-lived hiding place.

There was no time to read them. Not there.

Returning to the last stall, he removed several rolls of toilet paper and paper towels from his cart, put the files down, and covered them with the paper goods.

Satisfied no part of them were visible, he wheeled the cart toward the hallway. If he could get back to his barracks while everyone else was at work, he could put them under his mattress. It wasn't the greatest plan, but it would have to be good enough for the time being.

As he left the privacy of the restroom, it became clear what the ruckus was all about.

Several men in blue jackets—FBI. IRS. Secret Service—had gathered up a number of individuals into a group. Anastasia, Brent, Eleanor,

Cooper, to name a few. Jim could only assume one of them was responsible for dumping the documents in the ceiling, but he didn't get a good enough look to know for sure. White shirt sleeves and brown hair described at least six of them.

The good news was, no one was looking at him. No one ever cared about the janitor.

For a second, he considered grabbing one of the agents. "I'm being held here," he could say. But not without his wife. They still had her, and if he caused that kind of commotion, he had no idea if he would ever see her again.

No. He'd stick with the plan. Bide his time.

Jim wheeled the squeaking, squealing cart down the hallway and toward the residential wing. Still, no one blinked an eyelid.

It was his lucky day, he thought. Though he couldn't say the same for Curtis Hammond.

CHAPTER 20

THE MUSTANG IDLED at the east side of the Publix Market parking lot in Palmetto. There was one other unoccupied car in the row. The clock read 3:58.

These were the instructions Blake had been given.

The location was about as random and non-descript as they came. With easy access to I-75 and no connection to either Blake, Haeli, or their contact, it would be a quick drop-and-go in the middle of nowhere. All in plain sight.

As clandestine transactions went, there was little risk in this one. To a layperson, the unit they were attempting to acquire would look like nothing more than a commercial access point or a beefier version of a Wi-Fi router you'd find at Best Buy. Even if they were stopped by the police, there was nothing illegal about possessing a piece of computer hardware.

All the risk was carried by the contact. Blake didn't ask, but there was no question in his mind that the guy was CIA. If he was caught, the repercussions would be severe.

Although not classified, per se, the Piranha device was highly regulated and only legally available for use by certain governments, including the United States. Lending it out to civilians without authorization would constitute a major breach.

"Do we know what we're looking for?" Haeli asked.

"I don't have a vehicle description, but he has ours. He'll find us. Should be an African American male, slender build. Khat said he looks like Griff, only not as pretty. And he's got different color eyes."

"That's unfortunate," Haeli said.

Blake knew what she meant. When it came to intelligence, especially in the field, the more forgettable the face, the better. If captured, it would be impossible to deny one's identity with such a unique physical characteristic. Contact lenses only get you so far.

"Is this him?" Haeli leaned forward to get a better view through the passenger side mirror.

Blake tracked the incoming car in the rear view. A gray Kia minivan rolled up and stopped, straddling the two empty spaces next to them. The driver, a slender Black man wearing sunglasses.

The man got out and approached Haeli's window. Haeli rolled it down.

"You got the cash?" the man demanded.

"Depends." Blake leaned toward Haeli to get a better view of the guy. "Can you see alright with those shades?"

The man paused for a moment, then lowered his sunglasses to the tip of his nose. One brown, one bluish green.

"What do we call you?" Haeli asked.

"Roger."

It was a fictitious name, but it helped to have some way to refer to him. Otherwise, they'd just have to make something up. "Two-tone," maybe.

"Alright Roger, we've got the money." Blake reached behind his seat and grabbed the stack of 300 Benjamins. "Thirty Thousand."

Roger stepped back and reached through the open driver's side door of the van. He came out with a black metal box. There were antennae sticking out from the top and wires wrapped around it. "You know how to use this?"

"I do. It's been a while, but I'm sure things haven't changed that much." Blake said.

Roger slapped the finned aluminum casing. "Battery should last a few days. This unit can connect eight access points at once. It's got two twenty-watt amplifiers, so you should have no problem overpowering the existing access points. There's also a thirty-two-watt jammer built in to knock your targets off their existing connections. And it's fully weatherproof. Whatever your need is, this thing can probably do it. Grab credentials for any app, cloud service, whatever. I swear, you don't even need skill anymore."

Roger was right. The tech had become so good, it was scary. No computer or device had ever been safe, but in the past, it'd at least required someone like Blake to be behind the keyboard. Now, anyone with a decent computer background could do it. Any device, account, content, anytime they wanted would be at their fingertips.

"Got it." Blake handed the money to Haeli, who handed it to Roger. Haeli took the device and placed it on the floor under her feet.

"You've got three days max. Understand?"

"We do," Blake said.

"Our mutual friend trusts you, and I trust him. But if you don't show up with this unit, you know what happens next."

"We do," Haeli replied.

"I'll send the login for the 4G link to our friend after I leave. Other than that, enjoy."

Roger got in his car, Haeli rolled up the window, and they parted ways.

On to the next step. Deployment.

"HI." Blake greeted the man at the front desk. "My wife and I are looking for a basic room for the night, maybe two."

"Do you have a reservation?"

"We don't."

The inn was inexpensive but offered a surprising number of amenities. In excellent condition, the exterior was painted ocean blue with white trim, giving it a Caribbean feel. From what they could see online, the rooms were spacious and decorative—nicer than their room at the

Fenway, even. And there were resort type activities on the property, an RV park, and a pool.

But it wasn't comfort they were after. Or a place to stay. The motel was located across the street from the concrete wall along the back side of the Church's property. It was more than close enough for a signal and with the help of a "Do Not Disturb" sign, it would be the perfect staging point for the Piranha.

"I'm sorry, we are booked up. I have something next month if you'd like."

"That's not going to work for us," Blake said. "Do you have anything at all?"

"No. Like I said, we're completely booked."

"Are you sure?" Haeli asked.

If they were in a courtroom, this would be the moment the lawyer objected. "Asked and answered," and even that would be unnecessary. The man behind the desk didn't seem to have any intention of repeating himself.

"Thank you for your time." Blake walked away.

Haeli followed him outside. "What now?"

Blake needed a second to think. He stood in the lot, surveying the area. Across the street was a farm stand. The small building sat near the southernmost edge of the compound, separated by the thick wall surrounding the entire property. At least, Blake assumed the wall continued along the entire border. With the thick cover of trees to the north of the stand, it was hard to tell.

It got him thinking. "This thing is weatherproof. There's no need to be inside. Look at that tree line over there. What're the chances anyone has been in there in the last year? I say we put it right behind their wall."

"You're right," Haeli said. "We're overthinking it."

"We pull right in. You go distract whoever's there, ask some questions about vegetables or something, and I'll slip into the woods. Done."

"Sounds like a plan."

CHAPTER 21

"YOU THINK we should have shown her how to use the shower?" Fezz laughed, but he was only half-joking.

Ian didn't laugh at all. "Thank you for doing this," he said.

"Of course."

If Fezz were honest, when Ian had first suggested they try to help Jodi out, he'd wanted nothing to do with it. Not that he's heartless, but they didn't need any more complications.

Then, he'd met her.

Seeing the way she lived, how smart and sweet she was, he couldn't help but feel bad for her. He was glad Ian connected with her. If anyone could begin to understand what she'd been through, it was him. And vice versa.

"We can't really let her put those filthy clothes back on," Fezz said. "Let's take a run across the street and see what they have. Maybe we can find something for her to wear."

"Across the street? The gas station?"

"No, not the gas station. The horse place. The sign says they have clothing. Sure, maybe it's chaps and spurs, but it's worth a look. It'll take us five minutes."

"Okay." Ian said.

It didn't take much to convince Ian of anything when it came to

Jodi. Ian would jump through hoops to help her, but somehow Fezz couldn't decide which one of them was more invested—Ian, or him.

The trip took less than a minute, door to door, walking at a spirited pace. Inside, there was more clothing than Fezz anticipated, including a wide selection of western boots.

Now came the hard part.

"What the hell do either of us know about what to buy a girl?" Fezz chuckled.

"I don't know. Girl clothes, I guess." Ian was being a wise ass, but he had a point.

They found the women's section and Fezz thumbed through a rack of sundresses. He picked up a couple and eyed them with a picture of Jodi's height in mind. "How about this one?"

"I don't know." Ian's nose scrunched as if he had gotten another whiff of the cow manure bagged-up outside the entrance.

"Come on, this is cute."

Did he just say "cute?" Fezz would have smacked himself if it wouldn't have drawn attention. He needed his head examined. *Cute.* Next, he'll be baking brownies for Thursday night PTA meetings and inviting the neighbors to Tupperware parties. Still, it kind of was —cute.

"Maybe jeans and a t-shirt are more her thing." Ian pulled a pair of Lee's off the rack and picked up a tiny peach colored tee that said "Denver" on the front. "Something like this."

Fezz considered the options. "How about this idea? We get both and let her decide."

"Okay. Shoes?"

"She's got shoes," Fezz said.

"But they're old and have holes in them."

"Fine. Shoes too. We'll pick out a pair of boots for her."

Ian shook his head. "Not boots. Sneakers. She's wearing sneakers."

"Look around, bud. See any sneakers here? She's gettin' boots."

There were a few pairs that looked small enough and had a feminine style. Fezz picked one, then grabbed three pairs in different sizes. "We'll just get a few and she can see what fits."

Balancing three boxes of boots and a blue flowery sundress on top, Fezz headed for the checkout counter.

"Wait. Socks and underwear," Ian said.

"Oh, no." Fezz peered over his payload. "Socks, fine. But underwear, she's on her own. Besides, they don't have any here."

As it turned out, Fezz was only half right. They didn't have girl's undergarments, but they did have a rack of Duluth Trading men's boxers and briefs.

After some debate, Fezz agreed to get her a pack of small briefs, even though he knew they would likely be too big—not to mention, a tad bit baggy in the front.

With every base covered, Fezz forked over the $598.90, which was about $500 more than he intended to spend. But at least he learned something—boots were damn expensive.

Despite being rushed, Fezz thought the outcome was pretty good. And by the time they got back, they could still hear the shower in the adjacent room through the wall.

"When the water turns off," Fezz said, "you go next door and knock. You can leave the stuff outside the door."

Ian did just as Fezz suggested. Like an Olympic athlete in a timed event, the moment the water stopped, Ian gathered the bags and darted outside.

IAN WAITED TO HEAR A RESPONSE. Should he knock again? Or should he just leave the clothes, hoping she heard him?

The door cracked open as far as the chain would allow it. Jodi, wrapped in a towel, poked her head in the gap.

Hair wet, face reddened, she looked like a different person. She was beautiful.

"I'm not ready yet," she said.

"I—I know." Ian stuttered. "Um—we got some things for you." He squeezed the clothing through the small opening, then reached down into each box and passed one boot at a time. "We didn't know what would fit, so we got some options. And sorry about the underwear, it's all they had."

Jodi took each item and piled them at her feet. "I can't believe—" Her eyes welled with tears.

Ian wanted to sneak through the gap and hug her. She could use it. And so could he. "See you after."

Holding her towel at her armpit with one hand, she bent down, picked up the sundress, and passed it back to Ian.

CHAPTER 22

CURTIS TOOK in the doorway of the accounting office, surveying the scene. Where mini-computer towers had once sat on every desk, there were now only scraps of paper and empty file folders. Much of the paper deemed irrelevant had been tossed to the floor, giving the area an aura of natural disaster.

Peter approached from behind. "What a mess."

"Are they all out?"

"The last of them were just loading up. No one's left in the building."

"How did this happen? Every avenue was covered."

"They're fishing," Peter said. "Trumped up charges on one little mistake in the filing and they're getting as much mileage as they can out of it."

"We had a deal. A lot of money was paid to make sure this didn't happen." Curtis could feel blood pressure pounding in his upper arms.

"You had a deal with Wagner. There's a new attorney general, remember? The one you pissed off."

Lest he forget. There were always going to be enemies. The Church was no stranger to legal battles, only they were usually the ones bringing them. "We have a round table with the attorneys in an hour. Will you be there?"

"Which ones?" Peter asked.

"All of them."

"Right. I'll be there."

"Good." Curtis moved Peter into the hallway. "Is everyone accounted for?"

"Yes. I pulled everyone from their posts after the Feds showed up. They're sequestered in the barracks."

"Thank you." Curtis said. "I appreciate your diligence."

"Do we know what they got?"

"Still sorting that out. We should receive an inventory in a day or two."

"That's not what I mean," Peter said. "Are we exposed regarding the other files?"

"No." Curtis smiled. "I got a heads up before it all happened. Just enough time to make sure that part was taken care of."

"Excellent. The rest we'll work out."

"We will." Curtis turned to leave, then turned back. "Are you going downstairs?"

"Yes."

"Have Anastasia track down Cooper for me. Send him up to my office."

"No problem."

Peter left and Curtis headed back to his desk.

Inside, the story was much the same as the other administrative offices. When the Feds had arrived, Curtis directed everyone to be as cooperative as possible. He himself had turned over many documents and even opened his personal safe for them. While normally he'd have made them work harder for it, simply out of spite, he knew that if they found what they were looking for, they would have no need to force themselves further into the facilities. There were several high-profile guests staying in the celebrity center and the last thing they needed was the Feds poking around the barracks, talking to the disconsolates.

Sitting down at his desk, he gathered the sheets of paper and rearranged them into a stack, all face up. He didn't have to read them to know they were inconsequential internal memos. He could tell by the format. And besides, they'd been left behind.

Curtis flicked the mouse. Of course, the screen remained dark. His computer was the first to go.

He knew what would relieve his tension, but he couldn't have it at that moment. A quick viewing of his favorite movie, starring his favorite starlet. Adrianna.

Luckily, even though they took the on-site servers, their video surveillance footage was stored in the cloud. He'd have a new computer by the morning—the IT department was already on it—and he'd be back in business.

Cooper poked his head in. "Sage?"

"Come in."

"Um. Sir, there's a problem."

"Look around Cooper, there's a lot of them."

"You know the files you gave me and told me to hide?"

"Why do you think I called you here, for tea? You can retrieve them now. I'll put them back—"

"That's the thing. I hid them in the ceiling of the women's bathroom. I didn't know which bathroom you wanted, so I put them in the one by the lobby."

"Doesn't matter which bathroom, just go get them."

"I did. I mean I tried to. But when I went back, they were gone."

Curtis froze. He met the younger man's concerned gaze. "Gone?" He shook his head frantically. "No, no, no. Go look again."

"I pulled all the tiles down. They're nowhere."

Curtis stood. "For shit's sake. Are you sure you have the right restroom?"

"Yes. I swear."

"Those bastards found them?" Curtis smoothed his hair back with a shaky palm. "How is that possible? How could they have known to look there?"

"It's not possible. I was down there the whole time. None of them went in there."

"Cooper, listen to me. I want you to check every bathroom in this building and hope that your puny little brain is mistaken."

"Yes, Sage."

"Go."

As Cooper fled in fear, pain surged from behind Curtis' eyes. He clenched his jaw.

"Stop it," he said into the ether. "Just stop this!"

Whatever he had done to anger the Universe, to bring bad energy upon him, he was sorry. He was sorry, and he'd do better. He was broken, in so many ways. But not defeated. He would stand up and fight, with however much he had left in him.

Curtis picked up the phone and dialed the front desk. "Anastasia. Get Peter and Evie. We are going to turn this place upside down."

CHAPTER 23

"ALMOST THERE." Blake tapped away at the keys on his laptop. "Another minute."

It had only been twenty-two minutes since he and Haeli had gotten back to their room. In that time, he'd set up a tunnel through the hotel's Wi-Fi and acquired the software needed to utilize the Piranha. With its own 4G radios, the Piranha was already online. He only needed to connect to it.

Haeli bit her lip.

"And—" Blake slammed the last keystroke. "Done. We are up and running."

Haeli knelt on the floor beside Blake and rested her arms on the bed in front of the laptop.

A grid of black boxes appeared on the screen, each replaced with a live video feed in random order.

"Recognize any of this?" Blake asked.

"Some, yeah. The windows are so tiny it's hard to tell. But this is the garden here." She clicked her fingernail on the plastic screen panel. "Can you enlarge this?"

"Double click," Blake said. "You're driving."

Haeli pressed twice on the mousepad and zoomed in on the exterior shot. "Hold on." She got up, grabbed the hotel-branded notepad and pen from the nightstand, and kneeled back down. After a few scribbles, she had drawn a rough map of the compound's layout.

Rough was an understatement.

"Where's the main door?" Blake asked, then pointed at his best guess. "Here?"

"Yes. This video is from here, looking that way." She drew an X on the map and an arrow facing the top of the page. "There should be a door directly underneath it. And several more along this wall."

"What's this building here?" Blake pointed to another box toward the right side. "Or is that not a building?"

"It is. Recreation. This is the residential wing here as far as I could gather. Admin offices here on the first and second floor. Hammond's office is on the second."

"Take me through the camera views. I need some context." Blake scooted the laptop closer to Haeli. "Two-finger click to zoom out to the grid. Swipe to move to the next camera."

Haeli double clicked on the top left box. "This is the front parking area, you know that." She swiped. "And the lobby you know." And again, several more times. "Lobby, lobby. This is where I met Hammond. It's just off the main entrance."

As Haeli continued to swipe, Blake made his own mental map. He tried to visualize himself moving through the buildings. To relate one place to another in three-dimensional space.

The purpose and location of some areas were obvious. A kitchen or dining hall, for example. Others, like hallways and offices, were arbitrary. Haeli only recognized some.

Many of the offices were a mess, not what you'd expect from such a high profile and well-appointed space. There were papers everywhere. Closets open. Chairs pushed into piles. If there weren't people around, he'd say the place had been deserted.

It was the people he was interested in. Over the course of the next day or two—or three if necessary—Blake intended to track the movements of everyone he could see. To understand their schedules, protocols, and habits. Only then would the full picture come into focus.

Haeli continued to scroll through the impressive array of angles, devoting no more than five seconds to each. Blake couldn't be sure, but he thought he saw something—someone—he recognized.

"Stop," he said. "Go back one."

Haeli swiped. "This one?"

"Yeah." He slid the laptop in front of him, pulling the screen six inches from his face.

There were large men in black polo shirts, similar to the ones who'd shown him the door two days earlier. They were following two older men down a corridor. Blake zoomed in further. "That's my father."

Blake was sure of it. He was older, more withdrawn, and his eyes had dark circles under them, but it was him.

"Let me see." Haeli said.

Sharing the screen, Blake watched as the four men left the camera's field of vision. "Can you follow him?"

"I don't know." Haeli fumbled with the trackpad. She returned to the grid view and searched for another angle. She saw it at the same time Blake did.

"There."

Four men approaching a set of windowless double doors. Haeli zoomed in.

One of the security guards fobbed in and held the door. Blake's father and the other elderly man entered, but the guards didn't follow. Instead, one pushed the door closed and tugged on the handle, as if double checking it was secure.

Haeli rushed to find the next feed. With two more swipes, they were inside what looked like a barracks. Racks of bunks lined both sides of the large room. It was reminiscent of boot camp.

Multiple people of varying age, gender, and race milled about. Some laid on bunks, others grouped together. There, off to the right, were the two men who had been escorted there, a minute earlier.

In the well-lit room, any possible doubt was removed. This was his father. Jim Brier. In the flesh.

"What is this?" Haeli asked.

Blake squinted. Looking right at it, he couldn't get his head around what he was seeing. Is this how they lived? They left their condo for these conditions? It made no sense. "I was hoping you could tell me."

"Well, I didn't catch this on the tour, that's for sure. They locked these people inside. It's like cult prison."

"Maybe it's part of the whole thing," Blake said. "Swearing off material things to focus on whatever they focus on. Like a convent."

"I don't know. From what I got, the entire doctrine is *based* on material things. Achieving more. Having more. These aren't ideologues."

"You make a point."

"I don't know what it is," Haeli said, "but I think I know *where* it is." Haeli swiped back to the hallway where they first saw Blake's father. It was empty. "Look out these windows," she said. "That's Admin at the other side of the garden. This is the second floor, leading to the residential wing. That means if you follow this hallway around the horseshoe, you would get to Hammond's office."

"Put it on the map."

Haeli found the spot and drew a rectangle, tracing the outline four or five times until it was bold. "I think we found our target."

Blake took the laptop and returned to the view of the barracks. He zoomed in on his father, now sitting on a lower bunk.

It was surreal to see him at all, but more so to see him looking so vulnerable. One of the things that had always defined his father, in Blake's eyes, was strength.

With one answer came many more questions. But right now, only one needed asking.

"Haeli," he said. "Where is my mother?"

CHAPTER 24

IAN PACED outside Jodi's door. Fezz got a kick out of seeing him so nervous. For a kid who never showed any emotion, he was a basket case.

"You alright, bud?"

"Yeah. Of course."

"I talked to Ernie."

Ian's shoulders sank. "Our truck is fixed, isn't it?"

"Actually, no. The parts never showed up. It's going to be at least another day."

"Really? That's great."

"That's not what I was thinking. But I had a feeling you might be alright with it."

Jodi opened the door and stepped out.

"Jodi," Ian said. "You look..."

"Pretty." Fezz nudged Ian. "Doesn't she?"

"Yeah. Very pretty."

Jodi gave a meek smile and pawed at her hair. "I didn't have a brush."

"You look great." Fezz said. "You hungry?"

"I am," Ian said.

"I know you are, Ian. You're always hungry. Come on, let's walk over."

Fezz hung back as Ian walked, shoulder to shoulder with Jodi. With Fezz out of view, she was much more talkative. She seemed like any other kid in America. Amazing how a bath and clean clothes could change a person. Or at least the perception of them.

At the restaurant, Ian sat across from Jodi. Fezz next to Ian.

There were more patrons than he'd anticipated. The place wasn't fancy by any means. Most of the folks in there fell into three buckets. Kids, obese people, and people wearing sleeveless shirts. Many fell into two of those categories. A few, all three. Not that he was judging.

The waitress dropped off chips and salsa and promised to be right back.

"Do you guys know what you want?" Fezz asked.

"Is this for us?" Jodi pointed at the complimentary snack.

Fezz nodded. "Have some if you want."

Jodi reached in and grabbed a handful of chips. One at a time she used each chip as a backhoe, shoving gobs of salsa into her mouth. Red sauce splattered on the table and ran down her chin.

"Slow down." Fezz laughed. "We're going to be here for a while. You can chew."

Jodi paused like a deer in headlights, then finished chewing her mouthful.

"The food is pretty good here," Ian said.

Fezz knew Ian was struggling for something to say. To break the ice. But he wasn't wrong. Despite the deceiving atmosphere, the food was solid. "I have an idea. Let's order a bunch of everything for the table. And you can have whatever you like. This way, no one has to choose. Sound good?"

Jodi nodded, finished chewing, and swallowed. "So, where are you from?"

Fezz and Ian both looked at each other. Fezz guessed Ian was thinking the same thing he was—Jodi asked a question. Not just that, she'd started a conversation.

"Go ahead Ian, tell her."

"Um. We're from Rhode Island. Have you ever been to Rhode Island?"

"No. I've never been anywhere, really."

"It's nice," Ian said. "We lived right on the ocean. And we had some really cool friends."

"That must be nice. I never really had any friends."

The truth was, Ian never really had any friends either, not the way she meant. He had never gone to school, lived most of his life locked down in an apartment in the United Arab Emirates, and then was surrounded by a bunch of heathens like Fezz.

"What about in school?" Fezz figured he knew the answer, but it was worth asking anyway.

"I never went to school."

"I didn't either," Ian said.

"Look at you two," Fezz said. "The smartest people I know, and neither of you went to school. Doesn't say much for the education system, does it?"

Jodi munched another chip. "My Auntie Bern said school was for losers. I think she just wanted me around to help her."

"So you lived with your aunt? Where is she?"

"She died. My mom didn't want me, so she sent me to live with Auntie when I was six. Then she got sick and died, too. I never met my dad."

Ian perked up. "Really? I never knew my—"

Fezz kneed Ian in the thigh. "He never knew his aunt, who we talk about a lot. So is that your Aunt Bern's trailer?"

"It's mine now," Jodi said. "She said I could have it when she died. When she got sick, she couldn't leave home as much as before. She used to collect books. She said I could have those, too."

One step inside Jodi's trailer and it was clear Auntie Bern had been a hoarder. She'd known she was dying, but left Jodi high and dry. Then again, if the books made Jodi happy, they turned out to be something of an inheritance after all.

"I used to read a lot, too," Ian said. "And I got to play video games sometimes. You probably never play video games, but they're really fun and you have to try it. Maybe you can visit me and I can show you."

Visit him where? As of the moment, they were homeless. Fezz wondered what fantasy world Ian was concocting for himself. One in which his new friend Jodi would pop over to hang out and play games? Ian was in for a big letdown, and Fezz was only feeding into it.

"We're going to California," Fezz said. "After Ian's mother—my wife —died, we decided to give the west coast a shot. You know, start over. You know we're only here for a couple days, right?"

"I know." Jodi said. "Ian told me."

The waitress came back and Fezz placed the order. As promised, one of almost everything on the menu. Tacos, enchiladas, fajitas, tamales. A smorgasbord.

Fezz waited for her to move out of earshot. "Jodi, Ian and I were talking. We, or I, noticed there are a few things that could use fixin' around your place. Maybe, if you want, we could come by and do a little work before we leave town. Just to make sure you're all set when winter rolls around again. Does that sound good?"

"That sounds nice."

The roar of bike engines from outside drowned out the chatter inside the restaurant. Through the many windows, Fezz could see four motorcycles pulling into the lot. He recognized two of the riders.

It was possible they were going to the motel. A fifty-fifty shot.

He thought about grabbing the kids and getting out of there, but it was too late for that. They would have to walk right past the gang of riders.

Fezz remained calm, hoping not to upset the kids. They were talking about something, but Fezz wasn't listening. Instead, he focused on his peripheral vision.

It was as he feared. The four men walked straight into the restaurant, whooping, cussing, and generally causing a scene. Ian and Jodi turned to see what the commotion was. Everyone did.

"Looky what we have here," Snake said. "A cozy little dinner for three. Who are the tykes?"

Fezz ignored Snake, instead looking at Ian and Jodi. He spoke in a low and measured tone. "Just ignore them. Stay calm, it'll be alright."

Snake came closer, moving behind Jodi. He pulled out the empty seat and sat, draping himself as if he were made of Jello. "Mmm. What a lovely gathering." He reached over and with his index finger pushed a lock of Jodi's hair behind her ear.

Jodi jumped out of her seat and rushed behind Ian.

Fezz leaned forward and looked Snake in the eyes. "You're scaring the kids."

Snake looked over his shoulders at the three men who had gathered behind him. They were laughing and snarling like animals. "Hear that boys? We're scary."

"I didn't say you were scary," Fezz said. "I said you were scaring the kids. Now, how about you and me take this outside and let the rest of these people enjoy their tacos?"

"Oh, we're not here to fight. We're here to deliver a message."

"Is that right?" Fezz planted his hands on the table and stood up. "What message is that?"

Snake smiled. "I think you got it already."

The waitress emerged from the kitchen. Noticing the goons, she barreled over to Fezz's table like her hair was on fire. "Snake, get outta here. What the hell you doin?"

Without taking his eyes off Fezz, Snake rose out of his chair and waved the other three men to follow. "We were just leaving."

The room remained still and silent for several seconds after the group left. Until the four Harley motors fired up and faded.

"What was that all about?" Jodi asked.

"You know those guys?" Ian added.

"We've met. But listen, they're gone and we're about to have a lot of food to eat. Everyone relax. There's nothing to worry about."

Of course, it was a lie. Fezz knew it wasn't over.

He shouldn't have been surprised. Ernie did warn him.

CHAPTER 25

"SORRY I'M LATE." Cathleen grabbed a chair and set it in the circle.

"We're just sitting down," Evie said. "Everything alright?"

"I was just giving Roberta instructions. Nathan has a sinus infection. He's on antibiotics. Three times a day."

"The ladies will take good care of him," Evie said. "Roberta's always on top of it. You know that."

Cathleen nodded, her expression still pensive.

Roberta was the longest serving nanny. She had been with the Church for over fifteen years, and had raised many of their children from birth. Like the advanced tutors for the older age groups, the nannies looked after those under eight years old and taught their reading, writing, and math lessons when they grew old enough.

"The wives club," as they called themselves, had seventeen children in total—not counting any they might have from their past lives. The Church only acknowledged those fathered by Curtis Hammond. They were commonly referred to as "the heirs."

"Let's jump in," Evie said. "I'd like to start by addressing the elephant in the room. I'm sure you have all heard about the FBI's presence in the building yesterday. Let me say there is nothing to worry about, but I want you to feel free to ask any questions you have. I'll try to answer them."

"I have one," Jessica said. "Was the Sage arrested?"

Jessica, the youngest of the group at twenty-nine years old, was trembling. Evie understood why the girl was nervous. All of them relied on Curtis for their survival and that of their children. Jessica had two—eight-year-old Birch, and four-year-old Rose. She knew she couldn't care for them without her husband's support.

All of them believed this same premise, but it wasn't true. It was the Church that provided for them, not Curtis. And as long as Evie was around, she would make sure they were all taken care of, no matter what.

"No, Jessica. He wasn't arrested."

"Then why was the ceremony canceled last night?" Amanda asked.

"It wasn't canceled," Evie said. "It was postponed. The Sage regretted that he became indisposed and told me that he had every intention of communing with you all in a few days' time."

The ceremony was something the wives looked forward to. Each month, they would gather for an extravagant meal, a meditation circle, and an affirmation of their vows. At its culmination, Curtis would choose which would share his bed for the following month.

Of course, all were welcome in his bed at times, but only one would sleep beside him each night. A true wife for the month. Technically, Evie was eligible. Happily, since taking up the position of Den Mother, she hadn't been picked. He wouldn't have dared.

"Will he be arrested?" Cathleen asked.

"I'll be honest with you," Evie said. "I don't know. But I do know that he has done nothing wrong. The government has decided they want to pick on us for some reason. That's fine. But it doesn't change anything, and it's nothing any of you have to worry about."

Cathleen raised her hand. "Is that why he's been acting so strange lately?"

"I don't know what you mean." Evie knew exactly what she meant, and she wasn't wrong. There were several factors triggering Curtis—that she knew of—but none she wished to air out in this forum.

Jessica chimed in. "Cathleen's right. He's been acting strange, like he's depressed or something. Please don't tell him I said that."

"You know this is a safe space. All of you know you can speak freely here." Evie wasn't just placating them. These women were her responsibility, one she took seriously. And although she didn't let on, she was concerned with Jessica's assessment. As the wife chosen at the last ceremony, she would have the most intimate knowledge regarding Curtis' mood. She could read between the lines and guess that what Jessica was really trying to say is that he had been uninterested in engaging in his husbandly duties.

"It's obvious what's going on," Amanda said. "Are you all stupid? He brought that new girl here. That's why he's been ignoring us. He's more interested in her than us. Tell me I'm wrong."

Evie could have dismissed her concerns. After all, Amanda was only upset because she was convinced that she would be the one picked if the ceremony had happened as planned. But she made it a point to never lie to them. Not unless it was critical, or she was forced to do so.

"It is true that the Sage considers Adrianna to be a possible candidate. I would have thought you would all be happy. She's beautiful and seems like a sweet woman."

For whatever reason, Cathleen couldn't speak without raising her hand. Evie had told her it was unnecessary a million times, to no effect. She held it high as she spoke. "I'm okay with it. She looks fun. I call dibs."

"No one's got dibs, Cathleen. Now, is there anything else about the raid, or can we move on? Anyone other than these three wish to speak?"

Silence.

"No? Okay, then." Evie opened her planner. "Let's go through the schedule for this week."

CHAPTER 26

"RIGHT THIS WAY." The hostess grabbed two menus and led Blake and Haeli to a window booth.

The lively breakfast crowd contrasted with the low-key atmosphere. All in all, it was what Blake expected.

Haeli had wanted to have breakfast on the patio at the Fenway. Blake was all in until they showed up and saw Counterfeit Coverdale in his usual spot, this time with a single Asian girl. Unlike the previous run-in, Coverdale was drunk and being loud and obnoxious. Blake had been in no mood to deal with it.

The diner was the recommendation of the kid at the front desk. "Best breakfast burritos in town," he'd claimed. The jury was still out.

"Nice to have a minute to catch our breath, isn't it?" Haeli pushed the condiment tray to the side and put her hands on the table, palms up.

Blake took her hands in his. "I know you've been wanting to get away, just the two of us. I promise when this is all done, we'll go somewhere. Wherever you want." Blake paused. "Except Switzerland. Or France. Or Germany. Or Israel. Or Botswana—"

"Okay, okay. I get it. I'm an international pariah."

"You haven't pissed off anyone in the Caribbean yet," Blake chuckled.

Haeli scrunched her brow and bowed her head.

"No. The islands too?"

Haeli cracked her wise-guy grin. "I'm just kidding." She laughed. "The Caribbean sounds good."

"What can I get for you folks?" The waitress seemed to appear out of nowhere. Blake read her name tag.

Niki.

"Mornin' Niki. I think we're both going with the breakfast burrito." Blake checked with Haeli. "Right?"

Haeli agreed.

"Two breakfast burritos." Niki wrote on her notepad. "Grits on the side?"

"Sure, why not? And coffees."

"I'll bring a pot. That all?"

Blake looked at Haeli and found no objections. "Yeah. Thanks."

"Hey, I meant to ask you," Haeli said. "Anything new on Fezz?"

"Not that I'm aware of. I texted with Griff for a couple minutes last night. He didn't mention anything."

The waitress came back carrying a silver carafe and two ceramic mugs. As she placed the mugs down and started pouring, Blake touched her on the arm.

"Can I ask you something?"

"Sure, hun."

"You know anything about that Church down the street?"

Haeli kicked him under the table. He waved her off.

"Why, you lookin' to join?"

"Maybe," Blake said. "Are you a member?"

Niki laughed. "Shit no. And if I was you, I'd steer clear of that place —no pun intended."

Blake glanced at Haeli. She frowned back at him. "Steer clear? Is it that bad?"

"Worse." Niki put both of her palms on the table and leaned forward. Her head swiveled between Blake and Haeli. "Most people around here wouldn't even say nothin'. But I don't care. Look at me. What are they gonna do to me? Those people are weird and they're freakin' everywhere. Probably half the people in here right now. Don't even get me started."

Getting her started was exactly what Blake was trying to do. Although, given what she said, even he thought she should keep her voice down.

"So what are they? Some kind of cult?" Blake knew damn well what they were. He had no idea where he was going with the line of questioning, but he hoped she might tell them something they didn't already know. Sometimes it just took starting the conversation.

"Don't know about no cult, but they all think they own the place, I can tell you that." She lowered her voice to a whisper. "You see that girl, the waitress over there? Sarah. She's one of them. Total bitch. I mean, where does she get off? Miss high and mighty. Last I checked, we're both working the same shit job. I'm tellin' yas, she is weird with a capital W. They all are."

Wow, Niki, tell us how you really feel.

Blake glanced over his shoulder at the woman their waitress called Sarah. She was attractive, probably in her thirties, and didn't seem all that weird from a distance. But she did seem perturbed. Now staring in their direction, there was a good chance she had heard Niki's less than stellar assessment.

"Anyways, like I said, stay away from them and you'll be good. Your food should be out in a minute." She walked away.

"Interesting woman," Haeli said.

Blake kept his eyes forward. "The other waitress behind me. Is she still staring?"

Haeli checked with a quick glance behind Blake as she brought the cup of coffee to her lips. "Yep."

"I think we should talk to her."

"We're not talking to her." She set the coffee mug back on the table. "Mick, the only thing it does is get people riled up. We're not going to learn anything more than we already know."

"You're probably right. But she's not staring for nothing. It's like there's something she wants to tell us."

"Look." Haeli pointed over Blake's shoulder. "She's leaving. Can we drop it now?"

Blake looked. Haeli was right. She was carrying a pile of dishes into the kitchen.

"Please."

Blake sighed. "Consider it dropped."

SARAH DROPPED the plates in the basin, wiped her hands and pulled her cell phone from her apron pouch. With the phone to her ear, she opened the back door and stepped outside.

"Hi. Anastasia. It's Sarah again. Can I talk to him?"

She listened to the fabricated response.

"That's fine. Just have him call me back. Tell him it's about the ginger."

CHAPTER 27

FEZZ HUFFED along North Main Street. Salon, post office, firehouse. This was only his second-round trip jaunt, and the scenery was already getting old.

When he'd left, he'd instructed Ian to stay at the motel. This time, with Jodi already there, there was a good chance he'd obey.

After the incident at the restaurant, Fezz figured the party was over. Jodi would take her first opportunity to escape, and Ian would be a nervous wreck. But to his surprise, the rest of the evening hadn't been derailed at all. They ate and talked and even laughed together for two more hours before heading back to the motel for the night. Ian and Jodi seemed to have a connection. Fezz had to admit, he was becoming fond of her, too.

This morning he'd tried to call Ernie, but he wasn't picking up. It was worth the ten-minute walk to check on him. Call it peace of mind.

As he approached, he noticed there were no motorcycles parked out front.

Off to a good start.

The garage bays were closed, which meant the shop was probably closed. Fezz figured Ernie was shorthanded and had to take the wrecker out.

Just to be sure, Fezz tried the door. It was open.

Inside, there was no one behind the counter.

"Ernie?" Fezz remembered the last time he'd popped in. It wasn't quite so tranquil. He opened the interior door to the garage. "Ernie, you here?"

Empty.

Behind and to the left of the counter was Ernie's office. The broom closet-sized room was open, and it was clear no one was inside, unless Ernie was on the floor. The thought did occur to him that he should check.

Fezz peeked in. No Ernie, but there was something that caught his eye. On the wall was a shadowbox frame. Inside were three medals, and a placard engraved with the name "Ernest R. Campbell." Fezz recognized the awards.

Purple Heart. Distinguished Service Medal, and a Silver Star.

Ernie, you sly bastard.

At no point since he'd met Ernie would he have guessed the man was a veteran. Then again, this was often the case when it came to true warriors. Look at Blake. And himself.

In Fezz's experience, the more dangerous a person, the more unassuming they were. The loud, cocky guys with their military bearing—pussycats. Chances were, Ernie was the real deal.

One of the humblest soldiers involved in the Iraq conflict was an Army Sergeant First Class named Dillard Johnson. Stateside, Johnson could be found spending time with the family, surfing, and volunteering with no outward indication of his service. As the commander of a Bradley Fighting Vehicle nicknamed "Carnivore," however, Johnson had personally racked up 2746 confirmed kills. Which also made him the deadliest soldier in United States history.

"Ray," Ernie said as he came through the garage door. "Sorry, didn't realize you were waiting here. I was out back."

"No worries," Fezz said. "I just stopped in to see how everything was going."

"With what? Your truck or the Demon Squad?"

"The Demon Squad? Don't tell me that's the name of their little gang."

Ernie laughed. "Not little. The Demon Squad is a big deal down south. Based in Texas."

"So, what are they doing up here?"

"Who knows? But they opened a clubhouse here. About a mile out. This guy named Butch Gossamer is the president of the chapter. A real ass. Calls himself Hawk, if you can believe that."

"So this Butch guy is from Byers, or just showed up?"

"He's from Byers, I think. Then he was in Texas. Odessa. Mind you, this is just what I heard. He petitioned to open a chapter here and took a bunch of guys with him. I don't know if he got booted from down there or what. But he's been a pain in our asses ever since."

"Who's Snake then?"

"Snake is Gossamer's buddy. Another winner." Ernie rolled his eyes. "When they first came into town, nobody paid much mind. Guess they were busy building the clubhouse, bolstering membership or whatever. Everyone knew what they were doin' in there. It was all about booze and women—you know. But then, as time went on, they started messin' with the residents. Going to the businesses and offering protection—from what, I don't know. And it just got worse and worse."

"I don't get it," Fezz said. "I don't mean to pry, but I noticed your medals. In your office."

"You saw that, did ya?" Ernie averted his eyes and snorted. "Past life."

"Marines?"

"Scout Sniper. Desert Storm."

"How are you letting these guys come in here and run over you? No offense, but I mean—"

"They're not worth it. I came back here to be left alone. I'd seen enough. Before I went in, I loved working on cars, machinery, fixing anything and everything. When I got out, I decided I would open a shop, mind my business. I know Byers isn't the most exciting place, but I wouldn't want to be anywhere else."

"I understand. Not trying to overstep, I'm just trying to wrap my head around how these knuckleheads have such a hold over this town."

Fezz shook his head. "They paid me and my son a visit last night. Just harassed us, but they're treading the line."

"At first, most of us pushed back. Pay them for so-called protection, not a chance. Then, Jackie's liquor store down on forty burned down. With Jackie in it. Everyone knew the Demon Squad was responsible, hell they made it a point to make it known. There was never enough proof to arrest anyone. The Fire Marshall couldn't determine arson. Said it could have been a faulty space heater. So, they skated."

"And everyone else fell in line."

"Including me. It was just easier to pay than to deal with them. I'm not in this business for the money. I'm just trying to keep a roof over my head and food in my belly. Other than that, what else do I need?"

Ernie had a point. Fezz was a magnet for trouble, but maybe he brought it on himself. Not every wrong needed to be righted. Anyway, he was out of the vigilante game. He'd be leaving the hero act to Blake and Khat and the others.

"So is that why you came down here?" Ernie asked. "Or did you want to know about the truck?"

"Did you get her done?"

"No." Ernie laughed. "Parts still aren't in."

"Tell me the truth, Ernie. Should I just buy a new truck?"

"Listen, if you do that, I'll take the old one off your hands. Give you a fair price, too. She really is a beaut."

Fezz laughed and shook his head. "Just call me when it's done."

CHAPTER 28

"PETER, HOW ARE YOU?" Evie put her arms out, ready to accept her hug.

Peter acquiesced. "I'm fine. They told me you needed to see me."

"I asked Matthew if you were around, that's all. It wasn't pressing."

"Well, I'm here now. What is it?"

"I wanted to talk about your father."

Peter chuckled. "In that case, I think we'll to need to set aside the afternoon."

"I'm serious, Peter. I'm worried about him."

"Everyone's worried about him." Peter shrugged. "What do you want me to tell you?"

"I could use your help. The wives are noticing he's not been himself. And now he's obsessed with this woman, Adrianna. He's not sleeping or eating well. And with this whole investigation going on—honestly, I think he's on the verge of a mental breakdown."

"It's not just us who's noticing," Peter said. "There's been rumblings from the membership. You know as well as I do, that's the bigger problem. Look at what's going on. He hasn't been meeting with the members. He blows off scheduled sessions. It makes a difference. Numbers are dropping. Retention is suffering. I'm doing my best to hold it together."

"I know you are, and I'm not saying any of this is your fault. I'm just trying to figure out what to do about it."

"Get him to do his thing," Peter said. "Shake some hands. Dole out some bullshit wisdom. Be the 'Sage.' You know they all look to him—even if we're doing all the real work behind the scenes. I've got my hands full keeping the wolves at bay. You know better than anyone what I'm dealing with. I'm running out of beds and we're getting dangerously close to losing control of them. There's only so many we can handle at a time."

"I agree, but we don't have a choice. Curtis is half the problem. Sometimes I wonder if it wouldn't be better if he just faded off into the sunset. Retire to the Keys with the girls. We could handle this. Get it back on track."

Peter put his hand on Evie's shoulder. "The time will come. Have faith."

"You know I do. I ask the Universe every day to give me the strength to see this through. And to look out for you. I worry about you, too."

"Don't worry about me," Peter said. "I can take care of myself."

Evie outstretched her arms and moved in for another hug. She squeezed him tight. "You're my son. Of course I worry. It's a mother's job."

CHAPTER 29

"THE KID WAS RIGHT," Haeli said. "Darn good burrito.

Blake flicked on his signal and waited for a break in traffic to turn left. "Not bad at all."

"Want to take a walk or something? It's a beautiful day."

"I'll pass." Blake took the left and then another onto Bayshore Boulevard. "I want to keep an eye on the cameras. With any luck, my mother will pop up. Plus, we only have the unit for a couple days, we need to take advantage. The more intel we have the better."

Haeli groaned. "We spent the whole night looking at it. Don't you want to stretch your legs a little? Just for a bit? Then we go back to it."

"You can take the car," Blake said. "Or take a walk on the beach out in front of the hotel. I just don't want to waste any time."

"Fine." Haeli pouted.

It was a small miracle she didn't put on her cutesy voice and pull her sing-song shenanigans. He was grateful. Mostly because it would have worked.

Bayshore turned into Broadway. After a right and a quick left through Marina Plaza, they were on Edgewater Drive.

Blake peered into the rearview mirror. "Haeli. The sedan, two cars behind us—was it in the lot outside the restaurant?"

She twisted around and looked through the rear window. "I'm not sure. Why?"

"It's been behind us for a while. Staying back, like he's trying not to be conspicuous."

Haeli took another look. "There's two people in the front. Men, looks like."

"Ya know what, I'm going to take the long way. Just in case."

Although the hotel was only a few blocks up, Blake didn't want to take the risk of leading anyone to where they were staying. Instead, he took an abrupt left onto President Street. He slowed down and waited for the car to pass.

Only it didn't. It turned onto President Street and slowed to match their speed.

"Not good," Haeli said.

The average person might not have thought much about it. A mere coincidence that they were going to the same place. It wasn't out of the question, after all. But it wasn't where the car was going so much as how. Slowing until other cars passed and slotted in between them, adjusting their speed to match Blake's, and even the fact that both occupants appeared to stare straight ahead. All telltale signs. Normal people talk, they're animated, and the passenger looks at the driver or out the window. But not in the car behind them. This was a tail if Blake ever saw one. And he had seen more than his share.

"Be ready," Blake said.

"What's the plan?"

"If we find an opportunity, we should bail. Let 'em come on foot. All I need is to create a big enough gap." Blake slammed the accelerator. The big V8 screamed and the car shot forward. He blew the stop sign and made a hard right onto Douglas Avenue, then opened it up again.

Behind them, the sedan fell out of sight for several seconds. Blake checked the mirror and could see it turning toward them. On the left was what looked like a driveway, cutting into a small condo complex of four buildings. It had a private street sign. "Douglas Place."

"Hold on." Blake jerked the wheel left and jammed the brakes, sending the back end of the car sliding to the right. He hit the apron, and the car bounced forward.

In twenty feet, he jerked the wheel again, this time to the right.

Ahead and at the end of the four small buildings, Douglas Place ended at a tee with another cross street.

"You go right, I go left, we meet in the middle." It was all Blake had time to say before reaching the intersection.

He assumed the tail had seen them turn, which meant in another second they'd be coming around the corner. At least, he hoped so.

Screeching to a stop, Blake flung his door open. "Close the door," he said as jumped out, whipped his own door closed and headed for the edge of the building. Behind him, Haeli was heading off in the opposite direction.

Blake circled around the outer perimeter, headed north, and cut back west through the walking path between the two east side buildings. Across the street, he could see Haeli crouching in her own identical alley. Of course, she had beaten him there by a mile.

On the street, the sedan was pulling behind the running Mustang. Two men, both busting out of black polo shirts, got out.

Blake peered around the corner. The men were approaching the car, and it didn't look like they were planning to deliver well-wishes. He gave Haeli the signal and the two of them sprinted onto the street and up behind their pursuers. The predators had become the prey.

On the driver's side, Blake came in hard, striking the man with a tucked fist in the kidney.

A few feet away, Haeli jumped on the other man's back, wrapped her legs around him, and squeezed her forearm against his neck.

Blake's guy spun around with a haymaker. He ducked and returned an elbow to the man's eye, knocking him to the ground and opening a gash on his brow.

Riding him like a bronco, Haeli held tight as her man bucked and stomped his way around the front of the car.

Before the other could get to his feet, Blake dropped a knee and straddled his opponent. Blood gushed down the man's face. He delivered several more punches, straight down into the man's mouth and nose. Beside them, the human bronco fell like a sack of cement, Haeli still clamped down on his neck. He was out cold.

Both Blake and Haeli climbed to their feet and brushed themselves off. The bleeding man groaned and whimpered.

Sucking wind, they got back in the Mustang.

Before putting the car in drive, Blake put one arm out the window and leaned over the side to better see the bleeding man on the ground below. "Tell your boss he's going to have to do better than that. Or he can come see me himself."

Peeling out, they turned onto Lyndhurst and headed east toward the Fenway. Each took a silent moment to catch their breath.

"Well, that was unexpected." Blake snickered. "I guess we're playing full contact now. Fine with me."

Before Haeli could respond, her phone rang. She dug it out and looked at the screen. "It's Hammond. I'm not getting it."

Blake pulled the car to the side of the road and stopped. "Pick it up."

Haeli mumbled something unflattering, then hit the speaker button. "Hello?"

"Hi, Adrianna?"

"Curtis?"

"I hope I'm not bothering you. If you're busy I—"

"No. Not at all. I'm just relaxing by the pool. Trying to finish my book." She looked at Blake and scowled. Her voice was as bubbly as could be. "How are you?"

"I'm great," Curtis said. "I was wondering if you'd be interested in having lunch with me."

"Today?"

Curtis chuckled. "Yes, today."

"Um..."

Blake bobbed his head and waved his hands like a lunatic. In his mind, he was screaming, "Yes. Say Yes." In his opinion, there shouldn't have even been any hesitation.

"Okay, sure."

"Great," Curtis said. "I can come pick you up if you want."

"No, that won't be necessary," she blurted. "I can meet you at your office."

"Suit yourself. Can you be here around noon?"

"Sure. I'll be there at noon."

"See you then." The phone disconnected.

"What timing," Blake said.

Haeli glared at him. "I told you I didn't want to do it again, Mick."

"I know but hear me out. This might be our only shot. When these goons get back and tell their story, it's only a matter of time before they put two and two together. They'll be suspicious, at a minimum. We have a decent enough plan and I think it could work. This plays right into it."

"I thought you wanted to wait until we found your mother."

"I did. But the timeline changed. After this, they're not going to stop coming, and once they know you're with me, we lose our *in*. We have to act quick, Haeli. You know it's true."

"This is the last time, Mick, seriously. If this doesn't work, I'm not going back. Not with Hammond."

"If this doesn't work, meeting up with Hammond will no longer be an option."

Haeli smirked. "You have a point."

"Let's get back and run through it from start to finish. We don't have much time."

Blake pulled onto the road and hit the gas.

Haeli threw her head back against the headrest and sighed. "What I do for love."

CHAPTER 30

"I'M TIRED." Ian trudged along, wading through the tall grass. Almost as far as he could see were flat open fields. "Where are we going?"

"I told you, it's a surprise," Jodi said. "You complain a lot."

"It's just—we weren't supposed to leave the motel. And now we're so far away and it'll take forever to get back and we're going to be in trouble when—"

Jodi stopped and pressed her index finger to his lips. "It'll be worth it, I promise. Anyway, it's right up here. Two more minutes."

Ian looked around. *What's right up here?* There was nothing but grass and a couple of distant silos. Regardless, he kept pushing forward. She could have led him to Mexico and he would have followed.

"What do you want to do when you grow up?" she asked.

"Me? I don't know." For a second, he considered telling her what he really wanted. But Fezz's voice rang in his ears—"Ian, don't do it." Anyway, it would be hard to explain how he wanted to be a part of his fake dad's friend group, who hacked computers, shot guns and jumped out of planes for fun. He wanted to be as good a hacker as his mother had been, which meant he had to be just as careful. If there was one thing he'd learned from her, it was how to stay off the radar.

"I want to be a detective," Jodi said.

"Really?"

"Yeah." She smiled and her eyes seemed to twinkle. "Like Sherlock Holmes or Phillip Marlow."

Ian had heard of Sherlock Holmes, but Phillip Marlow? He decided to play along and hope she didn't ask if he knew who Marlow was. "Cool."

"Here it is."

From out of the grass appeared a pond, hidden in the flat landscape until they were standing on its bank.

"A pond?"

"I told you it'd be worth it."

Ian wasn't sure what made her so excited about a big puddle in the middle of nowhere, but if she liked it, who was he to judge? "Nice. Are there fish in there?"

"I don't think so. Never seen any."

"Alligators?"

Jodi laughed. "No, there's no alligators. It's a swimming hole. You never seen a swimming hole?"

Ian had spent most of his time at the edge of the largest "swimming hole" in the world—the Atlantic Ocean. But swimming in it wasn't his cup of tea. Whenever he did go in, it was because he had fallen off his paddle board or flipped the kayak. No, he'd stick with the pool. There was nothing that could eat you in a pool.

"Well, what are you waiting for?" Jodi started taking off her cowboy boots and socks. "You said you were worried about the time."

"What are you doing?"

"Going in. Whatta ya think I'm doing?"

Ian hadn't planned on this. He thought he was going to look at something interesting and then go right back. He got more than he bargained for. "We don't have our bathing suits."

"You just go in your underwear, silly." Jodi dropped her jeans, revealing the pair of boy briefs. She then turned away from him and pulled her shirt over her head.

Ian took a gasping breath. Butterflies filled his stomach. There she was, standing almost naked, with her arms across her chest and her bare back in full view. Embarrassed, he felt it appropriate to look away.

But he couldn't help it. He dropped his chin, but let his eyes rise. She was the prettiest thing he'd ever seen.

Jodi ran and jumped over the edge splashing into the water. She went under, then popped back to the surface and pushed her hair back. "Your turn."

"No, not me."

"Come on, you can't come all the way out here and not come in. Don't you want to swim with me?"

He wanted to do everything with her. But he was self-conscious about undressing in front of her and would rather avoid the murky water.

A weird thought occurred to him. How was he going to be on the team someday, trusted to handle himself and have the others' backs if he couldn't even jump into a pond in his underwear? If she could do it, he could too.

As Ian kicked his shoes off, Jodi began cheering him on. She was laughing. Not at him, but with him. It was infectious and soon he found himself giggling as well.

He stripped down and jumped in, splashing her. The water was as warm as the air.

"Woo! Come on." Jodi began to swim further toward the center of the pond.

Ian bounced until he reached the edge of where he could stand and stopped.

After a minute, Jodi flipped around and headed back toward Ian. "Can you swim?"

"Yeah."

"Can you?" She goaded. "Do I need to carry you?"

Jodi scooped her arms under Ian and took a few steps toward land. Ian broke free and grabbed her. He ducked down and then picked her up over his shoulder. She whooped and howled in laughter. He dumped her back into the water.

For an hour they played and talked and goofed and laughed. Ian laughed so hard his stomach hurt. He was exhausted, but he couldn't ever in his life remember having as much fun.

Near the bank where their clothes lay spread out in the grass, they found a submerged boulder. Up to their shoulders in water, they sat together, side by side. Ian felt Jodi's hand brush his. Then she slid her fingers between his.

"This is my favorite place," Jodi said. "No one ever comes out here."

"How often do you come here?"

"A lot. I can get clean. Or sometimes I wash my clothes. Mostly, I sit on the edge and read."

Ian nodded, letting a silent moment pass. "Do you miss your aunt?"

"Sometimes. But I miss my Mom more. I can barely remember her, but I miss her anyway. I always wonder if she's still alive. I think she is, and I think I'll see her again when I'm old enough to find her."

"I can help you find her someday."

"You would do that for me?" Jodi smiled.

"Of course. I'll be able to do it, too. I'll be able to track anyone down. That's what we do, we help people who need it. If it was my Mom, I'd want someone to help me too."

"Were you very young? I mean, when you lost your Mom."

"I was—" Ian didn't know what to say. Did he tell her it had been less than two weeks? How would he explain what had happened to her? Did he even want to talk about it? "It was recent."

"Oh. I'm so sorry, Ian. What happened? Was she sick like Auntie Bern?"

Ian took a deep breath. Vivid images flashed through his head. Images he had imagined when Fezz told him. Images he couldn't get out of his head. "There was an accident. I don't really want to talk about it."

"I understand. I mean, I really do. But if you ever do want to talk..."

There was an awkward silence. Ian looked out at the water. He could feel Jodi looking at him but when he turned, she was facing away. He had one thought on his mind and he couldn't help but say it.

"I don't want to leave here."

"I don't want you to leave either," Jodi said. "It's really nice to have a friend who knows what it's like. It's really nice just to have a friend."

"Yeah, it is."

Both looked out at the landscape. The silence was back, but it didn't feel as awkward.

Then, it happened. Jodi leaned over and gave him a peck on the cheek.

Ian sat frozen, his mouth hanging open. Unable to move a muscle—to properly celebrate the greatest moment of his life.

"We—we should—you know, start heading back." Ian stood up and leapt onto the bank. He gathered his clothes, holding them at his waist, and stared back at Jodi.

She laughed. "I'll come out, but you've gotta turn around."

"Oh, right. Sorry." Ian turned his back.

Behind him he heard the splash as—the very naked—Jodi hopped from the rock onto the grass. He pulled his shirt over his head.

When he was dressed, he stood still, waiting for the okay to turn around. After a minute, Jodi walked up next to him. "That was fun."

Ian looked her in the eyes, built up the nerve, and then leaned in and kissed her on the cheek.

Jodi smiled, took his hand, and headed home.

CHAPTER 31

HAELI PEELED the silk blouse away from her chest. The humidity was high and even the short walk had caused her to work up a sweat. It wasn't the look she was going for, but something told her Curtis wouldn't be dissuaded.

"Adrianna, welcome back." Anastasia popped up from behind her desk the moment Haeli walked in. She abandoned her acrylic cockpit to greet Haeli face-to-face. "He's expecting you."

"Sorry I'm a few minutes late. Not feeling well," Haeli said. It wasn't true in the slightest, but the notion would become critical to the plan. Best plant the seeds sooner than later. "Stomach bug or something."

Anastasia paused as if searching for the appropriate response, but it never came. Instead, she addressed one of the two security guards posted nearby. "Ronan, would you watch the desk for a minute? I'm going to take Miss Adrianna upstairs."

The guard took the cue and moved to take up Anastasia's usual position.

"Follow me."

As they moved up the stairs and into the administration hallway, Haeli peeked into each office as they passed. Things had seemed to calm down since last she saw. Much of the mess had been cleaned up, but there was an eerie stillness impregnating the cool, climate-controlled air.

"It's nice to see you back," Anastasia said. "I trust your tour was informative?"

"That's one way to put it."

"Good. We're glad to have you. You will see. This is a wonderful place to be. There are so many wonderful people here."

Haeli took a step in front of Anastasia and stopped, turning toward her. "Can I ask you something?" She checked her surroundings. "Do you really believe that?"

"It's the truth. Many people's lives have been changed by our wonderful programs. The Sage is a miracle worker."

Wonderful.

English wasn't Anastasia's first language, but that wasn't the cause of her lack of vocabulary. It was like she was reading off a script. "Wonderful" or not, Anastasia didn't believe a word that came out of her own mouth. As her father had always said, if you can't say something nice, don't say anything at all. For Anastasia, it wasn't an option.

"Maybe, but that's not what I asked. Do you believe it?"

Anastasia opened her mouth, but no words came out for several seconds. Her uplifted cheeks and wide eyes sagged. "I don't know what you want me to say, ma'am. I just work here."

"I don't want you to say anything. But if you are going to speak, say something real. We're both smart, capable women, right? We both know what this is."

Haeli knew she had to tread lightly. Her mission was to string Curtis along, not to offend him. But Anastasia wasn't Curtis. She had no stake in his game.

"Prostitute," Anastasia blurted.

"Excuse me?" Not expecting Anastasia to lash out with name-calling, Haeli was taken aback by her tone. There was a little bitterness under the saccharine, after all.

"You wanted me to say something real. That's real, right? You're here to trade sex for money and fancy things. It's not like you're the first. Or the last."

Haeli smiled. Anastasia was dead on. Of course, Haeli had no intention of following through, but Anastasia didn't know that.

"And you're okay with that?" Haeli asked.

"I'm still here, aren't I? It's none of my business what you do. And I don't care. He asked me to bring you, I'm bringing you. Are you okay with *that*?

"I am."

"Wonderful." Anastasia carried on down the hall.

In a weird way, Haeli liked her. One of the many casualties of that screwed up place, perhaps. On the other hand, she embodied everything wrong with it. A bright, optimistic exterior with sheer disregard lurking below.

Upon reaching Curtis's office, Anastasia gave three rapid knocks.

"Yes?" Curtis said from within.

Anastasia opened the door and gave a curt announcement. "Adrianna for you."

"Nice talking with you," Haeli said.

With a sarcastic smile, Anastasia put on her sweetest voice yet. "Have a wonderful time."

"Adrianna," Curtis said, "Please, come in."

CURTIS TOOK IN THE VIEW. Adrianna was a sight to behold. The neckline of her silk top plunged low and her skin glistened. His body shivered with anticipation.

"I'm glad you accepted my invitation," he said. "It's a pleasure to see you again."

"The pleasure is all mine. To be honest, I was hoping you would call."

"That's good to hear. After our last time together, I wasn't sure if you had gotten weirded out by our—how do I put it–our lifestyle. For some people, it's a lot to take in."

Adrianna waved him off. "If you mean the polygamy thing, it

doesn't weird me out at all. I'm kind of a free spirit that way." She giggled.

"I could tell that about you. From the moment we met. I said, 'this woman has a special kind of energy. She'd fit in perfectly here.'"

"So funny, I thought the same thing. After I left, I was like, 'I don't know what it is about this man, but I feel like I have to be open to him. I have to listen.' Of course, you probably get that a lot." She fluttered her eyelashes.

"It's true, I do. But despite what people think, I'm only the messenger. The real power is within *you*—if you're open to it, and it sounds like you are. The first step is walking through the door, and look, here you are."

"Right? I have to tell you, I have not been feeling well today. Something I ate, or a little bug, I don't know. I didn't plan on going anywhere. But when you called, I knew I had to come. It's like something was drawing me here. Something saying, 'you have to go.'"

"Always listen to your gut." As they were talking, he noticed Adrianna's collar was bunched, causing it to flair on one side. Taking the opportunity, he closed the distance between them. "Your collar. Here let me."

Curtis stepped closer and ran his fingers under the silk flap, from the back of her neck to her collar bones.

"There," he said as he slid his hands to her shoulders and down her arms.

Adrianna leaned in and pressed her lips to his. He could taste a hint of cherries. Curtis pulled her close and kissed her deeply, lost in the enchantment of her scent. She ran her hands down his back, to his hips, and then his buttocks. With force, she pinned his pelvis to hers.

Then, she pulled away, wiped her mouth and giggled. "I'm sorry. I hope that wasn't too forward. I couldn't help myself."

"Please, don't be sorry." He adjusted his trousers. "The feeling was mutual."

"So—" Adrianna clasped her hands and wiggled one foot. "Lunch?"

"Yes, of course. As promised. I know a very nice place, I think you'll enjoy. Much less stuffy than this office. Very private. We can get to know each other a little better. I'm interested in hearing more about you."

"Before we go," Adrianna said, "I'm afraid I need to find a restroom. I'll just be a few minutes."

"Of course. I have a private bath right through that door." He pointed over her shoulder. "Feel free. I'll let my driver know we'll be leaving shortly."

Adrianna's eyes widened, and she swallowed hard. "I'd rather—uh, this is embarrassing. My stomach isn't well. What I mean is, you're right here and—is there a ladies' room nearby?"

"Ah, yes. Straight down the hall, follow it left and you'll see it. Take your time. I'm all yours this afternoon."

"Thank you. I'll be right back." Adrianna scurried out the door.

Curtis enjoyed the view on her way out.

HAELI CLOSED Hammond's office door behind her. She scanned the area. The coast was clear.

Instead of heading straight, she darted to the left, following the route she had committed to memory. At the end of the hall was a window looking out into the courtyard. To the right of it, was a staircase. Exactly as she remembered.

Haeli bounded down the stairs. Before busting out into the first-floor atrium, she peered through the one-by-one mesh-lined window. The angles were limited, but she didn't see anyone.

She opened the door a foot, stuck her head through, and took one last look. The bright corridor, lined with windows on one side and hanging art on the other, was empty. At the other end, was another door. This one leading to the outside. On the other side of that door was the moment of truth.

If Blake was successful in scaling the wall next to the produce stand —and thus defeating the spear-like tips of the wrought iron fence crowning the high concrete barrier and avoiding the cameras covering most of the courtyard—he would be waiting for her at the door. If not, she'd be having lunch with a sleazeball. Either way, she'd know in a few seconds.

One last sprint in the open and she drove her hip into the latch release bar. When the door flung open, Blake slipped inside.

"Thank God." Haeli let out a breath she hadn't realized she was holding. "Get to the stairwell."

The two ran back the way she'd come and ducked into the cover of the first-floor landing.

With a flourish, Haeli produced a keycard and handed it to Blake. "Don't ask me what I had to do to snatch this from his pocket. You're welcome."

Blake kissed her on the cheek. "I owe you one."

"You know where you're going?" she asked, even though she knew the answer. They had run through it fifty times together.

"I'm good," Blake said. "Stall him as long as you can."

"I will. Just hurry." Haeli rushed up the steps.

Blake hung back. He would have to go the same way once Haeli got back to Hammond's office.

When she hit the second floor, she slowed, caught her breath, and prepared herself. Then she strolled back into the office.

"Ready to go?" Hammond asked.

"Would you mind if we hung here for a couple more minutes? I might have to use the ladies' room one more time. I'm really sorry about this."

"No problem." Hammond walked to the leather sofa and slapped one of the back cushions. "Here, have a seat. Relax for a minute. Would you like a drink?"

"Sure," Haeli said. "A drink would be perfect."

CHAPTER 32

BLAKE REACHED THE SECOND FLOOR, took a quick look down the hall, and then started walking. He imagined himself completing a mundane task—seeing Sheila in accounting or getting ready to clock out for the day. It was a strategy he'd used before. Sometimes the best way to avoid detection was to not avoid it at all. The mind was a powerful thing. Believe you don't belong and your body responds with furtive movements—little cues intuitively picked up by everyone around you. But believe you do, and poof—you're invisible.

He'd used the tactic outside of legitimate operations as well. Once, he'd snuck backstage at a Soundgarden concert with his late buddy Bonzo. They milled around, talked to a few people, even bullshitted with the band for a couple of minutes before they went on stage. No one ever asked what their job was or who they were. They'd gotten so cocky as to tell one of the security guards to let in two blondes hanging around by the stage door. The guard had listened. Why wouldn't he? Some random person wouldn't be doling out orders, would they?

This was no different. Chances were, anyone who worked in the building would have no idea who he was. With a few notable exceptions—Anastasia, the two goons who'd tossed him from the lobby, and the two others who were probably still nursing a couple of pretty bad headaches. Other than them, he had to assume Hammond himself would recognize him. But Haeli was taking care of that much.

The issue would arise on the way back. If he could find his father and mother—assuming his father knew where she was being held—their group would definitely be noticed. He had to hope he could find a way to keep them hidden.

He walked around the horseshoe, ready to give the obligatory wave or "afternoon" to a passing colleague. None materialized.

One left turn, and then another.

Ahead, past the windowed bridge connecting one building to the other, were two double doors. Blake recognized them from the video—or at least, they matched his expectation.

With no offices along the stretch, he picked up his pace to jog. Upon reaching the dead-end, he keyed in with Hammond's credentials and barged in.

Inside, he was met with two dozen curious stares. He was in the right place.

"Jim Brier," Blake announced. "Jim Brier, I need you to come with me."

His father stood up and froze. Blake could see the recognition in his eyes.

"What's this about?" another man asked.

The rest of the room remained quiet.

"It's alright Freddie." Otherwise completely still, Jim raised a hand toward the man. His face was void of any expression.

"Now, Mister Brier," Blake said.

With shuffling steps, Jim walked to Blake. The room watched intently.

"How did you—" Jim's face contorted. His eyes were glassy.

Blake whispered. "I'll explain everything. But we need to go. Right now."

As if carried by an apparition, Jim moved into the hallway.

"You." Blake pointed at the vocal man. "Freddie is it? Come here."

Outwardly cautious, Freddie obeyed.

"Hold this door."

Blake stepped out and Freddie took his position, holding the door three-quarters open. Blake turned his attention to his father.

"Where's Mom?"

"Mom? I don't know."

"Is she here? In the building?"

Tears filled Jim's eyes. "I don't know."

"Did something happen to her?" Blake raised his voice. "Is she alive?"

"Yes, she's alive." Jim's voice cracked, and a tear ran down his cheek.

Blake barely recognized the feeble man in front of him. Whatever he had been through over the past two decades, it had broken him. "Then we'll have to come back for her. We *will* come back for her."

"Is this your son?" Freddie whispered. "You can't get out of here. There's nowhere to go where they won't catch you."

"I wouldn't be so sure," Blake said.

While it wasn't foolproof, Blake had a plan for extraction. At the local hardware store, he'd purchased two chain fire ladders and a six by three sheet of heavy rubber. After dropping Haeli off, he'd gotten on his laptop and used the Piranha to disable all on-site cameras and jam all other Wi-Fi signals. Then, he'd gone to work in the wooded area behind the compound, setting up the route over the wall. The rubber, folded over the wrought iron spikes, gave a solid enough base to hook the two ladders—one on either side. With luck, his father would have the strength to climb them.

Blake turned to Freddie. "Do me a favor, give us a two-minute head start. Then do whatever you have to do. The door is open. The rest is up to you."

Grabbing his father's arm, Blake led him down the hallway. The fact that Jim didn't protest was confirmation enough that he wasn't, for some reason, living in the locked-down barracks voluntarily.

Peeking around the corner, he decided to cross the next section of corridor. A few more legs and they'd be in the stairwell, on the way to the courtyard. And as soon as his father was on the other side of that wall, they would be home free.

"Wait," Jim said. "I have to go back. I need to get something."

"There's no time," Blake said.

"Blake." His father's eyes became stern. Much like the man he remembered. "I'm going back. Wait for me here."

FROM BEHIND THE COUCH, Hammond handed Haeli her drink. He leaned over so his mouth was close to Haeli's ear. Haeli could feel his hot breath on her neck. She fantasized about throwing her elbow into his throat.

"So you wanna do it right here? On the couch?"

Haeli didn't respond. There was only so far she would let this go on. If he touched her again, she couldn't be responsible for what she did to him. Anyway, Blake would probably agree, unconsciousness would trump distraction.

"No?" Hammond laughed. He walked around to face her. "Don't want to take one for the team?"

"What's that supposed to mean?"

Hammond cackled. "Did you really think I was that stupid? That I didn't know what you're doing here?" He checked his pockets and feigned surprise. "Oh, no. My keycard's gone. I must have lost it. Gee whiz."

Haeli sat back and smiled. The gig was up. But it didn't matter. By now, Blake would be on his way out. At least she didn't have to keep up the charade any longer.

"Well, this is awkward," Haeli said. "And we were having such a nice time."

"We were." Hammond's smug grin melted. "All of us. Including your boyfriend. Security should be giving him a warm welcome as we speak. Had a feeling we might know where he was headed. So we set a little trap for him."

Haeli figured he might get suspicious at some point. But this? She couldn't say she'd seen it coming. "How did you—?"

"I found it interesting that you always seemed to show up here on foot. Made me wonder, where you were coming from? Does she live close by, I wondered? I watched the recordings from when you came for the tour—watched you come from somewhere over a block away. So I went back to your first visit. Lo and behold, there you were getting out of a black Ford. Blake Brier's black Ford."

Took you long enough.

"Then, of course, I get a call that Blake was at a diner with a woman, described as attractive and petite with dark hair—that would be you. And Peter's men, who ran into the two of you out in town—they said the same thing. I figured, best to stay one step ahead of you."

"Good for you," Haeli snarled. "You win the prize."

"I have. You. And your boyfriend. You see, I knew what Blake Brier was after. And once I knew you were working together, I knew what your game was, too. But I have to hand it to my son, this little ruse was his idea. If we allowed you access—allowed you to think you had the upper hand—you'd both come barging in here like the arrogant fools you are. And now, you'll be our guests on a more permanent basis. So enjoy your drink, because you won't have another for quite some time."

———

BLAKE GLANCED AT HIS WATCH, then peeked around the corner.

If his father wasn't back in thirty seconds, he was going to get him. With each minute that ticked by, the chances of someone coming their way increased.

Footsteps approached from behind him.

"Okay, I got it." His father was carrying a stack of manila folders.

"Whatever that is, it better have been worth it. Now let's go."

Blake went first, making sure his father stayed close. At the next corner, Blake stopped and edged his way out until he had a clear view. He snapped back behind cover. "Two security guards."

"Are they coming this way?" Jim asked.

"They're standing in the middle of the hall, with their arms crossed. Like a blockade."

"You think they know we're coming?"

Blake shook his head. "How would they? I knocked the cameras out."

From behind, more footsteps approached. This time, there was more than one set.

"Two more," Jim said.

"I can see that." Blake took his father's arm and pulled him around the corner. "Stay with me."

Ahead, the faces of the two security guards lit up. They planted themselves firmly, and both dropped their arms to their sides.

Blake moved toward them at a steady pace. When he got about a foot away, he looked down at the floor, then exploded upward with a fist to the chin of the man on the left, followed by an elbow to the cheekbone of the man on the right. Both buckled over, grabbing at the pain.

Yanking his father by the arm, Blake pulled him between the two guards. "Run!"

Blake let go, and both men sprinted down the corridor. Behind them, two pursuers passed their injured brethren and continued giving chase. The other two fell in behind them.

Jim hobbled, pushing himself to what Blake assumed was his absolute max.

The men were catching up. And there was no doubt Blake was about to be tested. Maybe past his own limits. Four on one weren't very good odds.

"We're not going to make it," Jim huffed.

"No Dad," Blake pushed harder. "I don't think we are."

"I THINK I'll go ahead and pass on the offer." Haeli got up and moved toward the door. Hammond didn't try to stop her. "I've had enough of this place for a lifetime. I'll see myself out."

Haeli opened the door. Behind it stood two large men wearing black polo shirts. Neither had time to register what was happening before Haeli had kicked one in the groin and pulled the other's legs out from under him. As he hit the ground, she delivered a flurry of kicks to his skull. His head bounced back and forth without any tension. He was unconscious.

The second man was doubled over, holding his groin and groaning. She grabbed his head with two hands and slammed it into the door-frame. Still feeling pushback, she did it again. This time, the man went slack, and he tumbled over face first.

Hammond had worked his way around to the back of the couch as he watched the massacre unfold.

Coward.

Haeli ran toward him, planted a foot on the couch, and launched herself at him. Like a spider monkey, she grappled him to the ground and latched onto his neck. Cutting off the blood supply from the carotid artery, he passed out in mere seconds. She left him where he lay.

Looking around the office for something she could use as a weapon, she noticed a sliding door behind the sheer drapes. A possible escape route.

Muggy air flooded in as she cracked the slider and stepped out onto the balcony. She peered over the edge. Only one story.

The jump would be easy. And once on the ground, inside the fenced perimeter, she could make her way to Blake's extraction point.

But not knowing if Blake had been ambushed, she couldn't leave the building. He might need her help.

Haeli returned inside, stepped over Hammond's snoring body, and headed for the door.

Before she could climb over the two meatheads, she saw it. A human freight train was coming her way. Blake, his father, and an angry four-man caboose.

BLAKE LOOKED OVER HIS SHOULDER. The men were gaining on them. Focusing ahead, he saw Haeli standing in Hammond's doorway. Two piles of muscle at her feet. She waved him toward her.

"This way," she yelled.

Blake put his hand on his father's back and pushed. He gave it everything he had.

As he and his father stepped over the two men, crossing the threshold to Hammond's office, Haeli moved out of the way, kicking the door shut behind them. She turned the lock.

"Out there!" Haeli pointed to the open door, exposed by the sheer curtain blowing in the breeze.

From the hallway, the men smashed and banged. The door rattled, barely resisting the force.

Blake and Jim went first, and Haeli followed.

There was no question, at any second the wooden door would give way and four men would come spilling into the room.

Swinging his legs over the railing, Blake jumped. He hit the grass and rolled to break his fall.

"Dad, come on, I've got you." Blake held his arms out. When his father dropped down, Blake would wrap his arms around his falling body to lessen any impact.

Jim was reluctant.

"Trust me."

Jim climbed over the railing and then sat down on the edge. Then he slid forward, letting himself drop. Blake caught him.

A loud bang from within sent Haeli leaping over the railing. She landed and dropped to her knee.

"This way, around back," Haeli said.

By the time the men breached the door, they were half-way across the courtyard. On their way to freedom.

CHAPTER 33

IAN HOPPED on one leg to expel the water from his right ear. It didn't work.

Up ahead, Ian could see the back of the trailer park. Unlike the walk out, the way back went by in a flash. They talked about books and music, even though the only music Jodi knew was whatever they played on country radio.

It occurred to Ian that after all he had been through, his experience still didn't stack up to hers. Fending for yourself was a whole different ball game.

She'd never had to answer to anyone. Never been berated for not being where she was supposed to be. Funny, he thought. In a few minutes, she would no longer be able to say never.

"He's gonna be pissed," Ian said.

"No, he's not. We didn't do anything wrong."

Ian moaned. "Maybe you didn't."

"We'll just tell him I needed to go to my place to get something, and I didn't want to go alone. I do need to stop on the way back, anyway."

"Look at us," Ian said. "Our clothes are wet, he's not going to buy that. And we don't have time to stop."

"I need to."

"Why?"

"It's a girl thing."

"What's that mean, a girl thing?"

Jodi grunted. "Stop asking questions. Just come with me. It'll be quick. We're going right by there, anyway."

Ian didn't know why Jodi was acting so strange. What was the big secret? She was right though, they were going right by. At this point, what was a few extra minutes?

Out of the field and over the berm, they were at the side of her trailer.

"Can I come in with you?" Ian asked.

"Yeah, I just need to grab something."

Ian followed her. The spring-loaded door crashed closed behind him. "Ya know, when my dad said that he and I were going to help fix this place up, he really meant him. I don't know how to do any of that."

Jodi ducked into the back room and responded to him from there. "That's okay. You're strong and smart, I bet you'll be great at it." She emerged with nothing in her hands. "You gotta learn this stuff for when you grow up and get married and have a house, right?"

"I'm not getting married," Ian blurted.

"Why not? Don't you want to have children someday?"

"Do you?"

"Of course I do," she said. "Three. And a cute house and a big strong husband that's nice and kind and has money and doesn't leave me and the kids."

Jeesh. She's got it all worked out.

Ian didn't know where he'd be tomorrow, and she had her whole life planned. Not that it didn't sound nice, but his path was different. Married to the mission, as Fezz said.

He didn't want to offend her. And the truth was, if he ever was going to marry someone, she would be his choice. "You're right. That does sound—"

Outside, the rumble of motorcycles shook the trailer. They got louder and louder until it sounded like they were inside. Then, they staggered to silence.

Jodi went to the window and peeked outside. Ian squeezed in next to her.

"Darlene," she said.

In the middle of the dirt road, Darlene was talking to one of the biker men. He was fat and had a shaved head with tattoos on his scalp. Darlene was pointing, and the man looked over to Jodi's trailer.

Jodi and Ian ducked and stayed low.

"Just stay quiet," she said. "They'll go away."

"Is the door locked?"

She shook her head.

Ian crawled across the floor, reached up, and turned the latch. "Is that locked?"

"You shouldn't've done that. It's broken. Now we're gonna be stuck."

"Better than them getting in."

Jodi seemed to agree.

After a few minutes of quiet, a ruckus sounded outside. One of the men was yelling, although Ian couldn't make out what he was saying. Then a few men were yelling at once—whooping and laughing. Ian couldn't understand what they were doing. What did they want with them?

Ian scooted over to Jodi and sat next to her with his back against a chest of drawers covered in books.

Jodi huddled in close and he put his arms around her.

He could feel her jump as one of the motorcycles fired up. Then came another, and another.

Before they knew it, the whole gang was riding away.

Jodi got to her feet and peeked out the window. "They're gone."

"Darlene, too?" Ian asked.

"Yeah. Her too."

Ian got up off the floor. "What was that all about?"

"Who knows? Darlene's probably still pissed at me. The guy with tattoos on his head, I think that's Darlene's old man."

"Like, her father?" Ian asked.

"No, like her boyfriend. I don't know, she calls him her old man. If you ask me, she looks older than him."

"If you think they're really gone, we should get back. It's getting really late now."

Jodi went to the door and twisted the lock back to its original position. She tried the door, and it didn't budge. "Told you."

Ian gave it a shot. Same result.

"Come on," Ian said. "This just keeps getting worse and worse. Fezz is gonna kill me."

"Who's Fezz?"

"Uh. That's just something I say. Never mind. Is there a way to get it open?"

"Last time I used a knife. It was a year ago. Slid it in right there. Took a while, but I got it."

"Do you have a knife?" Ian asked.

Jodi went to a drawer in the kitchen area. When she opened it, Ian thought he smelled something like burnt wood. Like a campfire. "What's that smell?"

No sooner than he spoke the words, smoke began billowing in from underneath.

"It's on fire!" Jodi screeched.

"No, no, no," Ian repeated. "We have to get out of here." He kicked the door. It didn't open. He kicked it again.

The smoke got thicker. It started filling the inside of the trailer, fast. It was becoming hard to breathe.

Ian stepped on a box of books and pulled at the window. After a few attempts, he got it open. Smoke rushed out, but not much air filled in.

"This way." Ian coughed.

He could hear Jodi coughing but could barely see her. When he stepped off the box, he could tell that she had knocked all the books off the dresser and was crawling around as if she was looking for something. She was coughing violently.

"Come on, Jodi." Ian coughed again, this time it was a fit. He stumbled, steadying himself on the small table attached to the wall. Under his hand he could feel cloth, like a sweatshirt or a towel. He grabbed it and tied it around his face.

Jodi stopped coughing.

"Jodi?"

Blind, he took two steps toward where Jodi had been and began feeling around the floor. When he felt her, he hooked his arms under her limp body and dragged her toward the light. The open window.

With all his strength, he hoisted her against the sill, then grabbed her legs and tipped her out. She went head over heels. Then, he went the same way.

Hitting the ground, he got to his knees, grabbed Jodi's legs, and dragged her away from the flaming trailer.

She coughed. He coughed. They coughed together.

He laid down beside her and stroked her hair. "You're okay. You're going to be okay."

Jodi's body bucked. She turned to the side and vomited. In her left hand, she clutched a photograph. A picture of a woman.

CHAPTER 34

PETER ACCOMPANIED security while they escorted the last two escapees back to the residence.

While several had made a break for the front doors, Zhào Yan and Mark Cooper had decided to hide out in the building, hoping everyone would think they were already gone and would stop looking for them. Peter knew better.

Yan was clever. It was no surprise he'd try to take advantage of the breech. But Cooper? He hadn't even been in lockdown for a full twenty-four hours.

Peter swiped his card and opened the double doors. Security shoved the two men inside.

"You're just adding time onto your sentence, you know," Peter said.

The two men trudged back to their bunks, defeated.

"Are we all accounted for?" Peter addressed the group. "I don't know what it's going to take to make you all see that you're only hurting yourselves. This organization is ready and willing to accept you all with open arms. All of this is for your benefit, and still you spit in the eye of the Church."

Alex Humbolt stood up and moved to the dead center of the room. His fists were balled, and he held his head high. "Because we're fed up."

Peter's brow furrowed. "Watch yourself Alex."

"I'm done watching myself. I'm done playing your games." Alex turned 360 degrees. "If any of these people were telling you the truth, not one would say they believe any of this is somehow in our best interest. Have you forgotten why we're here? We're the ones that have woken up. Who see things as they really are."

"Clearly Brother Alex has not made much progress," Peter announced. "Starting right now, we will be on a forty-eight-hour lock down and introspective fast. A gift from Alex. You will be provided water and nothing else. No meals. No coffee. Perhaps tonight, you might wish to give Alex a gentle reminder of how his actions hinder your progress. However you see fit."

Alex laughed. "You don't think they know what you're trying to do. You're a bully, plain and simple. What all these people don't realize is they can walk out of here anytime they want. You know as well I do that you can't hold us here. It's called kidnapping and we're not going to stand for it anymore." He turned to the group who were watching with blank stares or open mouths. "Who's with me?"

Not a soul budged or made so much as a peep. Peter expected nothing less.

"You will be released when you have proven that you aren't a detriment to yourself. Just like everyone else. Now I suggest you take a moment to reflect. Ask the Universe for peace and guidance. It will provide."

"Fine!" Alex shouted. "If none of you will stand up, I'll do it myself." He stormed up to Peter and stared him in the face. "I'm walking out that door and I'm going to the cops. Your ass is going to jail."

Peter bowed his head, then stepped around the disgruntled man. "Brothers and sisters. I have never given up on any of you. Like my father, I have given my heart and soul to help every single one of you achieve greatness. No matter how mixed up you might have become, you all deserve the chance at redemption. It pains me to say it, but I'm afraid brother Alex may not have the capacity to control his inner demons. I don't want to let you all down, but for the first time ever, I may have to admit defeat. Brother Alex might very well be a lost cause."

"I'm the lost cause?" Alex sneered. "Laughable."

Peter stepped aside. "Brother Alex, you are free to go."

"What do you mean? You're going to just let me leave? Just like that?"

"Of course. I've told you all many times. All of this is for your benefit. You may not understand it, but sometimes we are all in need of an intervention. Ninety-nine times out of a hundred, the person being called on the carpet is forever thankful that someone cared enough to invest time and energy into them. To save them from themselves. But there is always that one. One who is so damaged, he is incapable of ever seeing the truth. I believe that's you, Alex."

Alex glanced over his shoulder one more time, as if trying to gauge the reaction of his roommates. Maybe even trying to determine if he *was* the fool.

The crowd gave him nothing.

"I wish you well, Brother Alex. And know that our doors are always open." Peter swiped his card on the interior access sensor and pushed the door open. He waited.

With leery movements, Alex moved past Peter and faded down the hall.

Peter offered a solemn moment of silence, then addressed the group one last time. "Please do not condemn me for giving up on Brother Alex. I am dedicated to all of you. I will not give up on you as long as a single ounce of hope remains. Now, it's been a trying day for everyone. Try to get some rest."

"Peter?" Sandy's high-pitched voice rang out from the back. "Do we still have to fast?"

"No. That won't be necessary. You may all report to work tomorrow."

Peter stepped out and let the door latch. He chuckled to himself. Sometimes the ridiculous crap that came out of his mouth was too much for even him. *Brother this and Sister that.* Ludicrous. *Ask the Universe for peace.* Crap, his father would say. Not that he was a skeptic. Far from it. He believed in the program and was committed to its success. It was just that his approach was different from his father's. More practical, say.

As Peter rounded the corner into the next corridor, his men were already bringing Alex back. "Look what we found, boss."

"Tell them!" Alex squirmed. "Tell them you let me go!"

"You must be mistaken," Peter said. "Would I let someone go who challenged my authority in front of everyone? Who threatened to have me arrested? Doesn't sound like me."

"Bastard," Alex snarled. "You're evil. Pure evil. Mark my words, you're going to get yours."

"Maybe. But you first." Peter broke eye contact and then continued down the hall. "Take him to the infirmary. Strap him down. I'll check on him later."

"No!" Alex cried out from behind. Peter could hear him struggling as his men dragged him away.

Peter sighed. Some days, he felt like burning it all down. Today was one of those days.

CHAPTER 35

HAELI STRUTTED into the Don CeSar hotel and charged toward the front desk, a wireless earbud in her right ear. Her role was simple. As the executive assistant to a wealthy businessman, she was responsible for booking accommodations and ensuring a smooth travel experience.

On the way south from Dunedin, Blake had asked her to look up the most expensive hotel she could find, at least forty-five minutes away. At $786 a night for a standard suite, the Don CeSar Hotel in St. Pete's Beach fit the bill.

Blake's reasoning was three-fold. First, the more expensive the hotel, the nicer the area and the less chance of running into any trouble. Two, the resort-like property, with its pools and beachfront activities, seemed to cater to the out-of-town vacationer—less likely for Jim to get recognized by someone associated with the Church. Three, and most important, after the conditions he had endured, Jim deserved a bit of luxury. Haeli agreed with Blake on all counts.

Of course, there was still risk. If they could have, they would have stashed Jim in St. Petersburg, Russia, rather than St. Petersburg, Florida. But until they could locate Blake's mother, Tampa Bay would be their home-away-from-home.

"I can help you ma'am." The young man's raspy voice carried a distinct Australian accent.

Haeli held out her index finger. "Yeah. Uh, huh. Listen, I have to go, call me when it's done." She tapped the earbud and then addressed the man in front of her in a rapid, nonstop cadence. "Adrianna Cruz, pleasure to meet you. I'm looking for availability for the next few nights. A suite with a king, preferably. And if I could have fresh flowers delivered and four bottles of Pellegrino, chilled. The room will be occupied by my boss, Angelo Romano, but you can put it under my name. Here's my ID. And here's my AMEX for the room and any incidentals. Mr. Romano doesn't like maid service during his stay, so if you could be a dear and inform the staff. You know what, on second thought, scratch the flowers. I'll take care of them myself. Did you get all that?"

"Not a problem, ma'am. We can certainly accommodate, although we only have double bed suites. Will that be alright?"

"If it's all you have, it'll have to do for now."

"How many nights?"

"Make it four, to be safe."

"Great, I'll get that booked for you." The clerk inserted the credit card into the reader and spoke as he typed. "There we are. One suite, four nights for Mister Angelo Romano. I will just need his ID on arrival. Hotel policy."

"Of course, I will personally make sure of it."

"Then you are all set." He pulled a sheet of paper off the printer and handed it to her. "I hope he enjoys his stay."

"One more thing," Haeli said. "Can I get a key? I need to set up the room before he arrives."

"I'm not really supposed to—"

"Nonsense. That's my AMEX you've run up thirty-two hundred dollars on."

"I like my job, Miss Cruz. I'd like to keep it."

Haeli gripped the edge of the counter and leaned toward the man. "You don't understand. Mister Romano is very particular. I like my job, too, and I'd also really like to keep it, ya know what I mean? It's not like you don't know who I am. You have a picture of my license for shit's sake."

The clerk looked around and then lowered his voice. "Fine. But make sure your boss checks in." Grabbing a blank card, he ran it over the magnet.

"And they said chivalry was dead." Haeli winked. "Thank you. I'll be back. With flowers." She parted ways as fast as she could.

Outside, Blake and Jim waited in the car. As Haeli approached, she could see they were engaged in conversation. Blake wasn't smiling, but by the lack of tension in his jaw, she could tell he was relieved. Both men were playing it cool, but it was clear to her how much they cared about one another.

Haeli got into the back seat and passed the key over Jim's shoulder. "Hope you like Pellegrino."

"You didn't give them my name, right?"

Haeli chuckled. "Not our first rodeo, Jim. The room is under Angelo Romano. That's you, in case anyone asks. We'll have to go in through the side door. Whatever you do, avoid the staff. They're going to be looking for your identification. With any luck, they'll forget about it when the shift changes."

"Are you two staying as well?"

"No," Blake said. "The further we are from you the better. They've been tracking us down for days. Anyway, we're already settled in at the Fenway and it'll be better if we're closer to the Church. Unfortunately, since we had to pull the Piranha, we no longer have eyes inside."

"When are we meeting the contact?" Haeli asked.

"Don't know yet. I have a call in through Khat. He'll get back to me."

Jim twisted around to face Haeli. "Piranha?"

"Long story," Blake said.

Haeli leaned forward, so she was between Blake and Jim. "I have to say, it's really great to meet you finally. I've heard so much about you."

"A less than flattering portrayal, I'm sure." Jim glanced at Blake. "Nor should it have been. I was an ass. All these years wasted—" His voice wavered, and he cleared his throat. "I'm sorry, son. I'm so sorry about everything. I can't say it enough."

Blake took his father's hand. "We both made mistakes. Forget about it right now. We need to focus on getting Mom out of there."

"I need to talk to you about that," Jim said. "Your mother and I…"

After several agonizing seconds, Blake spoke up, as if he could no longer take the anticipation. "You what? Split up?"

"No. Not exactly. But we were on different paths. I started asking questions and instead of getting answers, I got backlash. Mom wanted me to stop drawing attention, but of course, I didn't listen. She wasn't willing to get ostracized over it, so she started distancing herself. She was right, of course. I landed myself in lockdown. She maintained her good standing, as far as I know. She wasn't in there with me, that's for sure."

"Is she living at the compound?"

Jim nodded. "I've seen her during my shifts around the building. I know she saw me too, but she avoided me. She's scared, that's all. Scared to lose everything. And I get it, I feared the same for a long time. It's just that I finally woke up. Realized I was living a lie." He sighed, and looked out the window. "She's still dreaming."

"Are you saying she doesn't want out?" Blake asked.

"I don't think she—no, that's not true. I know she doesn't. When I was captive, I kept telling myself that I would rescue her. Somehow convince her to come with me if I could find a way to escape. I was fooling myself. Giving myself a reason to get up in the morning. But the truth is, she'll never leave."

Blake's phone dinged. He glanced at the screen. "Khat says the contact wants to meet in an hour. Same place. Dad, we'll have to take care of this. Why don't you go inside and get yourself settled. We'll stop back later."

Jim nodded. "Before you go—" Reaching under his seat, he pulled out the stack of file folders. "Take these."

"What are they?" Haeli asked.

"They're what almost got us jammed up." Blake grabbed the stack and passed it back to Haeli.

"They're receipts of some kind," Jim said. "Payments. Whatever they mean, the Church sure didn't want the Feds getting ahold of them. Some of them date back a little while, but I've never seen them." He opened his door.

"We'll take a look," Blake said. "Lie low, will ya? You need to be careful."

"I will."

"And don't be so sure about Mom. We'll get through to her."

"I hope so. I really do." Jim labored to get his feet on the ground and hoist himself out of the car. Then he bent over and stuck his head back inside. "I love you, son."

Blake looked right at his father but didn't say anything. Haeli felt trapped in the awkwardness of the moment, but she understood. She could almost read his mind. After all that had happened—all the betrayal—it was going to take more than a parking-lot-apology to mend what was broken.

Jim stood and pushed the door closed before Haeli could squeeze out of the back seat to join Blake in the front.

As Jim walked away, Blake bowed his head and squeezed the bridge of his nose.

He whispered.

"I love you, too."

CHAPTER 36

FEZZ BURST INTO THE ROOM, snagging the toe of his boot on a flap of carpet that was peeling away from the doorframe. He lurched but caught himself before taking a digger. "Ian? Jodi?"

No one was there.

Since Fezz had returned from Ernie's, he'd been scouring half the town, trying to find the kids. At first, he'd assumed they had disregarded his instructions, and either went to Jodi's trailer or to the supermarket. These were the first places he'd checked. Coming up short, he'd tried the restaurant, the feed store, and every shop along Main Street. No one had seen them.

As time went on and he became more frantic, he strained to keep himself from overreacting—from spiraling into the land of worst-case scenarios.

But now, he was left with little option but to sound the alarm. He would have to contact the police—the one thing he had been trying to avoid.

Ian was responsible and conscientious. There was no precedence. He would never have disappeared for hours of his own free will. Not unless something was wrong.

Fezz sat on the edge of the bed and gathered himself.

Before he involved the authorities, he needed to be sure. He needed to check Jodi's place one more time. The more the minutes ticked by, the more peril Ian and Jodi could be in.

Springing to his feet, Fezz hurried outside, determined to prove himself wrong. There, Ian and Jodi were limping through the parking lot toward him. Both, covered in dirt.

"Where the hell have you been? Get inside, now."

Fezz stepped inside and held the door open. So as not to cause a disturbance, he'd wait until they were behind closed doors before flying off the handle. He would rip into them beyond anything they'd ever experienced.

But as they crossed the threshold, Fezz's anger shifted to concern. They were shaken, possibly injured, coughing, smeared with soot, and reeking of putrid smoke.

"What happened? Are you alright?"

Before Jodi could get a word out, she broke down crying.

"I'm sorry," Ian said. "We should have listened to you."

"You're not answering my question, Ian. What happened? Was there a fire? Where were you?"

"Jodi and I went to a swimming hole in the fields. We were only supposed to be gone for a little while. Then we were coming back, and Jodi needed to stop at home for a couple minutes."

Jodi hacked and wiped her nose with the palm of her hand. "We heard the motorcycles, and we tried to hide. But Darlene told them we were inside."

"Motorcycles?" Fezz could feel the blood rushing to face. His ears started to burn. "What did they do to you?"

"We got locked in and then we smelled smoke." Tears began streaming down Ian's face. "They set fire to the place and we couldn't get out. Jodi almost died."

Jodi sobbed. "Ian saved my life. All I remember is it was dark, and I couldn't breathe. And then I woke up on the ground. If he wasn't there, I would be dead." She threw her arms around Ian and sobbed some more.

Fezz couldn't believe what he was hearing, but there was no doubt it was the truth. Their tortured expressions guaranteed it.

As traumatizing as it must have been, they were alive. And Fezz had never been more grateful.

"Come here." Fezz wrapped one arm around each of them and pulled them close. They each buried their faces in his abdomen. "You're okay. You're safe now."

"My books," Jodi blubbered. "They're all I had."

"I know." He hugged them tighter. "I know."

Until that moment, the Demon Squad was nothing but a nuisance. But now they had thrown down the gauntlet. If it was a fight they wanted, he thought, it was a fight they were going to get.

Ian was his charge, but even if he hadn't been, there was nothing worse than those who preyed on the innocent. Especially children. It was something they all shared—Blake, Khat, Griff, Kook—an invisible line, drawn at the feet of the pure, to be defended at all costs.

"They'll pay," Fezz mumbled. "Every last one of them."

"I want to go home!" Ian broke away from Fezz's embrace, stormed over to his bed, and sat down. Under the circumstances, Fezz afforded him the leeway to sulk without chastisement.

Jodi let go as well. She let her arms fall to her sides, and she stood staring at the wall behind Fezz, as if it were an endless void. The hollow look of profound pain.

Jodi had suffered a punch to the gut of an already challenging existence and, in all likelihood, it was because of him. An unintentional repercussion of his obstinance.

Fezz's muscles vibrated with rage and guilt. He took a deep breath. "How about you both take a shower? Get cleaned up. You'll feel better, trust me. I will handle this, okay?"

"What's Jodi supposed to do now?" Ian asked, tears still wetting his cheeks. "She has no place to go."

"Don't worry about that." Fezz crouched down and put his hand on Jodi's shoulder. "Look at me."

Jodi turned her head, but her eyes were still vacant.

"I promise you," Fezz said, "we will not leave you without a safe place to live. I will make sure of it. You have my word."

Maybe it was crazy—after all they had just met the girl—but Fezz would have given his life to protect her. Just as he had sworn to do for his country, once upon a time.

He knew what had to be done. And of all the people in that town, he might well be the only one crazy enough to do it.

CHAPTER 37

PETER CHECKED HIS PHONE. No missed calls. It was unlike Grady Larson to be late.

As dumping grounds went, the dirt lot was well-chosen. After all, Larson knew his way around the nooks and crannies of the city. But on the outskirts of downtown Tampa, it was busier than Peter liked.

Beyond the border of overgrowth, cars buzzed by in a non-stop parade. Sitting still with Alex's body in his trunk felt like a provocation. Tempting fate.

He could dump the body without Larson and let the chips fall where they may. He'd learned enough about the detective's thought process to give it a go. And once he was no longer in possession, who cared what happened afterward?

Alex was a nobody. No family, at least none who'd cared enough to visit or call, and no known estate. He had been attached to the tit of the Church for years. For this reason, Peter couldn't understand why Alex had become such a thorn in his side. One would think it'd behoove a person to show a little gratitude. Peter was the literal hand that fed him.

If it were up to his father, people like Alex would have already tanked the entire organization with their accusations, faux outrage, and twisted moral high ground. The Church took no more advantage of its members than its members took of it. It was symbiotic. Absent as he was, even the great Sage was savvy enough to know that much.

"All right Alex, looks like it's you and me."

Peter popped the trunk latch and stepped into the low, late-day sun. The glare off the glossy paint was blinding. He reached in and grabbed his glasses, then pulled a box of medical grade rubber gloves from under his seat. Already sweating, he struggled to pull the gloves over his moist fingers.

Out of the corner of his eye, he caught movement in the brush. By reflex, he swung his half-gloved hands behind his back.

A Crown Victoria cut through the break in the foliage, followed by a cloud of dust, kicked up by the back tires.

Larson pulled perpendicular and opened his window. "Are you serious right now?"

Peter went back to wrangling the bunched-up latex. "You're late."

"I'm only here because I didn't want to say anything else on the phone." Larson got out but stayed close to his car.

"I was about to start without you," Peter said. "Need gloves?"

"You're not hearing me, Peter. I'm not a part of this one. I'm not a part of any of them anymore."

"What's your problem?" Peter pulled open the trunk and then stepped toward Larson. "It's just like the others. Just set him up so we can get out of here."

"That's my problem," Larson said. "*It's just like the others.* How many others are there, Peter? How many more will there be? I'm not an idiot. There's no way this keeps happening; people just don't keel over and die on a regular basis. Young people. What are you going to tell me this time? He just didn't wake up for some reason, right?"

Peter raised his fist as if he were going to take a swing, despite being several feet away. He extended his index finger, waggled it, then dropped it to his side. "You're something else. Are you accusing me of something, Grady? Because that's what it sounds like."

"Stop this," Larson said. "Whatever you're doing, just stop it. I can't be a part of it. That's all."

"I can't believe that's what you think of me." Peter reached into the trunk, grabbed the back of Alex's neck, and lifted his body to display his face. "He was having a nervous breakdown and was sent to the infirmary for observation. Last I talked to him he was feeling better. He was given a mild sedative and was able to get some rest. When the staff left for the night, they checked his vitals and everything looked good. When I went back to check on him, he was unresponsive. He had removed his monitors and was lying on the floor. I administered CPR, but it was too late. I don't know what else you want me to tell you. I'm not a doctor. What else was I supposed to do?"

Larson's arms swung and his head bobbled. "Call a doctor! Call the ambulance. That's what people do!"

"Don't have a conniption." Peter knew his calm demeanor would only frustrate Larson more, but he couldn't help it. He didn't have it in him to play the distraught role. Not today. There was a simple job to be done, and he was going to do it, with or without Larson's help. "If you don't want to help, don't help."

Larson sighed and his shoulders dropped.

Peter levered Alex's body until his torso rested on the lip of the trunk opening and his head and arms dangled toward the ground. He pulled his legs, sending the entire body to the dirt with a thud.

"I'm going to say this once, so listen carefully," Larson said. "Don't call me again. If I so much as get a whiff that there's another body, I'm going to have the entire department on your ass. Do you understand me?"

"Watch it, Grady. Remember who you're talking to." Peter left Alex lying below the bumper and moved to address Larson face-to-face. "You forget that you're a part of this, too. I consider your threats against me direct threats against the Church. My father will see it the same."

"Does your father even know what you're up to?" Larson let out a frustrated laugh. "Don't worry, I don't expect you to answer that. But understand this. As of right now, I am no longer a member of the Church of Clear Intention. I'm done. And if you try any of your bullshit with me—the intimidation tactics, the smearing, or any of that heavy handed crap—your secrets become not so secret. You leave me alone, I leave you alone. Everyone's happy. We forget we ever knew each other."

Peter seethed, but he didn't show it. Under the circumstances, it was a decent deal. For the moment, it was in Larson's best interest to keep quiet. If, for some reason, that changed, Peter would be prepared to get ahead of it. To go on the offensive. But right now, the best course of action would be to cool things down. He was insulated, but not untouchable. At least not when it came to the outside world. And Larson knew it better than anyone.

In any position of responsibility there were things that had to be done. Nasty things that took courage and self-sacrifice for the greater good. Peter didn't regret anything, save one thing—trusting Grady Larson in the first place.

"It's a shame to lose such an ardent, blossoming member such as yourself," Peter said. "But perhaps it is for the best."

"Save the company rhetoric. Is that a deal?"

"It's a deal." Peter offered his hand. "I accept your resignation and wish the best in all your endeavors. No hard feelings."

Larson refused the handshake. His gaze carried a skepticism which, in Peter's view, bordered on loathsomeness. The feeling was mutual.

As Larson got back in his car and pulled away, Peter tried to put the affair out of his mind and focus on the task in front of him. He'd take into account lividity and injury, and as always, try to make it look like another homeless man who let a hard life get the best of him.

"Like I said"—Peter crouched down next to the warming corpse—"Just the two of us, you poor, stupid man."

CHAPTER 38

BLAKE TOSSED the paper bag on the desk and pulled the leather cube stool from underneath. He dragged the plush armchair over from the window for Haeli.

There were two things vying for Blake's attention at that moment—the documents his father had given them, and the giant Italian sub wetting the paper bag with its aromatic olive oil secretions. The sandwich had a clear lead.

Haeli kicked her shoes off and climbed over the back of the plush chair. She sat cross legged as she ripped into the booty. "Let me at it."

He had to say, her enthusiasm rivaled his.

On the way to Palmetto, Blake's stomach had already been growling. Hunger pangs had led to a discussion about Jersey Mike's, the chain sandwich shop they'd hit up in East Greenwich on occasion. The discussion had led to a temporary obsession.

First, they'd have to make a successful handoff of the Piranha. As expected, it went off without a hitch.

The contact had been appreciative that he was able to keep his job, his freedom, and the money. Blake was happy he'd avoided incurring another adversary.

As soon as they'd parted ways, Blake and Haeli had sought out the closest Jersey Mike's, but decided to hold off after finding that there was one on Main Street, just up the road from where they were staying.

"Delicious," Haeli mumbled with a mouthful of prosciutto and provolone.

For the next three minutes, they munched in silence. The effort only depleted an eighth of the payload. Enough to quell the craving and transition to a less animalistic pace.

"Was that awkward?" Haeli asked. "It seemed awkward."

"What? My father?"

"Yeah." She finished chewing, then swallowed. "You guys seem to be lugging around *a lot* of baggage."

"I wouldn't say it was awkward. It's funny, though. In some ways, it almost felt like no time had passed at all. But it also felt like we were meeting for the first time. Which is true, if you think about it. We're all just a sum of our experiences, right? So you could say we're totally different people than we were back then." He paused. "I know I am. For better or for worse."

"I really like him," Haeli said. "He's not what I expected."

"What did you expect?"

"I don't know. An older you, I guess. I mean, you look alike, a little, but not the same intensity."

"You didn't know him when he was young."

Haeli took a bite of her sandwich, then wiped her mouth with a paper napkin. "Do you think he's right about your mom? Didn't sound promising."

"I think he's given up. There's obviously been some bumps in their relationship. More than he's letting on. I say we don't draw any conclusions until I can talk to her myself. My guess is she's hiding from it. It would be like her to avoid dealing with something like that head on. But I know them. They're good together. Whatever the issues are, they can work through them."

Blake didn't say it, but the truth was he didn't know them. He *had* known them. There was a big difference.

In his opinion, there were two distinct issues here. The most important—the reason they were in Florida in the first place—was to make sure his parents were all right. To reconnect on whatever level possible, and maybe to help bring them together. Then came the second issue. Since they had arrived, he'd seen a nasty side to the organization his folks were wrapped up in. And he took personal issue with it on its face.

Predicated by a simple inquiry, Blake had been forcibly removed, stalked, and attacked. And that wasn't accounting for Curtis Hammond's attempts to prostitute Haeli.

The Church of Clear Intention might as well have been a crime syndicate or cartel. If what they had seen so far was any indication, the dirt went much deeper. Maybe, Blake thought, the documents would provide a hidden perspective. Or a place to start.

"Let's see what we have here." Blake opened the folder on top of the stack. He held his sandwich in one hand, and a stapled document in the other. "Higgins and Braniker. Law firm."

"Lawsuits?"

Blake put his sandwich down and turned the page. "Looks like a nondisclosure agreement. Whoever Jacob and Rose Yates are, they've signed an agreement to not talk about"—He turned another page—"well, basically anything to do with the Church. It goes on and on."

"Doesn't surprise me," Haeli said. "Pretty standard for a corporation. Although, it's not like they're working on proprietary tech. Not unless you can patent pseudo-religious indoctrination."

"There's a payment associated with it." He looked up at Haeli. "Three hundred thousand dollars."

"Okay, a little less standard."

"Ya think?" Blake selected another packet and thumbed through it. "Same thing here. NDA. Two hundred fifty thousand dollar payment."

Blake skimmed through several more. A trend emerged. All gag orders. All with high dollar amounts.

"What were they paying so much to hide?" Haeli asked.

"Don't know, but you can be sure it'd be something damaging if it got out. And that's exactly what we need."

"Maybe your father knows."

"If he knew, he wouldn't have risked going back for these. He knew they were important but didn't know what they meant. That I'm sure of." Blake stood. "I need to track these people down. Make a few calls and see who's willing to talk."

Haeli chuckled. "Isn't that sort of the whole thing with the NDA? Making sure they don't talk?"

"Wouldn't be the first time someone spilled," Blake said. "Bribes have a way of coming back to haunt you."

CHAPTER 39

FEZZ LAID STILL in the tall grass. Flies buzzed around his head. Peering through a gap he had created by matting down a section of grass with his forearm, his position was all-too familiar.

Although he had never been a true sniper, he had gone through reconnaissance training, which included similar skills. Stalking and detection avoidance being the most applicable—even if much of the curriculum had to do with camouflaging and took place in more abundant foliage. Still, he had no experience, even in simulated environments, with such an open landscape. The way Fezz saw it, the fundamentals were the same. Above all else, stalking required patience and methodology. Two things he could muster when needed.

Ernie had been right about the Demon Squad's clubhouse being easy to find, but hard to sneak up on. In the middle of acres of open land, there was no approach that offered adequate cover. On the plus side, the barn-like structure had few windows.

Fezz had taken several risks getting there. For one, instead of crawling all the way, he had traversed much of the distance on foot, out in the open. There were no signs of activity at the time and he figured the time savings was worth it. If he had been seen, he'd have found himself in a precarious position—unarmed with nowhere to run.

Aside from the personal risk, he'd left Ian and Jodi alone at the motel. He'd locked them in the room and instructed them to barricade the door, but without him there, they were vulnerable. He also didn't like the fact that they were together in a motel room without supervision. But it'd been the only option. Separating them into their own rooms would only serve to make them less secure and a whole lot more anxious. He trusted Ian. Jodi, he still wasn't sure about.

The sun hadn't yet dropped below the horizon when Fezz went face down in the dirt. Slow and steady, he low-crawled for what seemed like miles, dragging his payload with him every few feet.

Halfway to his destination, he heard the incoming motorcycles roaring by. At first, one or two, then many more.

Now dark, the building's exterior lighting illuminated the growing line of bikes parked along the front side of the building. A campfire burned in a ring out front. Several men stood around it, passing a bottle.

If Fezz had to guess, he'd say this was more than a few guys hanging out. They were gearing up for a meeting.

Watching the action from a vantage point only a few dozen yards away, Fezz knew the exhausting effort was worth it. Not only was he able to get a front row seat without being noticed, but his crawl had also carved a path through the grass. A route for egress. When he needed to slip away, he could escape without disturbing the upright grass around him. From the gang's perspective, there would be no indication anyone was out there. Especially in the dark.

He watched intently, ready for a long night. From a distance, he couldn't tell who was who. But there was no doubt in his mind that Snake was there somewhere. Hawk, too.

In his solitude, Fezz reminded himself that it was them who'd picked a fight with him. Not the other way around. *An eye for eye* was not only a personal code unique to him, his team, or even the Bible. It was a concept dating back to the beginning of civilization itself. An eternal law of man, memorialized by Hammurabi on stone pillars of ancient Mesopotamia.

In the distance, the growl of straight pipes trumpeting the exhaust of a big v-twin motor announced an incoming visitor. As it grew closer,

Fezz could see that it was two bikers, riding side by side. They pulled up to the end of the line of motorcycles and dismounted.

From inside, a man stepped out and whistled, then swung his arm in the air like he was spinning an invisible lasso. The others abandoned their campfire and hustled inside, leaving behind a welcome quiet under the stars.

Fezz deduced they'd been waiting for the last two stragglers to arrive before starting. It meant no more would arrive at this point. The meeting would likely occupy the group for some time. All Fezz needed was a couple of minutes.

Knowing he wouldn't get a better invitation, Fezz seized the moment.

He stood and surveyed the expanse. All quiet, he picked up the two 5-gallon jugs of gasoline. Careful to step over the standing grass at the edge of his hidey-hole, he walked toward the front of the building.

As he got closer, he could hear the rowdy crowd. Either there was a heated debate or a serious game of charades was going on inside. Whatever the case, it was nothing compared to the ruckus that was about to ensue.

Starting from the far end, Fezz moved along the row of motorcycles, pouring a healthy amount of fuel on each as he went. He hummed a made-up song under his breath.

The mere act of visiting each and every one gave him pleasure. A small piece of payback for what could have happened if Ian hadn't had the wherewithal to escape the burning trailer.

At the end of the line, Fezz finished off the second can by dumping its contents high on the corner of the building. It dripped down into a puddle in the dirt.

With a flick of his lighter, he set the corner ablaze and carried the empty cans back to his spot in the grass.

By the time he settled, the flames had spread up the wall and to the first two bikes in the line.

It would have been a good time to start making his way out, but he couldn't help but linger. Long enough to watch the fire pick up speed, ravaging the entire line of the gang's precious Harley Davidsons. Long enough to see the first man burst through the door and scream in horror. And long enough to see the entire gang gather in front of their engulfed clubhouse, wallowing in agony and disbelief. No sweeter nectar had ever been tasted.

Revenge wasn't just about the wrong of the day. It was about all the wrongs that had come before. Men just like these, all over the world, who took advantage of regular people. This was for Ian and Jodi, yes. But also for Ima and Wade and the Novaks and Anja and even Bonzo.

Most of all, it was for himself.

Right now, the fire department was gathering its volunteers. Later, the Demon Squad would be on the warpath. For Fezz, it was time to go. Permanently.

Spinning around on his stomach, he started his journey into the wide-open expanse with a smile.

CHAPTER 40

PETER CHECKED THE CLOCK. Close enough. He slipped on his shoes and opened his door slowly enough that it didn't creak. Heading down the dimly lit hall, he was as quiet as he could be. The kids were all sleeping, and he didn't want to draw any attention to himself. It was the only major downfall to living in the main residence.

Since he'd been a child, he'd lived in the same room—more than a room, the small apartment had its own bathroom. While it had been renovated to include an office a decade prior, it still felt like time had stood still within its walls. Stifling at times.

That wasn't to say that he wasn't dedicated to the family, or he would want to be anywhere else. But communal living had its challenges, and it was probably the main reason he could never maintain a serious relationship.

Still, it was worth it.

Call him crazy, but he didn't feel the need for a relationship or even companionship. Unlike his father, Peter was content focusing on the things that mattered. And nothing mattered more than the Church.

In the residence, he could be instrumental in the daily workings of the family. A positive influence on all his siblings. His real brothers and sisters—the heirs—would one day work together to carry on the legacy and help bring it to the proverbial moon.

He passed the children's quarters and the wives' rooms—paying special care not to wake his mother. This had to be done discreetly, given the high level of occupancy.

Down the back staircase and out the rear door, Peter stayed close to the building as he worked his way around toward the front lot. He keyed through the security gate below his father's office and stuck to the fence line until he reached the main gates.

Peter made it a point to be prompt, lest Jesus "Three Fingers" show up first and get any ideas about coming onto the property.

Jesus had earned the name Three Fingers for obvious reasons. The middle finger on his right hand was missing. How that happened, Peter didn't know. And never cared to ask. All he cared about was that Jesus showed up with his order and kept his mouth shut. For that, Peter paid a premium.

Once through the gates, Peter walked south. There were no pedestrians or even vehicular traffic in sight.

About an eighth of a mile down, he found a spot not lit up by a streetlamp or floods from the compound or the nearby marinas and lingered there in the shadow.

A car approached from the north. He bowed his head, turned toward the concrete wall, and shuffled along, just enough so that it looked like he was heading somewhere.

The car passed.

Several seconds later, headlights appeared from the south. Again, he made himself busy.

This time, the car slowed as it approached, then pulled over a few feet from Peter. He glanced over to verify that it was the gray Honda Accord he had been expecting.

Jesus flicked the interior light on and waved Peter over.

Peter got in. "Turn that light off."

"What's good?" Jesus offered his palm. Peter mimicked him, allowing Jesus to slap his hand and then hook three fingertips on his.

"Nothing is good. Do you have the stuff?"

"Hell yeah. Whatchu think, I came all the way out here to say what's up? I don't go round pickin' up shady white boys off the side of the road. You hangin' around in the dark like that—that shit is shady, for real."

"Alright, alright. Just give it to me."

"You got the scratch?"

Peter nodded, reached into his back pocket, and pulled out a loaded envelope. He handed it to Jesus.

Jesus thumbed through the bills. Satisfied, he reached under his seat and produced a plastic baggie containing an off-white-colored powder.

Peter extended his hand and Jesus was about to drop the bag into his palm but paused. "This shit is hot, just like you asked for. But my brotha, you gotta be careful with this shit, 'ight? You gotta step on it hard. Like, hard. You touch this with your bare hands, you as good as dead, you feel me? If you don't know what you doin, and you don't cut it right, whoever boots it gonna be real dead, too. You feel me?"

"I feel you." Peter's patience was wearing thin. He knew exactly what he ordered and how to handle it. Of course, he'd have to play nice. Jesus could easily rob him and leave him on the side of the road for dead. Consorting with guys like this was a necessary evil and not something Peter would do if there were any other option. "Can I have it now?"

Jesus let go of the bag. "There's lots more where that came from. You peddlin' to the fat cats up in here? You could be pulling in hella chalupa. I got you. You know how to hit me up."

"Sure." Peter opened the door and stepped out. He wanted to put as much distance as he could between him and Jesus, but there was one thing that was nagging him. "Can I ask you something?"

"Depends."

"What happened? The finger, I mean. Was it shot off or something?"

"This?" Jesus held up his fist. The nub of a middle finger protruded above his knuckles. "I flicked my mother the bird when I was a kid. She didn't like that much."

"Are you serious?"

"Na. I'm just playin'. Birth defect, bro." Jesus snickered. "Shot off? You watchin' too many movies my man. Be good."

"Yeah. You too." Peter closed the door and Jesus drove off.

Peter made his way back onto the property and around the building, with no particular urgency. The air had cooled down, and it felt good to be out in it.

He thought about Larson. What a liability the man had become. As one of his closest allies, he bordered on what Peter would consider a friend. Now, the mere fact that he existed burned a pit in Peter's stomach.

None of this had been part of a grand plan. It started as a quick fix to an unfixable problem. Maybe, if he'd stopped at one, it would have been something he could put behind him. Now, there was no point in backtracking. The damage was done, and it couldn't get any worse.

Peter returned upstairs and slinked his way by the sleeping children and reclusive women. Back to his boyhood home.

He opened his desk drawer and tossed the bag inside. He stared at it with reverence. How powerful a substance that can snuff out a life as fast as a bolt of lightning. Like Zeus, smiting his enemies, he wielded it with righteous purpose.

One day he would follow in his father's footsteps. And if he planned to play God, he might as well get his practice in now.

CHAPTER 41

AT DAWN, the park was bustling with joggers, cyclists, and dog walkers. Blake walked hand in hand with Haeli.

He loved the culture here. Active. Alert. Novak's native land, the Tampa Bay area was as vibrant a place as he'd been. Maybe he was just feeling optimistic. His father was safe and well-hidden. And there was the meeting they, with luck, were about to have.

Spending several hours on the phone the previous evening had been mostly fruitless. There were a lot of choice words thrown at him, the majority of which started with "screw" and ended with "off." But he'd stuck to it and was glad he had.

Radek Sławomir—a Polish immigrant judging by his name and accent—was the one and only person on the list who hadn't hung up on Blake. Even though he'd been standoffish, Blake had gotten the impression the man wanted to talk. He wouldn't say anything over the phone, but after Blake had stuck with him for twenty minutes, he'd agreed to meet in person.

Local to the area, Radek had picked the time and place. An exhibit of his eagerness, he'd chosen daybreak, mere hours from then. He'd described a particular bench in this particular park.

As Blake and Haeli wandered around, Blake kept his eye on the bench. Time would tell if Radek was serious or had told him what he'd wanted to hear to get rid of him.

"I should be running," Haeli said. "Haven't done any exercise since we've been here."

"That makes two of us."

Not a day went by that Haeli and Blake didn't work out. It was part of their ritual. To Blake it was a necessity. Without it, he felt ungrounded. Weakened mentally and physically. He imagined it was the same for her.

Grabbing a beach house in a place like Florida wouldn't have been a bad idea for them. Both preferred outdoor activity to being stuck in a stuffy gym. And neither were fond of cold weather. Now that the house was done, they had more leeway to travel during the harsh Rhode Island winter.

"What would you say about coming back down here when this is all done?" Blake asked. "To look for a place. Something small, as a getaway."

"I'd say you're onto something." Haeli smiled up at him. "Are you thinking about this area?"

"Anywhere down here. East coast, west coast. The Keys. Doesn't have to be Tampa Bay."

"If you believe Buck Novak, it's the best place on the planet."

"He did make it a point to tout its virtues quite often, didn't he?" Blake laughed. "Ya know, we've got to reach out to him soon. See how he's doing."

"A lot better than his predecessor, I'm sure."

"I didn't mean the job, although I have no doubt that's the case. I meant how he's dealing with everything."

"It's going to take more than a few weeks." Haeli paused. "To be honest, I don't think Ima has even set in for me yet. I still feel like we'll go home and she'll be sitting there with some of her ginseng tea, waiting for me to go to the spa with her."

"If only that were true," Blake said.

"The sad thing is, I knew her better than anyone else in the world," Haeli said. "All of those countless hours locked in that cell together—

she really opened up to me. I never did the same for her. I never gave her that."

"You were there for her. And Ian. Even when you didn't have to be. Ian's future—that's what you gave her. She would have given her life for it."

Haeli contemplated in silence.

Blake's mind wandered. He squeezed Haeli's hand. "If this guy doesn't show in the next, let's say, ten minutes, we should go over and check on my father."

Haeli smiled. "You miss him."

"I don't miss him, I just worry about him—"

An elbow to Blake's side forced his attention to the park bench.

"That's gotta be him," Haeli said.

An older Slavic-looking man had sat down. Hands resting on his knees, he looked around with nervous, shifty eyes.

"That's him for sure," Blake said. "Let's go make an introduction."

They approached, careful not to come on too forcefully. The man looked skittish enough as it was.

"Hello," Blake said. "Are you Radek?"

He backed himself into the corner of the bench. "Blake?"

"I'm Blake and this is Adrianna. Can we sit?"

Radek nodded.

"Thank you. We really appreciate you seeing us. I know it must seem unusual, us calling you out of the blue."

"How do I know you're not with them?"

"The Church? We wouldn't have called you if we were with them. But I have family who are. We're trying to—"

"You must get them away from there." Radek looked at them both with wild eyes.

"Believe us, we know," Haeli said. "You must have been through something horrible yourself, am I right?"

"My wife and I both."

"Is that why you broke away?" Blake asked.

"Oh, we weren't involved with them. It was my daughter, Marika. She was the one who worked there."

"I'm sorry, we just assumed—" Blake looked at Haeli for input. She offered none. "We're confused. I called you because we found that you signed an NDA with the Church. That was you, wasn't it?"

"Yes. I'm ashamed to say, I did. My wife was against it, but we needed the money."

Maybe it was too soon to pop the million-dollar question, but so far, Blake was grasping at straws. He needed clarification if they were going to have an intelligent conversation.

"I'm sorry to be so blunt, but I have to ask you. What was the NDA for?"

Radek sighed. He looked around, tapped his feet, and did anything but answer the question. Blake and Haeli waited until he worked up the courage to speak.

"Marika was an attorney, and she worked for these Clear Intention people. First, she was only a member, but I remember when she got the job offer. They offered much more than she was making at the time, seemed like a good opportunity."

"But it wasn't?" Haeli asked.

Radek shook his head. "Something wasn't right. We spoke every day. She would visit all the time. Then she started becoming, how do you say—far away."

"Distant?"

"Distant. Marika was a happy person, but after a while working there, she seemed sad and depressed. I think there was a lot of stress. When I asked her about it, she said she might have made a mistake. There was something going on. I think she was fighting with them."

"So, did she end up telling you what it was? Is that what the nondisclosure was about?"

"No. She had gotten into drugs, I guess to cope with the stress. She passed away from an overdose."

"Oh no," Haeli said. "I'm so sorry."

Radek cleared his throat. "It was horrible. My wife has never been the same."

"This happened at the Church?" Blake asked.

"I think so. Three lawyers showed up at our house and told us. They said she had been having struggles with addiction and that she overdosed. That's when they gave us the documents to sign. They said they would give us a check and that if we didn't sign now, the money would go away. There would be no other chance." Radek took a deep breath. "So I convinced my wife to sign. She cried and screamed, yet I still convinced her to sign."

"Why would they do that?" Haeli said. "Make you sign an NDA after your daughter's death."

"They said they didn't want anyone to know that someone who worked there was mixed up with drugs. They acted like she was some horrible person. But she was my daughter, and she was so good."

"I am so sorry," Blake said. "We had no idea."

Haeli put her hand on Blake's knee and offered Radek further condolences.

"I'm not supposed to be telling you this, but I've been feeling so guilty. They wouldn't even let us have a funeral. We had to have her cremated."

It angered Blake to see Radek's torment. There were still a lot of questions, but some of the pieces were coming together. "I hope this doesn't come off the wrong way, but did Marika have a drug problem in the past? I mean, was she recovering?"

"She never did." Radek straightened up, and his tone became more adamant. "Marika didn't use drugs before this. I know this. She was smart and successful. She hated drugs."

It was what Blake thought he would say, what any loving father would say about their child. But Blake believed him. In his first crack at an assessment, the Church had taken advantage of this family's naiveté. "Did you happen to see the medical examiner's report? The cause of death?"

Radek shook his head. "The Church took care of everything. We do have her ashes. We think they are hers. But how do we know?"

Blake nodded in acknowledgment of the question but didn't attempt an answer. "Mister Sławomir, I really appreciate you filling us in." Pulling out the small notepad from his back pocket, he wrote down his number, ripped off the sheet, and handed it to Radek. "If you need anything, call me."

"That's it?"

"No," Haeli said. "We're going to get to the bottom of this, I promise you. We'll be back in touch, okay?"

Blake and Haeli stood up. Radek did the same. Haeli leaned over and gave him a hug. He accepted it without protest.

"Thank you," Radek said.

Blake and Haeli left Radek standing by himself. A lost soul, with fewer answers than he'd started with. But if Blake's hunch was right, answers he would get.

CHAPTER 42

FEZZ PUSHED OPEN THE DOOR. There was no barricade to contend with.

On one of the beds, Ian was fast asleep. The other bed was mussed and empty.

Fezz grabbed their suitcase, opened the drawer, and shoveled all the clothing he saw inside.

He checked the clock. Eight AM. Later than he'd hoped.

After he had crawled the quarter mile along his original track, he was forced to hunker down and wait for the activity to die down. Men walked the road, screaming and shining flashlights. Police and Fire cordoned off the area. It was a miracle no one had come across the disturbed grass. The path would have led them directly to him.

Just before first light, Fezz had started to make his move. Needing the cover of darkness, he'd had no choice but to run, despite the few individuals lingering near the scene.

He'd hoped that they'd assume the blaze had been started by a malfunction of one of the bikes, fueled by the gas tanks of all the others. The improbability of not seeing anyone, despite being outside only minutes before, and the fact that they hadn't located anyone afterward, would only bolster the assumption.

Of course, once the fire marshal investigated, it would be clear the fire was intentional. And unlike the liquor store, they were unlikely to sweep it under the rug.

"Ian." Fezz shook him.

Ian opened his eyes but wasn't fully awake.

"Get up. We have to go. Now."

"Where are we going?" Ian murmured.

"Get your stuff. We're leaving in two minutes."

Ian sat up and rubbed his eyes. "We don't have a car."

"We'll hitch a ride up on the highway. We can get a car in Denver. Let's go. Where's Jodi?" Fezz moved to check the bathroom. The door was open, and the light was off. "Ian. Where's Jodi?"

Ian shot up in bed. "I don't know. She was here last night."

"Damn it. Get your shoes on. I'll be right back." Fezz stormed out and banged on Jodi's door. She didn't answer. He returned to his room to grab the key. "You were supposed to stay together."

"We were together."

Back to the adjacent room, Fezz keyed in and announced his presence before barging in.

Inside, the beds were made. The room was dark.

"Jodi?"

She wasn't there.

Ian appeared in Jodi's doorway.

"Where did she go, Ian?" Fezz's panic caused him to be short. "She couldn't have gone home. There's no home to go back to."

"Maybe the store? Last night, she said she didn't have any more money and was upset that she missed a day. She could be at her spot."

"Let's go. We need to find her. We'll take her with us to Denver until it's safe for her to come back. Until then, we can't be here."

Fezz shut the door to their room and took off, prompting Ian to keep up.

The Mexican joint, the bank, and DMV—it all whizzed by in a flash. As they rounded the corner into the parking lot of the set-back General Store, Fezz saw the very last thing he wanted to see.

In front, a group had gathered around a deputy sheriff's car. The officer, a large man with a gleaming bald head, spoke to them.

From Fezz's vantage point, there didn't seem to be anyone in the back seat. So far, so good.

"Is Jodi in trouble?" Ian asked.

"We don't even know if she came over here," Fezz said. "This is probably unrelated. Let's wait to see what's going on before jumping to any conclusions."

Fezz slowed his pace, not wanting to appear like a crazy man. Whatever was going on, running up, out of breath, was a sure-fire way to become a person of interest.

As they approached, Fezz's optimism evaporated. Although he was pretty sure Ian didn't notice, there was a cardboard sign lying on the ground near the picnic table where they had first encountered Jodi. She had been there. That much was certain.

Fezz and Ian joined the crowd, hoping to overhear something to dispel their fears. But it only got worse.

"I'm sure it's somebody she knew," the deputy said.

The woman wearing a store-branded smock was incensed. "I'm telling you, that's not what happened. I see the girl every day. I know her."

"Okay, what's her name?" The deputy held his pad at the ready.

"I don't know her name, but—" the clerk answered.

"So you know her comings and goings and all the people she might know, but don't know her name."

The clerk let out a frustrated grunt and walked inside. "Forget you."

Fezz hurried after her. "Ma'am."

"What?"

"Jodi."

"I'm Sylvia."

"No. Jodi is her name."

"Oh," Sylvia said. "Okay, Jodi then."

"What happened to her?" Ian asked before Fezz could.

"That poor girl was sitting there, like she always does. She was already there when I came in to open the place. All of a sudden, a van pulled up and a bunch of guys got out and grabbed her. She didn't know them, I swear to you. She was screaming. They threw her in the van and took off. I saw it with my own eyes. But this idiot deputy doesn't believe me."

They were too late. The worst-case scenario played out before their eyes. Fezz wanted to smack himself. Why hadn't he just taken the kids away from there sooner? Why did he have such a drive to get even? If he had been smart, this could have been avoided.

Fezz knew who'd taken Jodi, and why. But he asked the question anyway. "Did you recognize the men?"

"No. But they looked like dirtbags."

"Can you describe them?"

"Greasy. Tattoos. Leather jackets. Probably part of that biker club. I think I've seen a couple of them here before, but I don't pay them no mind."

"Thank you." Fezz took Ian aside. Sylvia returned to work.

"Those are the same men that burned Jodi's trailer, aren't they?" Ian asked.

"Yes."

"Why are they doing this to her?"

Fezz knew why. It was because of him. But he didn't have the heart to tell Ian. Anyway, it didn't matter why. What mattered was what they were going to do about it. He had started a war, and Jodi was in extreme danger of becoming a casualty. If she wasn't already.

"We need to talk to the deputy." Fezz headed back outside and pushed his way through the crowd. Ian stayed back. "Deputy"—He read the name tag—"Deputy Parks. I know this young lady, she did not leave here of her own free will."

The deputy stepped away from the group. "And you are?"

"The name's Ray. Ray Sutton."

"And how do you know what happened, Ray Sutton?"

"The woman inside just told me that the people that took her are part of the Demon Squad. The girl's in danger. But I bet you already know that."

"Now what would fellas from the local social club want with a girl, huh? You're not from around here are ya?"

"I'm not, but I've been around long enough to know those guys are no social club. So what? You're on the take too?"

"Watch your tone with me, boy." The deputy stepped in closer, pointing a finger at Fezz's chest. "You might be big, but I get a couple of my boys down here and we'll put a whoopin' on ya."

"Deputies, or your boys from the club?"

"I'm warnin' ya, you're goin' down a path you don't want to go."

"Fine," Fezz said. "How 'about this? Your boys want me gone? I'm gone. I'm taking my son and we're leaving, right now."

"That sounds like a good idea to me," Parks smiled. "Safe travels."

Fezz grabbed Ian by the arm and trucked toward the motel.

"You don't have to pull me," Ian said.

"Sorry." Not realizing he was still holding him, Fezz let go. "This town is something else."

"We're not really going, are we? We can't go, Fezz. We can't leave her."

"No, Ian. No we can't."

CHAPTER 43

PETER TAPPED AND LISTENED. Hearing nothing, he knocked harder.

"What is it?" Curtis said.

"Can I come in?"

Entering his father's bedroom was always a chancy proposition. There were better than even odds that someone was naked or engaged in a lewd act. Not that Peter was a prude, but this was his father, and any women involved were essentially de facto stepmothers. It was best to use caution.

"I said come in."

Peter entered. And cringed.

Curtis was sitting on his floor mat, cross legged. Almost worse than interrupting coitus, he had disturbed his father's meditation.

"I apologize," Peter said.

"I was just winding down," Curtis said. "Is something wrong?"

As flighty as his father could be, he was still perceptive. Or Peter's expressions were cartoonish. Either way, the Sage had once again made the correct assumption.

"We got a call from the Paulsons."

"The Paulsons?" Curtis released his legs from their pretzel configuration and leaned back on his palms. "Why?"

"They got a phone call from Blake Brier. He was asking about the non-disclosure agreements."

Curtis's forehead rumpled. "How the hell does he know about those?"

"My guess? Jim."

Peter could see the realization cross his father's face. Either Jim had found the documents in the ceiling, or someone else had handed them over. It was the only way Blake could have known about them. It also would explain why they'd never been found.

"You've got to be kidding me. That's just as bad as the Feds finding them." Curtis rocked himself to a kneeling position and stood. "How could you let this happen?"

"I wasn't responsible for hiding them, remember? Anyway, I wasn't the one who was distracted by the conniving little bi—" Peter caught himself. He always made it a point to be as respectful as possible. Not because he respected the man, but because Curtis was his father. An ethic that was becoming harder to uphold by the day.

"It was part of the plan, and you know it."

"Well, you could have clued me in ahead of time. I could've made sure my team was set up properly. They're my responsibility."

"They're *my* responsibility, Peter. Everything and everyone you see around you is my responsibility. Don't you get it? It's on my shoulders. Mine."

"So you keep reminding me."

"You are so entitled, Peter." Curtis scoffed and shook his head. "I'm sorry, but it's true. And you know, that's my fault. You've been handed everything. Authority you didn't earn. A legacy you didn't build."

"How can you say I didn't earn it? Do you know what I've done for this place? I've given everything to support you. Mom and I are the only ones who can keep your precious legacy alive. Maybe a simple 'thank you' once in a while? Would it kill you?"

Peter was ashamed that he had raised his voice. He stopped to allow himself to cool off.

After a few moments of silence, Curtis spoke in a more measured tone. "I shouldn't have said that. It's not true. I know you work hard and

I do trust you. But things just keep getting worse and worse. I've got my own struggles, you know? It feels like everything is falling apart. Now, the documents are out there, too."

"Look, I'm not trying to tell you what to do," Peter said. "But guys like that need to be put in their place. We can't let him intimidate us. We intimidate him." Peter touched his lip and glanced at the ceiling. "Hmm. Sound familiar? Who did I learn that from?"

Curtis rolled his eyes. "I get your point. The truth is, I never should have approved the coverups in the first place. We should have taken our lumps and moved on. But you're right. Now, we're backed into a corner. I know I was upset you went after him before, but..."

"I should send my guys back?"

Curtis dipped his head and closed his eyes. He opened them with renewed vigor. "Send them. But this time send more and don't screw it up. And get those documents back."

Peter knew retrieving the documents didn't matter. If Blake had half a brain, they would already have been copied, scanned, saved, emailed, or whatever. The important part was sending a clear and painful message. This time with his father's blessing.

"Consider it done. Talk to you later."

Peter turned to walk away, but his father's voice stopped him.

"Peter—"

He cocked his head, keeping his father in his peripheral vision. He waited *That's right. Say it.*

"Thank you."

Damn right.

CHAPTER 44

BLAKE ACCELERATED INTO THE TURN.

"Do you have to drive like a maniac?" Jim's knees bounced.

Haeli chimed in from the back seat. "Is there any other way?"

Gripping the top of the window frame, Jim spoke under his breath. "There's no rush, for cryin' out loud."

"This isn't rushing, trust me." Blake punched it a little more, half in jest and half in defiance. "We shouldn't be doing this at all. It's a bad idea."

"You're the one who agreed to it. I'm just along for the ride."

Blake grunted. There was no use arguing with the man.

After speaking with Radek, Blake and Haeli had popped into the Don CeSar to check on Jim—if the definition of "popped in" was twenty minutes of counter surveillance and twenty more of circling the neighborhood to make sure they weren't being followed.

Before they'd gotten there, Jim had been sitting by himself, reading the book he'd bought at the hotel gift shop. Afterwards, he'd all of a sudden decided he needed to go to his old condo to look for something he might have left there. A photo album, he'd said. Despite his current nonchalance about the matter, at the time he wouldn't take no for an answer.

"We thought you moved out of the condo." Haeli said. "Your neighbor told us—"

"We did."

"But your stuff is still there? Was it supposed to be temporary?"

"Not at all." Jim's jowls shook in opposition to his face. "We collected quite a bit of junk while we were living there. When we moved to campus, we couldn't take it all. They let us leave whatever we wanted until someone needed the place. As far as I know, no one has." He scratched his forehead. "I really thought I brought the photos with me, but I couldn't find them. They have to be at the condo."

Through Jim's tangent, only one word stood out to Blake. *Campus.* As if it were the University of Texas and his father was rushing Sigma Chi. He found it funny how the Church used nomenclature to normalize itself. "The Universe" this and "the mind's eye" that. They called their captives "disconsolates"—whatever that was supposed to mean. It was their own little language, used to soften the abhorrent behavior.

"So, Dad. Have you been consoled?" Blake asked.

"Huh?"

"Disconsolate—no? Consoled?" Blake paused for a beat. His father provided a vacant stare in return. "Never mind."

No one could say Blake wasn't trying, but making conversation wasn't easy. His father had barely spoken about his ordeal, Blake's mother, or his plans going forward. Even when prompted, Jim trailed off into his own little world of denial.

"I wonder what happened to the others," Haeli said. "Do you think anyone else escaped?"

"It'd be nice to think so," Blake said. "But somehow I doubt it."

Jim pointed at Blake. "That I agree with."

"Well, at least there's something."

Blake turned left onto Causeway Boulevard and headed west toward Honeymoon Island. Right back where he and Haeli had started. Full circle. Only missing the resolution. They were back to square one, in a way. But this time with context. And while they might not have had the best footing at the start of a new and treacherous climb, they now had the tiniest of crags to grab onto, thanks to Radek.

"I love this road," Haeli said. "It's like driving across the water."

There was no disagreement. Built on a narrow land bridge, the water was only feet away from either side of the road. A small gap, whether natural or dredged, was spanned by a drawbridge to allow boat traffic to pass through. While there were many vessels nearby, the bridge remained down and Blake was able to pass without delay.

Upon arriving on Honeymoon Island, Blake took the right turn and wound through the condo complex. No matter the country, terrain, or conditions, once he visited a place, his memory for layout and topography allowed him to navigate with ease. Such skills weren't necessary in this case, but they didn't hurt to have.

At Dunoon Place, he found an open parking space in front of his father's condo. It was labeled for another unit. It didn't matter. They wouldn't be long.

"I'll be right back," Jim said.

"Hold up." Blake opened his door. "I'm coming with. Don't want you running into any surprises."

"What do you think, they're hiding out inside? Waiting for me?"

Blake didn't think so. But now that his father mentioned it, it would make sense. If Blake was tasked with finding Jim, the condo would be the first place he targeted.

"I don't know. That's why I'm coming."

"Wait." Haeli pushed the driver's seat forward and climbed out after Blake. "I'm coming too."

"It's a party." Jim waddled up to the door, holding his key ring. He tried it in the door. "Still works."

Jim went in first. Blake and Haeli stayed close behind.

On the floor, just inside the door, were small hunks of sand. As if tracked in on someone's shoes.

"Dad, stay here for a second." Blake bent down and pinched some of the sand between his thumb and forefinger, then rubbed them together. "It's damp."

"From the beach," Haeli said.

With instant, unspoken acknowledgement, both Blake and Haeli darted to Jim's side and nudged him back toward the door.

"What are you doing?" Jim asked.

Blake put his finger to his lips and whispered. "We have to leave."

Without bothering to close up behind them, they urged Jim toward the car. Blake pushed the fob to unlock it.

Haeli squeezed into the back, while Blake helped Jim into his seat.

As Blake moved around the front of the car toward the driver's side, a man bolted through the open door of Jim's apartment and careened toward Blake.

Here we go.

Taking a fighting stance, Blake prepared for the clash.

Instead of using his momentum to tackle Blake, the man stopped short and raised his own fists. He danced back and forth.

It was unusual, to say the least. It wasn't often that an attacker squared up as if more interested in a fair fight than an expeditious one. Blake half expected a referee and three judges to appear.

Blake took the extra seconds he was afforded to size up his opponent. The man was large and muscular, but young. Inexperienced. The nerves were telegraphed by his jerky movements and extreme focus, even though nothing had happened yet.

Overall, it made little sense. Was this one young man all they had sent? Did he think he was going to overpower all three of them? Or was it just a scare tactic? Part of a longer harassment play.

There was another possibility. One that was solidified by the sound of squealing tires at the other end of the parking lot. This man was a lookout. A distraction.

Blake threw a quick left jab and followed it with a strong right to the man's chin. He fell backward, hit the ground, then jumped back to his feet. But not before Blake could hop into the driver's seat.

"Hang on!" He started the engine, threw it in reverse, and hit the gas. The mustang smashed into the front of the approaching Lincoln SUV, causing Blake's door to swing closed. He smashed the gear shift into drive and took off.

Haeli contorted her body to get a better view out the back window. "There's five of them. They're coming at us."

Blake pushed the Mustang to its limit, only braking long enough to nail the turns without losing control. The driver of the Lincoln was just as adept.

Out of the neighborhood and onto the causeway, Blake moved into the oncoming lane and passed two cars, then cut back in before colliding head-on with a honking Jeep.

The pursuers took their own opportunity and before long were close to being back on their bumper.

"There's nowhere to go," Haeli said.

"I know." Blake swerved, passing another slow-moving car.

Ahead, just off to the south of the roadway, Blake saw a tall sailboat mast. He focused on it long enough to gauge which direction it was moving. Then he slowed.

"What are we doing, Mick? Why are we stopping?" Haeli peered out the back window. "They're passing. You've gotta move."

Blake watched his rearview mirror, then checked the progress of the sailboat. When the SUV was within twenty feet, Blake swerved again, passed the two cars in front of them, and jammed the accelerator.

A hundred yards ahead, a truss holding the drawbridge signal lights spanned overhead. The lights were not yet activated.

Passing one more car, Blake drove under the truss, traveled another thirty feet, then jammed the brakes. He spun the wheel, causing the car to slide sideways before coming to a stop, perpendicular to the road.

The two cars between them screeched to a halt. The Lincoln's tires squealed behind them.

Looking over his shoulder, Blake could see the mast approaching fast. While he couldn't see the lights, the sound of the horn meant the bridge was about to open.

"Are you thinking what I think you are?"

"What does she mean, Blake?" Jim looked around. "Don't do anything stupid."

Blake turned the wheel and watched the bridge. "Trust me, Dad."

Haeli yelled. "Incoming!"

Two of the men had gotten out of the SUV and were approaching on foot.

"A few more seconds." As the men passed the last car, Blake could see one of them reach for his waistband. "Get down!"

Blake punched the gas, fishtailing until he could right the wheel.

Careening toward the bridge, he could see the Lincoln pushing through the stationary cars to give chase, leaving the two other men on foot.

Ahead, the deck began its slow rise.

With the accelerator pinned to the floorboards, they hit the grated roadway of the drawbridge. The tires hummed a high-pitched song. Up the slight incline, they hung on to whatever they could as the Mustang rocketed up and over the three-foot gap. It bottomed out on landing.

Blake slammed on the brakes as the back end of the car kicked out to the right.

On the other side of the widening gap, the Lincoln backed away from the edge and disappeared.

Jim sat stunned, panting, with his mouth hanging open.

"Everyone okay?" Blake asked.

"All good," Haeli said.

"Dad?"

Jim looked Blake square in the eyes. The lines on his forehead deepened. "Who are you?"

Blake chuckled as he pulled forward and set off down toward town. "Yeah. We've got a lot of catching up to do."

CHAPTER 45

IAN LAGGED BEHIND.

Fezz glanced back to find that the boy had stopped and was staring across the street, toward the fire station. In the yard was a mangled car. Its roof was peeled back, its glass was shattered, and its doors were missing. Judging by the horrified look on his face, Ian must have thought it was the scene of a tragedy. Of course, Fezz knew better. "Don't worry. No one was hurt."

"How do you know?"

"It looks like the firefighters were using it to practice extractions. Jaws of life training."

"Jaws of life?"

"A giant pair of hydraulic scissors that can cut through metal. See how they cut the pillars and folded back the roof? If someone was trapped inside and the doors couldn't open, they'd be able to get them out."

"Oh." Satisfied with the answer, Ian started walking again.

Fezz carried on, matching every two of Ian's steps with one of his. In a couple dozen more stride's they'd be at Ernie's shop.

"Do you think they're hurting Jodi?"

"No. I think they're just trying to send a message." It wasn't the whole truth, but what else could Fezz say? He wouldn't put anything past the Demon Squad.

"Are you going to kill them?"

"What?" Fezz put his hand on Ian's shoulder. "No one is killing anyone, okay? We're going to find Jodi and bring her back, safe and sound."

"I hate those men." Ian's eyes were glossy and his neck was tense. "I really hate them."

"I know. Me too."

Ian was a peculiar kid. Smart, blunt, dry, and tone-deaf. Often, people misjudged him as something of a sociopath who wasn't capable of empathy. Blake, Khat—hell, even him—had made that mistake at first. But Ian was a sensitive soul, with deep feelings and concern for others. He just didn't have an outlet to show it.

Since Ian had first landed in their laps, he had made huge leaps in that regard. He was learning to communicate without sounding like a robot. Learning to read the room and keep his curiosities tempered. Whether or not Fezz had anything to do with it, he was proud of Ian's progress in social situations. Jodi was evidence of that.

"Hope he's here." Fezz held the door for Ian.

Inside, Ernie was standing behind the counter, scribbling on a paper form. "Look who it is."

"Hey Ernie. Hope we're not bothering you, but I need a little help."

"No bother." Ernie winked at Ian. "Good to see you again, young man."

Ian acknowledged him with a smile but didn't respond.

"We've got trouble—"

"No. You? Trouble?" Ernie chuckled. "Well, if it's your truck that's troubling you, you can rest easy. The parts are here and we're about to start working on her. You should be all set to go by end of day."

"I appreciate it, Ernie, but we've got bigger issues right now. Listen, there's a girl named Jodi. Begs for money outside the market. Don't know if you've seen her."

"I think I know who you're talking about. Cute little thing. Looks like she went rollin' around in a pigpen."

"Yep, that's her," Fezz said. "She and Ian have been hanging out while we've been here. So we've gotten to know her a bit. Anyway, this morning she was taken. I'd bet my life the Demon Squad was behind it."

"Taken?" Ernie set his pen down. His expression of amusement turned to one of concern. "How do you know?"

"We were there. At the market, after the fact. The sheriff's department was on scene. The deputy was useless, but I talked to the witness myself. The Demon Squad took her. No doubt about it."

"Why? Those guys are assholes, but kidnapping kids? For what?"

"Retaliation. Ian and I took her out to dinner the other night. Had a little run in with our friend Snake. I'm guessing he sees her with us, and figures—I don't know what they figured, but they're using her to get back at me."

"Makes sense, I guess. I told you not to stir the hornet's nest, didn't I?"

"Yes, you did, and you were right. But look, this girl Jodi doesn't have anything to do with this. I need you to help me out by telling me where they might be hiding her."

"I would have said their clubhouse, but the damnedest thing happened last night. The place burnt to the ground." Ernie gave a tight-lipped smile. "You wouldn't know anything about that, would ya?"

Fezz looked at Ian, who looked right back at Fezz. He could tell the boy's gears were already turning.

As honest as Fezz tried to be with Ian, there were things he didn't want Ian to know. He wouldn't even have brought Ian along at all, if he'd thought it was safe to leave him at the motel. Fezz had made that mistake once. He wasn't about to repeat it. From then on, Ian would be stuck to his side. If it meant he'd learn the truth, then so be it.

"Alright," Fezz said. "I'll give you the abridged version."

"Come on, let's go out back," Ernie said.

Ernie led them to a dirt patch behind the shop. There was junk strewn everywhere. Old motors, tires. In the center was a fire pit and a couple of old couches, covered in plastic tarps. Ernie gathered the tarps, threw them aside, and offered Fezz and Ian a seat. Then he joined them. "Fill me in. From the beginning."

"Like I said, we ran into Jodi at the market and Ian and her hit it off. We both felt bad for the girl. She's got a terrible story, Ernie. Lost her family, fends for herself. I figured we could help her out a little. Snake showed up at the Mexican joint, and the next day a gang of them went after the kids. Jodi was staying in her dead aunt's broken down trailer, up behind the gas station. They set fire to it with the kids inside. They're lucky to be alive."

"So in return, you paid a visit to the clubhouse."

Fezz nodded. Then looked to Ian for his reaction. "I'm sorry, bud. They took her because of me."

"You burned their clubhouse because of what they did to Jodi's house?" Ian asked.

"Yes."

"Good." Ian crossed his arms and sank back into the couch with a scowl on his face.

Fezz was relieved that Ian was letting him off the hook. For the moment. But the truth was, if he hadn't gotten involved in the first place, none of this would be happening. His job was to protect Ian. And now Jodi too. The best way to have done that was to mind his own business.

"Hawk has a ranch, just outside of town," Ernie said. "Perfect place to hide out. Since they can't be at the clubhouse, the ranch would be my best guess. But you can't just waltz in there, Ray. They'll be expecting you."

"That's why I need one more favor. Well, two actually. I know it's a lot to ask, but if you would—I need guns and ammunition, and I need you to look after Ian. Just for a bit, while I handle this."

Ernie scooted forward to the edge of his seat and clasped his hands at his knees. "The guns are no problem. But I can't let you go alone."

"I'm not bringing you into this, Ernie. You've done enough. I started it. I'll finish it."

"I've got a couple buddies. Good guys. All I have to do is call, and they'll be here. We could provide support. Sideline stuff. Just to have your back in case it hits the fan."

"I can't ask you—"

"You're not asking. I'm offering. The sheriff won't mess with those guys. I don't know if they're being paid or just scared of them, but they won't touch it. If you want to get your girl back, you're going to need a different kind of help." Ernie stood up and offered his hand. "I'll make the call."

Fezz stood and shook his hand. As reluctant as he was to involve another innocent person in this debacle, he knew it would be near impossible to take on the entire gang by himself. Ernie was a rare breed. Much like the friends he'd left behind.

Ian stood up and joined the men. "I'm coming, too."

"The hell you are," Fezz said.

"Don't worry little man," Ernie said. "You're with me."

CHAPTER 46

"CLOSE YOUR EYES. NO PEEKING." Birch giggled, then bolted out of the room.

It was Jagger's idea to play hide and seek, even though Birch always won. He was good at squeezing his small eight-year-old frame into weird places.

They were all supposed to be reading, but after Roberta left the room to take a phone call, they decided it'd be more fun to do something else.

Birch counted in his head. If Jagger didn't cheat, he still had a few more seconds to find a spot.

He cracked the door to Peter's room. During the day, none of the adults were around. Peter especially. One of his favorite hiding spots was in the cabinet under Peter's bathroom sink.

From outside the room, Birch could hear Jagger calling out, then running and laughing. Someone was already caught.

Footsteps approached. Birch dove under the desk, just before the door opened.

Jagger, he assumed, came in and went into the bathroom. After a minute, he went back into the hallway and shut the door.

Too easy.

Birch got out from under the desk and sat in the high-backed chair.

One day, he'd have an office just like this one. With pens and staplers and a computer.

Opening the top drawer, he rummaged through its contents, looking for anything fun. A lighter, sticky notes, a key chain with a whole bunch of keys. Nothing very exciting. He did find a box of rubber bands. Maybe he could fling them at Jagger if he came back.

In the second, larger drawer, he found a bunch of wires and a plastic bag with something in it. It looked like sugar.

He picked it up and squeezed it. Adults kept weird things in their desks, that was for sure.

"ARE you supposed to be running around out here, Delilah?" Evie asked.

"No, ma'am."

"Where's Roberta?"

Delilah shrugged. "I don't know."

"Get back to the classroom," Evie said. "And if there's anyone else AWOL, tell them I'll be there in two minutes and everyone better be there."

"Yes, ma'am."

Evie continued down the hall, went into her room and picked up the manilla envelope from her dresser. The meeting with the event committee was starting in fifteen minutes—just enough time to grab the documents she forgot. Little did she know she'd discover lawlessness. She'd need to have a conversation with Roberta, but it would have to wait until she got back.

"Help!"

From somewhere down the hall, Delilah's high-pitched scream pierced the walls.

Evie jumped, adrenaline dumping into her bloodstream. Dropping her purse and the envelope onto her bed, she hurried into the hallway on a frantic mission to find the origin.

Toward the end of the long corridor, Evie saw Delilah standing outside Peter's doorway. Her arms were stiff at her side.

"What's the matter, Delilah?" Evie moved closer. Delilah didn't flinch. She stood frozen, staring into the room. "You scared the heck out of me. Didn't I tell you—"

With one glimpse inside, the source of Delilah's fixation hit Evie like a truck. "Birch!"

The limp body of the eight-year-old boy lay crumpled on the floor. His gray, frozen face carried no expression. His eyes, no life.

"No, no, no! Birch." She rolled the boy onto his back, leaving behind a puddle of foam on the floor where his cheek had been. "Go get my phone. It's in my purse on my bed. Hurry."

Tears streamed down her wrinkled cheeks and she pumped the boy's chest. "Come on, wake up!"

Delilah ran in and handed Evie the phone.

"Make sure everyone is back in class. Go now!"

Evie dialed 911. The operator answered in one ring.

"I need an ambulance. The Church of Clear Intention. He's unresponsive!"

"Ma'am, I need you to stay calm. I'm dispatching an ambulance now. Who is unresponsive?"

"His name is Birch. He's eight years old. I found him on the floor. Foaming at the mouth. I don't feel a pulse. He's not breathing."

"Do you know CPR?"

"I do. I'm trying. It might be too late."

"Keep trying ma'am. Is there someone who can go outside and flag down the medics when they arrive?"

"I'll call the front desk and have them bring them to me. I'm in the residence building. Just hurry."

As Evie hung up the phone, she noticed the open bag of white powder lying on the floor, under the desk. It all became clear.

What did you do?

THE OFFICER HANDED Evie a glass of water. She drank, then placed it on the kitchen table.

"I'm sorry, I just have a few more questions."

Evie steadied herself. She was so dizzy, she worried she might fall off the chair.

"You said that the girl found him, right?"

"That's right."

"Is it possible that she took something? I mean, is it possible the scene was disturbed?"

"No. I came right away. Delilah stayed outside the room. I went in."

"And you didn't see anything unusual nearby. Chemicals, cleaners, pills, anything?"

Of course, she did. But she couldn't very well tell him that. After grabbing a pair of oven mitts from the kitchen, she'd picked up the bag and dropped it in the toilet. She didn't know what had come over her. It was like she'd been on autopilot.

"No, I didn't. Why?"

"The medics think he may have been accidentally poisoned."

"Sir—" Evie paused, took a deep breath and braced herself for the response to what she was about to ask. "He didn't make it, did he?"

The officer gave her a solemn shake of his head. "No, ma'am. I'm sorry."

Evie's stomach turned and her head swam. She didn't know if she would vomit or keel over and die herself. How could this have happened? And what would happen now? "We need to contact his mother. She's at an outreach event in Sarasota."

"We will."

"He was such a sweet boy. A wonderful, darling boy."

The officer placed his hand on Evie's and let her cry. After a few minutes, she withdrew her hand and wiped her eyes.

Another man walked into the kitchen and handed the officer a piece of paper. He took it and placed it on the table. "This is a consent to search the residence. I need you to sign it so we can continue our investigation."

"I don't—I think I should wait for Curtis. I don't have the authority."

"You live here, correct?"

"Yes."

"Then you have the authority. It's just a formality ma'am. In case we find anything—that is—"

"In case you find evidence of a crime. You think someone did this intentionally."

"I didn't say that. In fact, I don't think this was anything but an accident. But we just need to cover all the bases. You understand."

She understood, more than he realized. By destroying the evidence, she had made herself an accessory. She had done a terrible thing.

But on the other hand, Birch was gone, and there was no sense in compounding one tragedy with another. Her action may have saved Peter's life. Saved Curtis from the embarrassment. And saved the organization from scrutiny. Or, not.

The truth was, Birch was dead and everyone in the world would know it. There would be an autopsy, and then everyone would know how. What had she actually accomplished? And to what end?

None of this had crossed her mind at the time.

It didn't matter now. What was done was done. She needed to shift her focus to supporting the family. Hard times were on them, and someone had to pick up the pieces.

"Can I use your pen?"

CHAPTER 47

BLAKE AND HAELI sat at the table furthest from the bar. At the moment, there was no one else on that side of the patio.

In such close relative proximity to the Church, there were bound to be sympathizers or tattletales lurking around the Fenway somewhere. In Dunedin, it seemed like everyone was watching them. It was enough to drive one mad. But, as Khat would say, "You're not paranoid if they're really after you."

Jim was tucked away in his room at the Don CeSar. Probably taking a nap. He'd had a stressful afternoon. And he looked drained.

Blake had been apprehensive about taking him back there. He'd considered changing hotels, but his father was settled in and there was no indication the location had been compromised. As always, they were careful not to be seen on camera or linger too long.

With everything at a lull, it was time for Blake to get back to the task at hand. Making sense of it all.

Haeli sipped her Mai Tai concoction—a well-earned respite, in his opinion. He passed on the afternoon cocktail and appetizers Haeli ordered. His laptop and the stack of folders would have to suffice as lunch.

"It's probably safe to assume that each of these NDAs is for the same thing." Blake paged through the folder, for the umpteenth time.

"Same language, same attorneys. I found a small write-up on Radek's daughter in the Tampa Bay Times. Another for Joseph Calhoun, which I believe is Cynthia Calhoun's ex-husband."

Cynthia was one of the subjects found in the documents. She was the first call he made. And the first to hang up on him.

"What's the article say?"

Blake clicked the browser tab to display the Calhoun piece. "Both are basically the same. Drug addicts. Homeless. Another casualty of the drug epidemic. You know, all the usual taglines."

"It doesn't sit right," Haeli said. "These families were paid a lot of money to keep these deaths quiet, or to not divulge any information the deceased might have told them. If so, it would have to be sensitive info."

"And if they were in a position to know such high-level information, what were they doing living on the street? How could it be a coincidence that this has happened multiple times?"

"Maybe the drugs are part of the culture," Haeli suggested. "Maybe that's what they don't want getting out. Hammond makes money selling dope to a captive audience."

"I don't know. If that were the case, my father would have known about it. Probably would be detoxing right now."

"So what then?"

"These people were found in random, secluded locations, miles away from the Church. But Radek says his daughter was living there at the time of her death. What if they died on site, then were moved and dumped?"

"Do the articles say they were 'dumped'?" Haeli eyed Blake as she took the last sip of her drink, then crunched on a piece of ice.

"Staged, then."

"It would make sense. If people overdosed at the Church, they might want to hide that fact."

"Yeah. Especially if they were responsible for it."

"That's a stretch," Haeli said.

At the bar, one person sipped a drink and stared up at two television screens set to the same channel. A tag in the upper right-hand corner of the image said that the news report was live. An attractive brunette held a microphone. Blake recognized the building behind her.

"Haeli, look." Blake got up and called to the bartender. "Can you turn up the sound?"

He and Haeli leaned on the bar, watching in amazement as the details unfolded.

"—left a young child dead. It happened here, at the Church of Clear Intention, in a residential part of the compound. Police haven't released an official statement, but sources inside the department say this is likely an accidental overdose. We've reached out for comment from the Church, but so far, there's been no response. Live on scene, I'm Ashley Dupuis, News Channel Eight."

Blake shot Haeli a look. "A stretch?" He headed back to their table.

"What a shame. Eight years old." Haeli sat.

"Here's my working theory." Blake paced behind his chair. "Every one of the people in these files died at the compound. They either were forced to take something or didn't know what they were taking, right? Stick with me for a minute. I'm willing to bet none had any history of drug abuse. What we need is access to police reports, toxicology screenings, medical examiner records."

"So, we need to involve the police."

"Well, yes. But not directly. I'll call Harrison."

"Harrison's in Providence. How's that going to help?"

"The Church was raided by the FBI. Dad saw it himself. So the Feds already have a case going. If I provide Harrison with these documents, he can pass them on to the right folks. They can force some of these families to talk." Blake clapped his hands. "They can also access all the information to link the cases together and to the Church. I can wrap the whole thing up in a bow and all they'll have to do is connect the dots. Whatever they're digging into, it probably pales in comparison to this. The best part is, we're out of it. Anonymous."

Haeli squinted. "Do we really think Hammond is intentionally offing people? I mean, he's a misogynistic creep, but he seems kind of soft. Ya know how you can just tell that some people don't have it in 'em? Hammond is one of those people."

"Seriously? He sent men to gun us down in broad daylight. I'd say he's capable. Sure, it could be someone else pulling the strings, but Hammond has to be involved. I imagine nothing happens under that roof without him knowing about it."

"This still doesn't help get your mother back."

"No. But if the whole place crumbles, there'll be nothing, or no one left to hold her there. She'd be free, whether she wanted to be or not. Until then, we just have to avoid running into a Lincoln full of thugs."

"After today, I think our first priority should be getting hold of a couple of pistols."

"It's on the list. But not first." Blake tossed his phone on the table, dialed Harrison's number, and pressed the speaker button. "This is."

The audio clicked. "Agent Harrison."

"Guess who?"

"Elton John."

"Close. Two of your favorite people in the world."

"Hi Andy," Haeli added.

"Something tells me you're not calling just to say hi." He paused. "I'm gonna go out on a limb and say you're looking for one of your famous favors."

CHAPTER 48

"HOW ABOUT THIS THING?" Ian asked.

"Oil pan." Ernie shined his light and tapped his greasy fingers against the cast iron contraption. "And this here's the gearbox."

Ian laid on a creeper, no doubt following everything Ernie was telling him. His feet and shins stuck out from under the truck. Fezz stood near the front bumper.

No surprise, Ian was engrossed in his lesson in the anatomy of the undercarriage. Even after question 247, Ernie displayed patience.

"Which part needs to be fixed?" Ian asked.

"The water pump. You can't see that from here. We have to take the cover off the engine. And we're going to have to remove the timing chain, which we'll be replacing too. But we're doing all of that from the top."

"Listen close, Ian." Fezz said. "You'll do this next time we're stuck. It'll be faster."

Ernie slid himself out from under. "Hey, if I had the parts, you'd have been on your way days ago."

Fezz laughed. "How much do you wish they'd been in stock?"

"I can't lie." Ernie levered himself off the dolly and stood up. "Very much."

At their feet, Ian scooted out and looked up at them. "Can I use the wrench?"

"Sure can. Later." Ernie went to the workbench and picked up his phone. He manipulated the screen for a few seconds. "The guys are a few minutes out."

While it was gracious of Ernie to offer help, Fezz didn't like the idea of needing it. Especially from strangers.

Before, help had been built in. Khat and the others were always there. They all had each other's backs no matter what. Now, things were different.

He had set out to find a new life. For him and for Ian. But it was just more of the same. Only the faces had changed. He started to think he'd made a mistake. There was no new life to be had. The cause was never the environment or the people around them—it was *them*. Even Ian. They were wired in a way which made them unable to turn the other cheek. Unable to do the one thing every other so-called normal person needed to do—submit.

"My mechanic Dale is coming in to start working on the truck," Ernie said. "I need to be freed up. Ian can stay with him if you want. No one should bother Dale. He's got nothin' to do with nothin'."

"Once I meet Dale," Fezz said.

"Right." Ernie opened the back door of the garage. "We'll meet these guys out back."

Fezz and Ian followed, and the three returned to their newly assigned seats on the ratty old couches.

There was a prolonged silence, filled only by the sound of a dog barking in the distance. Fezz decided he'd be the one to break through it. "Can I ask you a question?"

"Sure," Ernie said.

"Why'd you get out?"

"You wanna know the truth? I didn't like how easy it was."

Ian chuckled. "See, I told you."

At one time, Ian told Fezz he wanted to be an operator—a notion he must have picked up from one of his more testosterone driven house-mates. In an attempt to dissuade him, Fezz told him it was too hard.

Ian, of course, argued that if Fezz could do it, he could, too. He wasn't wrong. But that wasn't what Ernie meant when he said it was easy.

"At first, you know, it's a big major deal," Ernie said. "The first time you pull that trigger it's like the most monumental life-changing moment. The next time, less so. Till one day, you don't even remember how many there were. It shouldn't feel easy. Ever. So, I packed it up."

"Must have taken its toll," Fezz said.

"As if you don't know."

Ernie left it at that, but it was clear he had Fezz's number. He appreciated Ernie not asking more questions.

"The gang's all here," Ernie whooped, as two men rounded the corner. Ernie gave them a warm greeting. "This here is Ray and his son, Ian."

"Good to meet you, I'm Billy," the taller man in the sleeveless shirt said.

"I'm Noah."

Noah was almost as wide as he was tall. The African American man sported a thin mustache and an olive-colored t-shirt that read, "My safe space is 1500 yards in all directions." Fezz liked him already.

"I appreciate you guys comin'," Fezz said. "We've run into a little trouble with the De—"

"Ernie filled us in," Billy said. "We're in."

Noah smiled. "Any chance to screw with those guys is a good day."

"Did you bring the stuff?" Ernie asked.

Noah nodded. "In the truck. Brought an assortment. Rifles, pistols. Some smoke. A bunch of other crap Billy pulled out of his garage."

Fezz wasn't sure if these guys were ex-military, militia, or just run of the mill gun nuts. Not that it mattered. They seemed capable enough, and if someone with Ernie's background trusted them, he would too.

"So what's the plan?" Billy asked.

"Alright." Fezz clapped his hands and rubbed them together. "Here's what I'm thinking."

CHAPTER 49

"FATHER, YOU WANTED TO SEE ME?" Peter waited for permission to enter.

"Close the door." Curtis fidgeted with his shirt cuffs. There were no words to describe how he felt. Angry, saddened, desperate—all failed to encapsulate the full nature of his condition. It disgusted him that after all the years of tireless practice, he was no better at controlling his emotions than the next guy.

"How are you holding up?" Peter asked.

Curtis glared at his son and took a deep breath. "To be honest, I'm pissed."

"I get it. We're all taking this hard. He was my brother. And he had so much potential. It's such a tragedy."

"And you loved him."

"Of course."

"Say it." Curtis could barely stand the sight of Peter's smug face. *Potential*. Birch was a human being. An innocent boy. Peter showed no sign of remorse or caring. He spoke as if he were talking about a distant foreign leader he'd never met. "And you loved him."

"Okay," Peter scoffed. "And I loved him."

"Pathetic. Your mother told me what she did. She told me she hid the drugs."

"Drugs?"

"Don't play stupid with me, you brat! Evie accused me. But she knows. Just like you and I know. They were yours."

Peter's shoulders slumped. A scolded child and a caged animal, both at once.

"Why didn't you tell me you had a problem?" Curtis's eyes glistened. "We could have worked it out. How could you be so irresponsible? I thought you were the future. I thought you had it all together. You're nothing but a liability. A mess, Peter. A disappointment."

"You hypocrite." Peter's face reddened. His voice rose. "You want to talk about disappointment? Do you want to know what everyone is saying? They're questioning if you still have the ability to lead. They've lost faith. *I've* lost faith. That's why I have had to take matters into my own hands. It's Mom and I who have been running this place. Keeping everyone in line. You're too busy trying to get into some new girl's pants. I'm sorry, but you're the disappointment."

"At least I'm handling my shit without turning to drugs. It's weakness, Peter. And it cost an innocent boy his life. Why can't you see that?"

"I don't use drugs, you naïve fool." Peter balled his fists. "Were they mine? Yeah, they were. But they were a tool."

"So what then? You're dealing to the parishioners. Is that what this is about? Are you telling me my son is dead because you were trying to make a buck? Look around you Peter. What else do you need? Everything has been handed to you."

Peter laughed. "There you go again. Are you so blind? I'm not dealing drugs. I mean, what do you think I am? I'm in control of this place. Not you. You want to know the truth? Huh? You really want to know? Hell, you're complicit so it doesn't really matter does it?"

"What are you getting at?" Maybe it was the deadness of the eyes, the robotic laugh, or the sneering grin, but Curtis shivered. As if he'd seen a flash of pure evil.

"All those mysterious deaths. Do you really think they were a coincidence? It wasn't the Universe balancing things, I can tell you that. No, it was fentanyl. It was me, cleaning up what you couldn't."

Curtis's knees weakened. He stumbled, and dropped into his seat.

Was this true, or a ploy to gaslight him? Could he have really created this monster?

No, it couldn't be. It wasn't. "That's a lie."

"Believe what you want. But you're in this, too." Peter sneered and crossed his arms, looking down on Curtis, now the caged animal. "So I'd suggest pulling yourself together so we can get a handle on what's coming. Mom got the police involved, there's no fixing that. We have to all stick together now. Weather the storm."

"I—" Curtis shook his head. "I've failed you."

"Don't do that!" Peter yelled. "Don't pity me. I pity you."

Curtis sat in amazement and disbelief. There was nothing to say. No reasonable way to respond.

"I'm leaving." Peter said. "I've got a company to run."

Maybe Peter was right. Maybe he was the one who should be pitied. Curtis didn't recognize any of it anymore. Not the Church he'd built, not the people he knew. Not even himself.

His oldest son was a murderer. A cold-blooded psycho. And there was nothing that could be done to reverse it.

"Go, then," Curtis said. "Leave me alone."

Peter stormed away, muttering. "You're the weak one. You."

Curtis was left with Peter's words echoing in his ears. And for the first time in his life, he realized they were true.

CHAPTER 50

"KHAT? HANG ON A MINUTE." Blake flagged Haeli's attention and motioned that he was leaving the room.

She nodded.

"Can you hear me?" Blake took the stairs to the bottom, then popped outside. He leaned against the door to keep it from closing and locking him out.

"You got me now?" Khat asked.

"I've got you. Horrible service here." Blake pulled the phone away, making sure he had enough bars to stay on the call. "What's up?"

"You called me."

"Right." Blake chuckled to himself. So much had happened in the past couple of hours, he didn't know if he was coming or going. "I'm just checking in."

"Everything's quiet here. Kook's still not back. Griff's been in the basement for days, doing God knows what. Something about a computer learning model."

"How about Fezz?"

"Still off the grid." Khat sighed. "How's it going in sunshine land?"

"Making progress. We found some intel that I passed along to Harrison. He called me back within the hour to say his people in Florida were excited about the lead. Apparently, they have everyone on it. So, we'll see where that goes. Oh, and I found my father. Got him stashed away."

"No kiddin'? What about your mother? They were together, no?"

"Still working on that. The place is like Fort Knox. We got in once but had to jump through a lot of hoops. I don't think we're getting back in there anytime soon." Blake watched an SUV pass. The female driver didn't acknowledge his presence. "I'm banking on the FBI investigation to crack things open a bit. All in all, not the most relaxing vacation."

Khat laughed. "Hey. No one's trying to kill you. I'd call that a holiday."

"Yeah. About that—do you think you can hook me up with someone down here? Need a couple pistols. Nine mil. Glock if possible."

"You're in Florida, man. Can't you just go to Walmart?"

"Funny. Also true, but I'm looking for something a little less traceable."

"I'll get you someone. Should we come down there? What're the heaters for? I thought you were dealing with the business class crowd."

"I am. As well as their hired muscle. But there's no need for you guys to come down, we've got it. The sidearms are strictly for contingencies."

"Sounds good," Khat said. "Keep me posted. I'll shoot you a text with the contact info in a bit."

"Thanks Khat." Blake hung up, then headed back up the stairs.

When they first arrived, Blake didn't imagine they'd need to be armed. But seeing as how the second set of thugs weren't deterred by the beatings of the first two, it was unlikely they'd stop coming. And with more drastic measures. Better safe than sorry.

Before reaching the room, he took out his keycard. There was no need. The door was still cracked open from when he left.

"Good news, Haeli—"

As he pushed inside, his stomach sank, and his body surged with adrenaline.

It took a fraction of a second to get a grip on what he was witnessing. Like a reverse tornado, the questions and answers swirled at incredible speed and were sucked into his stunned brain. But from his perspective, the realization came in disconnected chunks, traversing his neurons in slow motion.

Who is this man? I recognize him. It's Peter Hammond. Why is he here? And why is Haeli lying on the ground at his feet? She's unconscious. He's attacked her. He's ambushed her.

Within the same second, Blake had already left his feet, leaping at Peter, and tackling him to the ground. They landed on the far side of Haeli, just far enough to avoid crushing her ribs.

Blake straddled Peter, pinning him on his back, and delivered two devastating blows to the side of his torso.

Peter wheezed before Blake grabbed him by the throat. "What did you do?"

In Peter's right hand was a hypodermic syringe. Blake caught a glimpse of it just before Peter could jab him in the thigh. Grabbing Peter's wrist with his left hand, he shook the needle free, then picked it up with his right hand and flung it across the room.

Peter laughed.

Blake dropped his forearm on Peter's throat. "What was in it? Heroin? What did you do?"

The gurgling sounds coming from Peter's mouth weren't helping. Blake needed answers. He released the pressure.

"Sorry—" Peter coughed. "She's not going to make it." He laughed again.

Blake hauled off with a hammer fist to Peter's face. His lip opened up. Blood covered his teeth.

"That hurt, brother."

Peter's calm demeanor angered Blake even more. "I'm not your fucking brother, you piece of garbage."

"Oh, but I beg to differ." Peter flashed a crimson smile. "See, my mother is Evie. And your mother is Evie. Right? Like I said. Brothers."

"Bullshit." Blake's mind swirled. Peter was a liar. And a criminal. "Where's my mother? What did you do to her? I will kill you."

"You could. But I wouldn't waste any more time." Peter turned his head and spit blood. "Your girlfriend's accidentally mainlined quite a bit of fentanyl. Probably doesn't have much time. I mean, if you'd rather spend it with me..."

Blake looked over at Haeli. He could see her chest rise slightly, then fall again into stagnation. She was alive. But Peter was right. Not for long.

His memory flashed back to the patio. Breakfast. David Coverdale. He had been revived by the hooker. He said he kept Narcan on hand.

What was his room? 350? 318? No. 315.

With one more blow to Peter's ribs, Blake jumped up, scooped Haeli off the floor, and ran into the hallway.

Halfway down, he encountered a maid, bending over to retrieve something from her cart.

"Comin' through. Look out!" Blake hollered.

The woman threw herself back against the wall to make way.

Blake spoke to Haeli even though he knew she couldn't hear him. "Stick with me. Almost there. Keep breathing. Three eleven, three thirteen, three fifteen."

He kicked the door hard. And kept kicking. Over and over, until the haggard half-naked man answered.

"Narcan. I need your Narcan!"

Blake placed Haeli on the floor and checked her pulse, while the occupant fumbled through a drawer.

"I love you, Haeli. Hang in there."

With eyes on Haeli, Blake held out his palm. As soon as the plastic bottle touched his hand, he grasped it, put it to Haeli's nose and sprayed. "Do I do it in both?"

He didn't get a response from the stunned onlooker.

"Do I spray it in both nostrils?"

"I-I don't know...."

"Screw it." Blake sprayed again. "Come on, wake up. Wake up."

After a few seconds, Haeli opened her eyes and gasped. No slow awakening, no groggy half-closed eyelids. Just instant consciousness, like she was waking up from a nightmare.

"Thank God." Blake pulled her close and hugged her tight.

"What happened?" Haeli asked.

"I'll tell you later." Blake turned to the wannabe rockstar, who was now as alert as Blake had ever seen him. The situation seemed to have the same effect on him as the antidote did on Haeli. "Call for an ambulance." He handed over the spray bottle. "Hit her again if she starts to nod out. I'll be right back."

"Where are you going?"

Blake ran out of the room and down the hall. When he reached his room, the door was closed. He found his key and burst inside, ready for a fight he knew wasn't going to happen.

Peter was gone. And with him, the answers Blake needed.

CHAPTER 51

FEZZ WALKED along the dirt road. Slow and methodical. Hoping he had already been noticed.

The wind blew up dust and swayed the adolescent cornstalks, which stretched out for what seemed like miles. It was a scene from an old western movie. The begrudged stranger waltzes into town for a final showdown. Sidearm on his hip, Fezz was the modern version of Doc Holiday.

Ahead, the ranch house loomed large. Not because it was extravagant, but because of its presence in an otherwise open landscape.

Fezz didn't fear the men inside, if they were even there, as Ernie had predicted. As much as they played their roles, they all had something to lose. The ranch. Status. Livelihood.

The most dangerous men typically fell into three categories. The professionals, the zealots, and the desperate.

These men carried no righteousness, nor cause. No conviction. They were the least threatening of all.

Whatever happened, Fezz was resigned to letting the chips fall. He had taken an enormous step by allowing Ian to play an important role, despite his realistic concerns. Ian had made his voice heard and showed bravery. He'd convinced Ernie and Billy and Noah that he was ready and capable. Fezz had to admit that he was proud. Now, he just had to trust.

As he approached the front of the house, he touched his hip where the grip of the pistol poked against his shirt. He found a spot, about thirty or forty feet from the front door, then planted his feet and squared his shoulders.

With a whistle, he summoned fate.

Seven men poured from the structure and gathered into a group.

Fezz held his ground.

The group approached, all brandishing firearms. As they came within a dozen feet, they stopped. One man stepped forward. A forty-five leveled at Fezz's head.

"Do you know who I am?" the man asked over the canted pistol.

"Hawk." Fezz left his arms at his side and made it a point to avoid any sudden moves.

"I don't know where you're from, friend, but 'round here, what you done is an act of war."

"I'm here to make a deal." Fezz said.

"That right?" Hawk glanced over his shoulder. "He's here to make a deal. Now what could you possibly have that we would want?"

"A trade. Me for the girl."

Hawk laughed. "Looks to me like we already got you, now don't it?"

———

IAN OPENED the gate to the back patio and closed it behind him, trying to be as quiet as possible. Through every step, he imagined what Fezz would do.

This was a big moment for him. The chance to prove himself. The chance to correct the course Fezz had set them on. But all he could think about was Jodi. Either way, failing was not an option.

On the back of the house, there were two open windows low to the ground, and a sliding door inside the fenced in patio. If it was unlocked, the door would be the way to go.

231

He pulled on the handle. As soon as it cracked an inch he jumped back. The giant head of a Rottweiler appeared, barking and growling and slobbering on the glass. Ian pushed the door all the way closed. There was no way he could contend with the vicious dog. But Fezz was counting on him. And there was a timeline. Retreating was never part of the plan.

Taking a moment to gather himself and look at the problem in a logical way, he had an idea. Obvious, after he thought of it.

He looked around for something long.

Against the shed, set back from the rear of the house, were a few tools. Shovels and rakes, mostly. Ian climbed over the fence and ran to grab a metal-toothed rake.

Standing to the side of the enclosed patio, he reached over and hooked the teeth of the tool onto the edge of the slider and pulled. The dog raced out and jumped at Ian, landing his paws against the chain link. It snarled and drooled but couldn't get to him.

Ian backed away and waited for the dog to put his paws on the ground. Then, he held the rake up like a lance and darted forward, knocking it broadside into the edge of the door. It moved a foot or two.

Again the dog lunged, this time Ian was nearly bitten before he could withdraw his arms from over the side of the fence.

One more.

He timed it again, jabbing the rake and stretching out his arms as far as he could.

The door shut tight.

He swung the rake, striking the dog in the neck. Then dropped it into the pen and backed away. The Rottweiler was unfazed but distracted just long enough for Ian to avoid becoming a meal.

While the animal carried on with flipping out, Ian pushed open the screen of the closest window and hoisted himself inside.

It was a bedroom. The door was open and Ian could see into the living room.

He crouched behind the bed and listened for voices. Hearing none, he ventured out.

Along the hallway were several doors. Two of them were closed. But

Ian noticed something peculiar about one of them. It had a deadbolt turned backwards—the lever on the outside.

Jodi.

Hoping he was right, Ian unlocked the door and entered.

There, sitting on a mattress on the floor, was Jodi.

She looked up at him with wide eyes. "Ian? How did you—"

Ian figured the shocking part wasn't that she was being rescued, but that Ian was alone. As if he'd somehow single-handedly defeated the entire gang. For that second, he was Superman. And he liked the feeling.

"I'll tell you after. Come on, we don't have time."

Jodi got up and threw herself into Ian's arms. She hugged him so tight, he thought she might break his spine.

"I knew you'd come. I just knew it!"

KEEPING his pistol trained on Fezz, Hawk leaned to spit a brown stream of tobacco juice on the ground. "There's not gonna be any deals, sorry to say. But we were hopin' you'd stop by. Prepared something special for ya. Search him."

Fezz slowly lifted his arms away from his sides, as two of the men approached and frisked him. They found the gun, took it, and handed it to Hawk, who tucked it in his waistband. Snake stood in the background with a smirk on his face, clearly enjoying the show.

"Now walk." Hawk pointed behind Fezz to a wide dirt path that cut through the waist-high corn. "I wanna show you your surprise."

Attempting to keep track of time in his head, Fezz hoped Ian hadn't run into any trouble. The gamble had been that if Fezz was alone, there would be no need for someone to stay behind to guard the girl. He would try to buy as much time as possible, which meant following Hawk's instructions.

Like a desert caravan, the entire group followed Fezz along the trail. Fezz didn't need Hawk to point out what they were looking for.

The hole was about eight feet long, three feet wide, and six feet deep. Its purpose needed no further explanation.

"Aww. You guys went to all this trouble for me?"

Hawk was unamused. "Get in."

"Can I say something first?"

"Say whatever you want, it's not gonna matter."

"If I'm going to get in, there's something you need to know." Fezz put his right hand behind his back and held out two fingers. "M. Forty."

"M. Forty?" Hawk glanced at Snake. "What the hell's that supposed to mean?"

From behind Fezz, a volley of six shots rang out in the distance. Three, then three more in rapid succession. Six 7.62 rounds, all delivered by three M40 sniper rifles in the hands of three expert shooters. By the time Hawk registered the sound and spun around, his compatriots were taking their last breaths, if not already dead.

Hawk screamed in horror, then turned to Fezz. Rage consumed him. Fezz could see it in every fiber of the man's appearance. His skin, his muscles, his eyes.

"Before you think about lifting that gun hand, I'd count the dots. Right there on your chest." Fezz pointed. "One, two, three."

Hawk looked down at the glowing red dots darting around like three dancing fairies.

Of course, the snipers didn't need laser targeting devices, nor did they use them or even own them. It was Billy's idea to take along the run-of-the-mill laser pointers. He thought they'd have a dramatic effect.

"Drop the gun. It's over."

His fingers slackened, and the pistol hit the dirt. Fezz reached into Hawk's waistband to retrieve the pistol Noah had lent him. "Get in the hole."

Hawk walked to the edge, then stopped. "I'm not doin' it."

"Then I'll blow your head off right here."

"You won't. You're not going to kill me, because if you do, my men are instructed to kill the girl. Call it an insurance policy."

"The girl? You mean that one?" Fezz motioned to his right, where Ernie had run over to meet Ian and Jodi as they fled from behind the residence. The three of them stood at the edge of the access road, looking back at Fezz and Hawk.

"You son of—"

"Come on now, Butch." Fezz brought the muzzle closer to Hawk's forehead. "You play stupid games, you win stupid prizes, right?"

"Don't kill me. Please. I'll do whatever you want."

Fezz glanced over at Ernie and nodded. Ernie wrapped one arm around Ian and one around Jodi, turned them away from Fezz's direction, and pulled them in close.

With a squeeze of the trigger, Hawk crumpled over and fell into the hole.

It was satisfying in the sense that it marked the end of their ordeal. Even though it was Snake who he really wanted to make pay, Hawk was the man behind the curtain and thus the most deserving of the grave he had carved out for himself.

Still, it was strange how Fezz had not so much as set eyes on the man before ten minutes ago, and yet, Fezz had taken his life.

Ernie was right. It was way too easy.

CHAPTER 52

"GOOD AFTERNOON LADIES." Curtis dropped his briefcase and unbuttoned the two top buttons of his shirt.

Evie was standing by the edge of the sofa. The other wives were all seated, dutifully awaiting his arrival.

"Sage, we're all very sorry," Bridget said. "How are you feeling?"

"You know," Curtis replied.

There was a moment of silence.

"The Sage remains strong in these difficult times," Evie added.

"Where's Jessica?" he asked.

Cathleen spoke up. "Still at the hospital, but they say she's feeling better. She'll probably be released tomorrow. Poor thing. I can't imagine."

"Uh-huh." Curtis nodded. "Um—Evie, I need to talk to you. Ladies, I'm sorry, we'll have to talk later."

Evie smoothed out her skirt. "Okay. But the women have—"

"Now, Evie. In my room."

Curtis walked out.

Evie addressed the room. "He's going through a lot. He'll be back. Give me a minute."

When she met Curtis, he was wandering around, staring at his shoes.

"Did you know?" he asked.

"Did I know what?"

"Did you know what Peter was doing?"

"The drugs?" Evie waved him off. "Peter isn't doing drugs. There's another explanation. I know it."

"Oh, there's an explanation all right. Peter told me plain as day, right to my face."

"What did he tell you?"

"He's been poisoning the parishioners. The disconsolates. That's why they've been dropping like flies."

"That's not true. He's just angry."

"It's true Evie." Curtis turned to face her, a desperate look in his eyes. "This whole time, he wasn't just covering up some unsightly PR problems, he was covering up murders. *His* murders."

"It's just not possible, Curtis. Peter's a good man. And he works hard. Ya know he looks up to you, even if you don't realize it."

"What does that have to do with anything? Don't you hear what I'm telling you?" Curtis paced. His brain burned. "Evie, it's all over. All of this. Poof. Gone."

"Nonsense."

"I'm a fraud, Evie. You know it. You've always known it. You should leave here while you can. Get away from Peter. Get away from me. Go back to your family. Your real family. Jim doesn't deserve this. He's out there. Blake, too. Go find them."

"What are you talking about? I'm not going anywhere. What has gotten into you?"

"Evie, sit." Curtis held her hand and sat with her. "I'm going to tell you the truth."

There was no argument. Just patient anticipation.

"Look, when we were young, I manipulated you. You were beautiful, and I was jealous of Jim. I wanted you for myself, so I undermined your relationship. Sowed the seeds of doubt until you were so fragile, I could scrape you off the floor. I treated you horribly."

"So you never loved me?"

"I'm not saying that. I'm saying I didn't love you, *at first*. After we had Peter, I wanted you to have better. That's why I encouraged you to make amends with your husband. Jim was a good man. Loyal and devoted to the organization. I owe him an apology just as much as I owe you one."

"Jim has made his peace with it, Curtis. Why are you bringing this up now?"

"Because the whole thing has been a lie. I made all of this crap up. I was hungry. I loved the money, the attention, the women. Especially the women." He let out a frustrated grunt. "But it was all a fraud. People listened to me like I knew what I was talking about. And I ran with it. I made it up as I went along."

Evie shook her head in disbelief. "You were brilliant. You *are* brilliant."

"Even now, you can't see your nose in front of your face. You're as naive as I was about Peter. And I don't know how else to spell it out." Curtis took her hands. "Look around you, Eve. Everything you see is a lie. We feed people line after line, sales pitch after sales pitch. We collect their money, but what have we delivered?"

"We give people hope. The power to take control of their lives."

"Do we? We can't even control our own lives. Even the rats know to jump ship. But even after the IRS, the FBI, and murder, here we still are watching the hull fill up and hoping the damn ocean will dry up."

"You're stressed. I get that." Evie put her hand on top of Curtis's. "I promise you everything is going to be okay. I will help you through. Peter and I, and all the wives and children are here for you."

"I'm sick, Evie." Curtis bowed his head. "I don't know if it's the conquest or just sex in general, but every woman I see..."

"You can get help. You can take a break. Get some rest."

Curtis sighed. "We've done terrible things. Those families. We paid them to shut up. We took their children and their wives and their grandkids, and then we just paid them off. How are we supposed to live with ourselves?"

Evie pulled her hand away. "Let me get you a drink. You can take a few minutes to decompress. We can talk more about it later."

There was no use. Years of indoctrination couldn't be undone in the blink of an eye. She couldn't see the truth about him, or about Peter.

He laid his head back against the top of the cushion and closed his eyes. "Go home, Evie. Please. Go home."

CHAPTER 53

BLAKE BANGED ON THE DOOR. When his father answered, he pushed past him. "Is there something you want to tell me?"

"What are you all worked up about?"

Blake could have exploded. Instead, he pointed toward oblivion and shouted. "I just got a visit from Peter Hammond, that's what."

"Oh. I see."

"Oh, you see? So it is true."

"Sit down." Jim took a seat and waited for Blake to do the same.

Blake ignored him. "He tried to kill Haeli. And if he'd stuck me with that needle, we'd both be dead."

"Needle? Slow down. What happened?"

"Is he my brother?"

The room fell silent. Blake could see the sadness in Jim's eyes. Or was it guilt?

Blake crossed his arms and stared his father down, refusing to let him off the hook until he answered the question.

After a few moments, Jim cleared his throat and spoke. "Let me explain."

To Blake, that was definite confirmation that his parents had been keeping from him the secret of secrets. For decades. "I'm waiting"

"Can you just sit? You're giving me agita."

Blake gave in. He was more hurt than angry, and if his father was willing to spill the honest truth, he was ready to listen. He shook his head, avoiding eye contact. "How could you keep this from me, Dad?"

"I'm sorry. I know it was wrong. But I was ashamed. I didn't want you to hold it against your mother."

"Is this why you left? Why we haven't talked in so long?"

"No. That part was you."

Blake wanted honesty. And he got it. But this wasn't about him. "Then tell me how? Why? Peter's a grown man. And a terrible one, at that. All these years I thought you and Mom were together. No wonder you didn't know where she was."

"We were together, son. Please, let me start from the beginning."

There were a thousand questions Blake wanted to ask. But Jim was right. It would be more productive to let him spill it all out before interrogating him any further. "I'm listening"

"I don't know if you remember. When you were about sixteen or seventeen, your mom and I had just gotten involved with the Church. Both of us were spending a lot of time with Curtis."

"I remember."

"We were very busy with everything, and your mom and I went through a rough patch. She thought I might have been cheating—which I wasn't. And she had this idea that I was trying to undermine her to keep her from her spiritual journey. Anyway, we separated for a bit, until we could figure things out. I didn't realize it at the time, but she got involved with Hammond. Technically, she was the first of the wives. The original."

"Mom was Hammond's wife?"

"It's not really a marriage. She and I were still married, theirs was more of a ritual thing. But yes, they had a relationship and your mom got pregnant."

Blake felt a tinge of nausea. "How could she do that?"

"I was angry. I felt betrayed. But eventually, I came to understand. Hammond was like a magnet. A beacon. We couldn't help but be drawn to him. Now, I look back and see how foolish I was. But I never stopped loving your mother."

Sweat beaded on Blake's brow. "I can't believe my whole life you've been separated, and I didn't know it."

"We were only separated a couple of years. Eventually, we reconnected. We worked things out, and I forgave her."

"Dad, she married another man and had his child!"

Jim raised his hand in an attempt to calm Blake down. "She married the idea. The mission. I tell you son, the Church of Clear Intention was special back in those days. It was pure. And when she came back to me, we were happier than ever. It wasn't until recently that things went south. Once she went back to the harem."

"That's where she is? Back in Hammond's bed?"

"Heavens, no. She's Den Mother. It's a prestigious job, looking after the household. The wives and children."

Blake scoffed. "You realize how sick that sounds, right?"

"I do now. Look, I get how it's hard for someone on the outside to understand how and why we subscribed to all of this in the first place. But to us, it seemed normal. Important. Until—it didn't."

"My half-brother, who I never knew existed, is a criminal psychopath. You must have known that much."

Jim nodded. "I did. He was the one who held us captive. I wanted to warn you, but I couldn't bring myself to tell you who, I mean, what he was. I really didn't want you to hold it against your mother. I hope you still don't."

"How could I not?"

"I know that it's not her fault. This wasn't any of our faults. We were brainwashed. Made to see the world the way Hammond wanted us to see it." Jim shrugged. "Then he got old and tired, and his magic wore away. That's when Peter took over. In a way, it was good that he did. For me, Peter was the lightbulb that went off in my thick skull. He illuminated the folly that was the Church."

Blake stood up and cracked his neck. "He has to be taken down. I don't care who he is to me. Or to Mom."

"I agree."

"And we need to get her away from them. She can be deprogrammed. You, me, we can be her lightbulb." Blake had been convinced he could persuade his mother to break away. Now, in light of the new developments, he wasn't so sure. At the very least, Peter's existence complicated things.

"Where's Haeli?" Jim asked.

"She's recovering, down the hall."

"Here?"

"We moved out of the Fenway." Blake nudged his father, forcing him to look Blake square in the eye. "Something's about to happen, Dad. Something that may change everything. We're almost through this. Trust me."

"I do, son. I always have."

CHAPTER 54

"THANK YOU." Fezz shared a handshake and a pat on the back with Billy and Noah. "I owe you."

"You don't owe us nothin'," Noah said. "We had no choice. They were dangerous. Woulda killed you and probably the girl, too. Anyways, we did this town a favor."

"The kid's happy, I'll tell ya that much." Billy aimed the comment at Ian, who was sitting with Jodi in Ernie's hillbilly living room, making googly-eyes. They were all relieved everything had gone as planned, but none so much as Ian.

"If you need me to stay and take the blowback, I will," Fezz said.

"I don't think that'll be necessary," Ernie said. "It was smart thinkin', spray painting that cryptic Sons of Silence stuff. One percent and all that. I wouldn't have thought of it, but I think you're right—the cops are gonna be chasing their tails for some time."

Fezz was betting on it.

When a clubhouse burns down and a pile of bikers are found dead, what was the first thing that came to mind? Gang war. And what bigger rival did the Demon Squad have than the Sons of Silence? Known for extreme violence, the Sons would be the obvious suspects, with or without the hints.

"We're takin' off," Billy said. "My kid's got a game. Don't be a stranger."

Fezz agreed and sent them off, knowing he'd never see them again.

With Ian and Jodi preoccupied, it was just Fezz and Ernie. "You guys are a hell of a shot. That second one—with a bolt action? Most guys couldn't get two off that fast with a semi."

Ernie smiled. "Like ridin' a bike."

"I know you keep the past under wraps and I understand why," Fezz said. "But I gotta say, I'd fight by your side anytime. You're the real deal, whether anyone ever knows it or not."

"Appreciate it, man. The real hero here is sittin' right over there, though." Ernie pointed at Ian. "That's one brave fella. Calm under pressure. And smart. He sprouts up, he'll be nasty."

"That's what I'm afraid of," Fezz said.

More and more, it was apparent to Fezz that Ian was cut out for what Kook often called "the life." It meant whatever the circumstances, whatever the goal, operating at the highest level of human capability. Mentally and physically. Always ready and never overwhelmed. Ian had it in him. No matter how much Fezz tried to change him, Ian would find his way back.

"Do me a favor," Fezz said. "Have your guys keep an eye on their checking accounts. There's gonna be a couple transfers from an offshore account. Let 'em know it's not a mistake."

"You don't have to—"

"I know. I want to."

"You don't know their account numbers."

Fezz shrugged. "I know a guy."

"Okay then. I'll let 'em know."

"Is the truck ready?" Fezz asked.

"Dale finished it an hour ago. Good as new."

"Good," Fezz said. "I wouldn't want you drivin' around in a clunker."

Ernie's brow furrowed, and then his face lit up. "Wait. You don't mean to—"

"She's yours. As a thank you."

"My God. You shouldn't—I mean, how are you going to—"

"We'll need a ride. If you don't mind."

"Anywhere."

"Denver will be fine."

Earnie shook Fezz's hand and gave him a hug. "Ready when you are."

"Ian. Time to go."

"Do you have to?" Jodi whined. "Can't you stay? For a little while?"

"I don't want to go," Ian added.

Fezz feigned confusion. "But the redwoods?"

"I don't care about the redwoods." He stomped his foot. "I don't want to leave Jodi. She's got nowhere to go."

"Hm. That is a problem. So, you don't want to go to California?"

"No!" Ian crossed his arms. The pout on his face was priceless.

"That's lucky," Fezz said. "Cause we're not going to California. We're going to Denver. Denver airport."

"The airport? Where are we going?"

"Home."

"Home? Like Jamestown, home? Really?"

Fezz gave him a nod.

Ian sprung to his feet and jumped up and down. "Yes!" His smile faded as quickly as it arrived, and his shoulders slumped. "Wait. What about Jodi? Can she come?"

"She doesn't want to come with us."

"Yes I do!" Jodi blurted.

"Oh." Fezz shot her a goofy face. "Well, in that case, what are we waiting for?"

"Really?" Jodi stood, uncoiling like a spring.

"Yes, really." Fezz laughed.

Ian and Jodi ran and jumped on him. Each wrapping their arms around him.

"Thank you, Ray," Jodi said. "I can't believe it! Thank you, thank you, thank you."

Fezz peeled their arms away and bent down toward Jodi.

"Listen, if you're going to come and stay with us, there's one condition."

"Okay. What is it?"

"For God's sake, call me Fezz."

CHAPTER 55

"ARE WE SURE THEY'RE INSIDE?" Agent Burnson asked.

"We've had eyes on since last night," the officer responded. "They're there."

"Who's got the face sheets?"

"Detective Simmons."

"Round everybody up. We're going in."

Burnson was taking point on the operation. Even though the arrest warrants were local, the charges played into the wider reaching federal case.

The past twenty-four hours had been a whirlwind. As much as he needed a nap, the arrests meant it'd have to wait. There would be interviews and searches and paperwork. But it was all worth it to take the Hammonds off the board. It would buy them time to build the tax evasion and now racketeering cases.

When Burnson's field office received the intel, it was an instant shot in the arm for an otherwise dying case. The previous search had come up shorter than they'd hoped and the Bureau was getting weary.

The big break came when it was discovered that a single Tampa detective had been the lead investigator on all the deaths associated with the hush money the Church paid.

Detective Grady Larson was quick to flip. In exchange for a guilty plea and his cooperation and testimony, he was only looking at a one-year suspended sentence and five years' probation. The benefit of being a guppy in a shallow pool of 300 pound tunas.

Larson was able to provide enough for the local department to secure the warrants. There was a lot more work to be done. Gathering evidence, toxicology, and witness statements in order to build a solid case. But at least, by getting Peter and Curtis Hammond behind bars sooner than later, there would be no more victims.

"Gather 'round." Burnson addressed the group of agents, officers, and detectives. "These are the two targets." He held up two color eight-by-ten photos. "Curtis and Peter Hammond. Now, this could go a couple ways. Chances are we can keep this civil. But use caution, especially with the son. Secure him quickly and watch his hands. If anyone is exposed to any substance, let us know right away on the radio and we have medics standing by. We have a tight perimeter, so no one's getting out without us knowing about it. Other than that, any issues or concerns?"

None were voiced.

"Then follow me." Burnson led the crew through the front doors and to the reception desk. The woman at the desk started to pick up the phone, but Burnson reached over the desk and forced her hand and the receiver onto the base. "We're here for these two men." He showed her the pictures. "The sooner we locate them, the sooner we're out of your hair. Is that understood?"

The woman nodded.

"Where will we find them?"

"Mister Hammond is in his office," she said with a Russian accent. "Just up the stairs, down the hall to the left. His name's on the door. Peter should be in the residence. I can show you the way."

"Fine," Burnson said. "Team A. Go with her. Team B, hang back 'til Team A can get into place."

Half the group broke off and disappeared through a set of double doors with the receptionist.

"The rest of you, come with me. We'll stage outside his office until we get the go ahead." Burnson led the team upstairs. From then on, they would refrain from speaking, relying on their earpieces for the next step.

It was likely that both Curtis and Peter knew they were there and were expecting an arrest. After all, they weren't discreet about gathering in the parking lot. But just in case, it was protocol to hit both at roughly the same time to avoid one tipping off the other.

"Making entry," the radio squawked.

Burnson tried the door. It was locked. He stepped aside and gave the signal to the officer assigned the battering ram.

With one strike, the door was blasted inward.

The team flooded the room. It was empty. The receptionist had lied to them.

Two officers checked the bathroom, while others checked under the desk and turned over the couch.

Burnson opened the glass door and stepped out onto the balcony. While there was no one there, he did notice something peculiar. Tied to the railing were what looked like a couple of neckties, dangling out of sight like a makeshift rope.

It was something out of a prison break movie. Had this guy escaped by shimmying down formal wear? Then again, with the perimeter, he wouldn't be getting far.

Burnson pulled the fabric. It didn't budge. As if it were staked at the bottom. He leaned over the edge.

Jesus.

A head of silver hair swung from the end of the tether. It was an escape, but not the kind Burnson had assumed.

"I found him," Burnson called out.

Several agents joined him on the balcony. Their reactions were the same as his own.

All the months of work, down the toilet. Curtis Hammond would never see the inside of a jail cell. Or anywhere else, for that matter. Ever again.

The radio chirped in Burnson's ear. "Team A on. One in custody."

Well, at least there's that.

CHAPTER 56

AN AGENT EMERGED from the building, carrying a pelican box. The crime scene and medical examiner personnel had already left, and most of the parking lot had cleared out. If the scene wasn't already wrapped up, it was getting close. Blake decided to flag the agent down.

"Excuse me? Are we able to go in yet?"

The man kept walking past them. "Be my guest."

Huh. Easier than expected.

"All right, Dad. Ready for this?"

"Nope."

Blake squeezed his father's shoulder and edged him forward. They walked side by side, toward the Church Jim had only days before been so desperate to escape.

In the lobby, Anastasia was in her usual spot. The security guards, however, were absent.

"Anastasia," Blake said.

"Mister Brier." She turned to Jim and smiled. "Mister Brier."

"I'm sure you know why we're here. Where is she?"

"She's in Mister Hammond's office. Or—her office, I guess. She thought you might come. You can go on up."

Blake shot his father a grin. The Hammonds had only been gone for hours, and the place already had a different aura. Maybe it was his imagination, but even Anastasia seemed relieved.

As they climbed the stairs, Blake whispered. "Wasn't too broken up about it, was she?"

"That woman doesn't care about anything, as long as she's getting a paycheck."

"Which won't be happening much longer, I assume."

"Don't assume," Jim said. "You heard what she said. Evie's taken over Hammond's office."

"Jim." A man's voice came from behind.

Blake turned to see an older man approaching. The same man he'd met in the barracks. What was his name?

"Freddie. You're still here?" Jim stopped to wait for him to catch up. "Figured you'd be halfway to the border by now."

"No sir. I'm sticking around."

What was it with these people? Inside these walls was like an upside-down world. One where you couldn't pay the prisoners to leave.

"Let's catch up later," Jim said. "I've got to talk to Evie."

"Good luck." Freddie walked away.

Jim turned to Blake. "I knew he'd never leave."

A minute later, they found themselves standing at the door, about to knock. Blake was going to see his mother, in person, after all these years. Funny, the only thing that crossed his mind was that he wished Haeli were there so he could introduce her.

Haeli had said she felt fine and offered to come, but Blake thought it best if she continued to rest. Plus, this was a family matter, and bringing in an outsider would only serve to complicate things.

Jim knocked, and the door swung open on its own, revealing the damaged door frame. "Evie."

She stood motionless as Blake entered and let out an audible gasp.

"Hi Mom."

Her eyes were wide. She was still unmoving. "Blake. You look —good.

He gave her a hug. She hugged him back but remained less than animated.

"Are you okay?" Blake asked.

"Fine. It's been a rough day. But we do what we can."

Jim broke through the reunion. "Blake knows about Peter, Evie."

"Oh, my." She fidgeted. "I ..."

Blake could feel her discomfort. It had been a rough few days for everyone and he wasn't there to fight. As much as she deserved to squirm after having kept such a secret for so long, he decided to let her off the hook. "It's okay Mom. I understand why you never told me."

Her steely gaze softened. "I wanted to."

"I know."

If she'd wanted to, she would have. Unless she'd signed an NDA, too. A distinct possibility.

"Honey. It's finally over." Jim reached out to her. "Curtis is gone. Peter's going to prison. We can go home now."

She backed away. "I'm not leaving. Have you lost your mind? Do you know how much work I have to do? This is a giant mess. And who do you think's going to have to clean it up?"

Blake wasn't surprised at her reaction. From talking to his father, Blake knew he wasn't either. But he had to hand it to the man. Jim Brier did not give up easily.

"Evie. Stop it. Can't you see this place is toxic? It's estranged our son. It destroyed our marriage. Twice. We can start over. All of us. All you have to do is walk away."

Blake stepped up and nodded, ready to support his father. "Dad's right. Even if you do things differently, you'll never be able to shake the stigma. The feds will keep coming until the whole organization crumbles. You don't want to be a part of that."

"Let them come," Evie said. "I was chosen. Twenty years ago. This is my destiny and I'll be damned if I'm not going to fulfill it. You were once a believer, Jim. I don't know what happened, but you've forgotten the mission. You have amnesia. Think back to when we were young. Both of us knew how important this was. We were in it together."

"We were impressionable. Look at our son, Evie. Look at him! We neglected him. Lost years getting to know him as a man. I refuse to waste any more time. I love you, Evie. And I've always stuck by you, even when you went outside our marriage. But you need to make a choice."

"Why does it have to be a choice?"

Jim had no answer. Blake couldn't think of one either.

"I need to do this," Evie said. "I've made a lot of mistakes, I know that. And I'm sorry. But there are people here that count on me. Women and children who have lost their father and husband. I'm all they have."

"We need you, too."

"No you don't. And you both know it." Evie turned her back. "I'm not leaving here. This is mine now. And I intend to see it through.'

Tears welled in Jim's eyes. "You asked why it had to be a choice, as if we're the one's setting the ultimatum. Everything I've done—all the humiliation I endured—was so you wouldn't have to choose between me and the Church. Like you did with Blake. It didn't have to be that way. But even now, even as you deny it, you're making your choice."

"I guess I am."

Blake was prepared to give his mother a heartfelt speech. To drill into her brain and drag her old self out, kicking and screaming. But as he watched and listened, he realized the truth. She was no longer the woman he'd once known. There was no getting through to her.

Worse, his father had realized it too. Though he was reluctant to say it out loud, Blake knew that inside, Jim was coming to terms with the fact that his wife was gone.

"I guess this is goodbye?"

"I'm sorry, Jim." She was cold and lacked any expression. "It was good to see you, Blake."

"You too, Mom."

It was hard to tell if she was, in fact, sorry, in any sense of the word. But he had a feeling that a day would come, somewhere in the future when she would be. In the end, everyone must face themselves.

The reunion had been a long time coming. Although she'd offered Blake no love or affection, she had given him the one thing he'd needed most. Closure. Another line through his short list of regrets.

He knew that when they parted, they would never see each other again. Because they would never need to.

"Come on Dad. Let's go."

Tears streamed down the old man's face as he shuffled toward his wife.

"I love you Evie Brier. And I always will."

Evie reached up and touched his cheek. "So will I."

CHAPTER 57

"THIS IS YOUR HOME?" Jim stood in the circular driveway, looking up at the house. "I had no idea."

"It's in my name, but we all share it." Blake said. "If you want to get technical, it'd be Haeli's. She's the one who made all this possible.

Haeli shrugged. "I came into some money."

"Come on in. Meet the guys."

The three made their way through the front doors and into the great room. The house was quiet.

Jim looked around in awe, then stared out the back windows toward the pool and guest house beyond it. "What is this, a resort?"

"We like to think so," Haeli said.

Blake hollered. "Khat? Griff?"

From upstairs, Blake could hear footsteps, followed by a personal appearance.

"You're back." Khat descended the stairs. "And in one piece!"

"Barely," Blake said. "Khat, this is my father. Jim."

The two men greeted each other.

"Where's Griff?" Blake asked.

Khat smiled and then stomped his sandaled foot on the floor several times. Ten seconds later, Griff emerged from the pantry. "Hey! You made it."

Blake turned to Jim. "This is Griff."

"His dad, Jim," Khat added.

"Good to meet you Jim." Griff gave Jim a handshake, Blake a fist bump, and Haeli a hug. After making his rounds, he looked around the room. "No Misses Brier?"

"Evie decided to stay behind," Jim said.

"That's a shame. Is everything okay?"

"Yes," Jim said. "Everything is fine."

"Great." Griff walked over to Khat and slapped him on the back for no particular reason. "So how long you in town, Mister B?"

Blake looked at Haeli. She wasn't willing to interject. "For a while. Maybe forever."

"Really?" The surprise was evident on Khat's face.

Blake put his arm around his father's neck. "I was thinking he could take Fezz's room. Or Ian's"

"Perfect," Griff said.

Khat was less enthusiastic. "You know they'll be back, Mick."

"I know you want them to. But I don't think that's going to happen any time soon. In fact, if you'd prefer to have your own space, Dad, we can set you up in Fezz's old apartment in Newport. It's a great spot. You'd be close but can still do your own thing."

"That's a better idea," Khat said. "He never used it anyway. Except when Buck was there."

Haeli stepped in. "We'll figure it out. Until then, we can get you set up in the guest house, right out there." She pointed out the window. "Best view around."

"I don't want to be a bother," Jim said.

Griff laughed. "Please. We need you. Someone needs to keep Mick in line. Let me give you the tour. Then you can just make yourself at home, all right?"

Jim followed Griff, and the two went off down the hallway next to the kitchen.

"Do you drink?" Griff asked.

"On occasion."

"Let me show you Artie's pub. You're gonna love it."

Khat waited until Jim was far enough away. "What happened with your mother, really?"

"She took over for Hammond," Blake said. "She made her choice and we're living with it. What else can I say?"

"Damn. Sorry."

"Me too." Blake said.

Haeli walked over to the couch and plopped herself down. "I never even got to meet her."

It wasn't a question, but Blake felt as though the comment was meant to elicit a response. He wasn't sure what he could add. On one hand, he was sorry Haeli would never know that piece of him. On the other, it was probably for the better. Anyway, they had only spent a few minutes with his mother. Not long enough for any kind of impression.

"What's next on the agenda?" Khat asked. "I'm starting to go stir crazy."

With a dramatic slide, Haeli fell to her side. Her hair spread out across the cushion. "I was kinda hoping there was no agenda. For at least a week."

Blake chuckled. "Something tells me you already have something in mind."

"There is something. Griff's been working on—"

As if a bomb went off, they all jumped at the sound of the front door opening.

"Honey, I'm home." Fezz's giant frame was silhouetted in the open door. On either side of him were two smaller figures.

A huge grin appeared on Khat's face.

"Miss me?"

"What do you mean?" Khat wandered toward him. "Did you go somewhere? I thought you were in the can."

"Funny."

"Come here ya big bastard." Khat hugged him.

Ian ran to Blake and hugged him around the waist. Then moved over to Haeli.

Fezz, Khat, and Jodi joined them by the coffee table.

"Everyone, this is Jodi. Jodi Foster."

"Like the actress?" Khat said. "Love your work. A lot younger in person."

Fezz laughed. "Yeah, she has no idea what you're talking about."

"Everybody, guess what?" Ian beamed. "Jodi's going to live with us!"

"Is that right?" Blake flashed a smile. "Well, welcome, Jodi." He looked at Fezz for more.

Fezz waved him off. "Long story. I'll tell you later."

Whatever the story was, it had to be a good one. Fezz, the guy who never wanted to be married or have a family, was now toting around two kids.

The important thing was he was back. And he looked well.

"Why don't you grab your stuff, Jodi," Haeli said. "I'll help you get settled in."

Jodi reached into her pocket, pulled out a photograph, and handed it to Haeli. "This is all I have."

"Oh. Who's this?"

"My mother."

"She's pretty."

"I'm going to help Jodi find her," Ian said.

"That's great." Haeli handed the photo back to the girl. Blake laughed to himself at her awkwardness. But she'd walked into that one, all on her own.

"So, this means you're back for good, right?" Khat asked.

"As long as I'm still welcome."

"I don't know. Mick was going to give your room away about five minutes ago."

Blake held up his hands. "Yeah, but that was when I thought you moved to Colorado."

"How'd you know I was in Colorado?"

Blake grinned. "Lucky guess."

"God, it's good to have everyone back together," Haeli said. "Almost everyone."

"It is. Really good." Blake reached up and squeezed Fezz's trap. "You missed a lot, buddy. My father's here. Griff's showing him around. In fact, why don't we go catch up with them? Jodi could use the tour. Griff's gonna crap himself when he sees you. I mean, not as much as Khat did, but—"

"Aww. Khat. You *did* miss me. That's cute."

"Sat at the window all day, every day, waiting for you," Blake said.

"Only 'cause you owed me money," Khat said. "Anyway, I told these guys you wouldn't last more than a week without me."

"You guys are funny," Jodi giggled. "I think I'm gonna like it here."

"Wait 'til you go in the pool," Ian said.

Fezz bent down, eye level with Ian and Jodi as if he were about to scold them. "Why wait?" He jogged to the atrium door and opened it. "Pool party!"

The kids looked at him with blank stares.

Without another word, Fezz ran outside and jumped into the pool, fully clothed.

Ian took Jodi's hand. They ran after Fezz, jumping into the pool, almost on top of him.

Fezz picked Ian up and tossed him, then went after Jodi. She squealed as she tried to get away.

Blake, Haeli, and Khat looked at each other and burst into laughter.

When the laughter died down, there was a brief pause before Haeli hollered. "Race ya."

Blake and Khat took off after her but had no chance of catching up.

One after another, they jumped in. Splashing and laughing.

Their family had grown, then shrunk, then grown again. Through the hardship and loss, they'd always hung onto what brought them together in the first place. Love.

Each of them would need to deal with their own demons, in their own time. Ian, losing Ima. Blake, letting go of his mother. Jodi, getting past whatever horrible thing had brought her there.

But for now—for this single moment—they basked in the glory of their reunion. On a sunny day by the bay, they appreciated what they had, and those they were fortunate to share it with.

And it was enough.

Blake's story continues in Quarry. *Pre-order now:*
https://www.amazon.com/gp/product/B0C7J4744H

Join the LT Ryan reader family & receive a free copy of the Jack Noble story, *The Recruit*. Click the link below to get started:
https://ltryan.com/jack-noble-newsletter-signup-1

THE BLAKE BRIER SERIES

Blake Brier Series

Unmasked

Unleashed

Uncharted

Drawpoint

Contrail

Detachment

Clear

Quarry (coming soon)

ALSO BY L.T. RYAN

Visit https://ltryan.com/pb for paperback purchasing information.

The Jack Noble Series

The Recruit (Short Story)

The First Deception (Prequel 1)

Noble Beginnings (Jack Noble #1)

A Deadly Distance (Jack Noble #2)

Thin Line (Jack Noble #3)

Noble Intentions (Jack Noble #4)

When Dead in Greece (Jack Noble #5)

Noble Retribution (Jack Noble #6)

Noble Betrayal (Jack Noble #7)

Never Go Home (Jack Noble #8)

Beyond Betrayal (Clarissa Abbot)

Noble Judgment (Jack Noble #9)

Never Cry Mercy (Jack Noble #10)

Deadline (Jack Noble #11)

End Game (Jack Noble #12)

Noble Ultimatum (Jack Noble #13)

Noble Legend (Jack Noble #14 - coming 2022)

Bear Logan Series

Ripple Effect

Blowback

Take Down

Deep State

Rachel Hatch Series

Drift

Downburst

Fever Burn

Smoke Signal

Firewalk

Whitewater

Mitch Tanner Series

The Depth of Darkness

Into The Darkness

Deliver Us From Darkness - coming Summer 2021

Cassie Quinn Series

Path of Bones

Untitled - February, 2021

Blake Brier Series

Unmasked

Unleashed

Uncharted - April, 2021

Affliction Z Series

Affliction Z: Patient Zero

Affliction Z: Abandoned Hope

Affliction Z: Descended in Blood

Affliction Z: Fractured (Part 1)

Affliction Z: Fractured (Part 2) - October, 2021

ABOUT THE AUTHOR

L.T. Ryan is a *USA Today* and international bestselling author. The new age of publishing offered L.T. the opportunity to blend his passions for creating, marketing, and technology to reach audiences with his popular Jack Noble series.

Living in central Virginia with his wife, the youngest of his three daughters, and their three dogs, L.T. enjoys staring out his window at the trees and mountains while he should be writing, as well as reading, hiking, running, and playing with gadgets. See what he's up to at http://ltryan.com.

Social Medial Links:

- Facebook (L.T. Ryan): https://www.facebook.com/LTRyanAuthor

- Facebook (Jack Noble Page): https://www.facebook.com/JackNobleBooks/

- Twitter: https://twitter.com/LTRyanWrites

- Goodreads: http://www.goodreads.com/author/show/6151659.L_T_Ryan

Printed in Great Britain
by Amazon